LAKES HOCKEY ONE

BEFORE WE CAME

SLOANE ST. JAMES

CONTENTS

Before We Came Playlist ... v

Chapter 1 ... 1
Chapter 2 ... 13
Chapter 3 ... 28
Chapter 4 ... 38
Chapter 5 ... 47
Chapter 6 ... 62
Chapter 7 ... 87
Chapter 8 ... 96
Chapter 9 ... 99
Chapter 10 ... 105
Chapter 11 ... 107
Chapter 12 ... 116
Chapter 13 ... 128
Chapter 14 ... 142
Chapter 15 ... 162
Chapter 16 ... 174
Chapter 17 ... 180
Chapter 18 ... 189
Chapter 19 ... 202
Chapter 20 ... 206
Chapter 21 ... 217
Chapter 22 ... 234
Chapter 23 ... 251
Chapter 24 ... 254
Chapter 25 ... 267
Chapter 26 ... 274
Chapter 27 ... 284
Chapter 28 ... 299
Chapter 29 ... 309

Chapter 30   325
Chapter 31   335
Chapter 32   338
Chapter 33   343
Chapter 34   358
Chapter 35   370
🌶 Chapter 36   380
🌶 Epilogue I   394
🌶 Epilogue II   404

More Books by Sloane St. James   413
Acknowledgments   415
Shameless Begging from the Author   419

🌶 One-Handed Reader Shortcuts

BEFORE WE CAME PLAYLIST

Old Leaves Ephemeral
Fire Escape Call Me Karizma
Formula Labrinth
Running Derik Fein
R.I.P. 2 My Youth The Neighbourhood
Hotel Room Blake Rose
Birthday Cake Dylan Conrique
Don't Let Me Go Cigarettes After Sex
Midnight City M83
Let It Go The Neighbourhood
I Feel Like I'm Drowning Two Feet
Ruin the Friendship Demi Lovato
Miss Movin' On Fifth Harmony
Hypnotic Zella Day
Hellraiser Illiterate Light
Power Over Me Dermot KennedyTwo
Summers One11Twenty
Treat You Better Shawn Mendes
Good For You Selena Gomez, A$AP Rocky
Pretty Bug Allan Rayman
Somebody to You The Vamps
Sirens Nylo
Constellations Jade LeMac

Nothing's Gonna Hurt You Baby Cigarettes After Sex

You're Somebody Else Flora Cash

Crash My Car COIN

Feel Something Jaymes Young

Say Something ColdWards

Memories Conan Gray

Meant to Be Ber, Charlie Oriain

Take It Out On Me Thousand Foot Krutch

3, 2, 1 24kGoldn

Take on the World You Me At Six

Lover Taylor Swift

Feel the Light Jennifer Lopez

To Mark
The calm to my storm

ONE

Birdie

I need to get out of bed. I'm trying to think of something that might motivate me to open my eyes, but I can't come up with anything. Maybe if I lie here a little longer, I can trick myself into falling back asleep. Or not . . .

Isn't there something I need to do today?

Oh, yeah. Mom's funeral. What kind of daughter forgets her own mother's funeral? This has to be her way of reminding me from the grave how much of a disappointing daughter I was.

To be fair, she wasn't winning any *Mother of the Year* awards either. It's not her fault, though, she wasn't my biological mom, and we never developed that unique bond most mothers and daughters have. My birth parents sent me away at a young age, so in some ways, I'm an old pro at being a disappointment.

My adoptive mom and I had a somewhat strained relationship. At first, I was jealous of the intimacy other girls had with their mothers, but after so long, it turned into a smug bitterness. We didn't need all that phony closeness. Didn't these women have anything better to do than grandstand with all the *I-love-you*s and *have-a-good-day-sweethearts*?

Then, as if she knew I was thinking about her, my mother's stern voice interrupts my thoughts, "*Everyone shows love differently, Birdie.*"

This became her catchphrase.

It was the routine response when she caught me waiting for a hug or some other form of tenderness, like after I'd painted her a picture or fell off my bike. I'll never be sure, but I get the distinct feeling she thought I was purposely trying to provoke her by wanting more affection.

As I finally open my eyes, my black dress hanging on the closet doorknob comes into view. A few tears leak from the corners of my eyes, and my stomach feels hollow and empty. I can't believe she's gone. This is the second time I've lost a mother, and in both instances, I never got to say goodbye.

———

This funeral sucks. I can only blame myself, though, since I'm the one who organized it. I can't tell if it's

Mom's that sucks, or if funerals suck in general. This is the only one I've ever been to, and I didn't have the money to hire professionals. I wonder how one gets into the business of funeral planning. *I'll have to Google that later.*

After she died, I was left to my own devices. At first, I wasn't even sure who to call, so I started by calling people in her address book that shared our last name, Fournier. Thankfully, one of her cousins, Barbara —*or was it Bonnie? Shit, I can't remember*—took mercy on me and said she would contact the rest of the family tree. God bless Cousin What's-Her-Name.

The minister gave a lovely eulogy for "*Juliet*" Fournier—mom's name was Julianne. I think everyone collectively cringed as soon as he uttered the wrong name at the pulpit. He said lovely things, although, I suspect it was cookie-cutter as far as speeches go. I didn't give him much to work with because Mom was private and didn't share many details about her life with me. I knew the basics. She was a teacher and an excellent cook.

Sometimes she would travel to visit people, though I was never allowed to go with her. She would tell me I'd be bored the whole time and would have no fun. I was already bored, but I enjoyed having the apartment to myself while she was gone. None of the other kids got to stay home alone at age eight. Probably because their parents knew better.

She went to church, wrote in her journals every day, and she shopped. A lot. That woman could blow through money like it was her job. I didn't tell anyone that it was mainly on The Shopping Channel. On occasion, her purchasing habits put us in a tight spot, but those little angel figurines with the chubby asses mollified her, so I wasn't about to protest her spending.

During the service, I said a few words but was relieved when some of her extended family stood up and spoke. Hearing people talk about my mom the way they did was bittersweet. So many of their kind words painted my mother as bubbly and cheerful, but that woman was a stranger to me.

I should have set out name tags. And maybe laid out a guestbook like a genealogy map so I could figure out how the hell we all know each other. Some guests are friends of my mom, but it's hard to tell the friends apart from the family when everybody's dressed in the same fucking color. I'm a Fournier, but my commonalities with these people stop at our surname. They all know Mom, but rarely did she talk about her family and friends.

After walking into the reception hall, I pull one of the Styrofoam cups from the stack and fill it with hot coffee. I'm not much of a coffee drinker, but it serves as a hand warmer in the depressing church foyer. The chill in the air seems to radiate from the dated commercial tiling under my feet. *I want to go home.*

The soft murmuring of conversation and stories echo in the room . . . I take a seat at one of the empty tables covered in a lace tablecloth. The yellowing coffee stains throughout tell me it's been used in many funerals before this one. A table runner features a Christmas pattern of snowmen and holly. Interesting choice, considering it's September. These must be the *nice linens*.

I peer across the room at my best friend, Freya McCoy, and smile. She goes by Micky; we grew up preferring our nicknames. Micky is my rock today—well, most days. She's wearing a huge grin and is regaling the guests with stories about my mom. The operative word being "stories." Micky never actually met my mother, so she's most likely telling people that Mom invented the selfie stick or was an underwater basket weaver. She's the best. We met in the Vancouver Culinary Academy dormitories and have been inseparable ever since.

Vancouver has been my home for as long as I can remember. I tried asking my mother where I was born. I think she was afraid I might try and find my birth parents and leave her. Mom was my only family in Vancouver. I ruminate on that a little longer as I run my thumb over one of the loose threads in the tablecloth. I suppose Micky is the closest thing I have to family now. In a way, she always has been.

I was only six when I was taken in by my adoptive

mom, and she always yelled at me whenever I brought up my life before moving in with her. She would get so angry. After a while, I stopped bringing it up. Then I stopped thinking about it altogether. I hated thinking about it. I was mad at my birth parents for making me live with Julianne. Eventually, those memories became fuzzier and fuzzier. When you're ripped away from home at such a young age and never allowed to talk about it again, it's easy to forget your childhood. I remember some things but details are hard. I remember there were pine trees in the yard, and we lived on Briar Lane, but I can't remember what city or province.

When I found out my adoptive mom died, my world flipped upside down. Mom wasn't my most extensive support system, but she was the only one I had. The coffee in my hand jostles when I'm pulled from my thoughts by an older couple who stop next to my chair. The woman's thin gray hair is pulled back in a barrette; her kind, aged eyes are brown and glassy. Her husband stands close by with his hand on her back and gives me a sympathetic smile. The woman takes my hand in hers and winces as she shares her condolences. I thank them for coming, and they turn to leave.

I have no idea who I just said goodbye to. I've heard "I'm sorry for your loss" so many times that the senti-ment has lost all meaning. Kind of like when you say a word over and over and it no longer sounds like the word anymore.

Sorry for your loss.
Sorey feryer laws.
Soar-ee fer yer laaws.

I stifle a laugh at the absurdity as I recite it in my head. The Canadian accent is strong with this crowd.

I take the elderly couple's exit as an opportunity to stand and move around; I'm a sitting duck if I stay at this stupid coffee-stained Christmas table. Maybe if I appear busy, people will be less likely to converse with me. I don't want to cry in front of strangers.

Despite not knowing anyone here, everyone seems to know me pretty well. Although it takes me a second to realize they are talking to me because they keep calling me by my full name, Elizabeth—I've been called by my nickname, Birdie, my entire life.

I walk over to a card table tucked off to the side displaying all the photographs. We didn't take a lot of pictures. I had a couple of us from when I was about six or seven years old, but the rest are of me in my teen years.

Luckily, the Fournier brood has a whole box of photos of my mom when she was younger, and some even have me in them—it must be soon after I moved in with her because I look young. I take in all the stacks and scrapbooks. Jesus, these people took a lot of pictures. I've never seen any of them before and can't help but notice how happy Mom seemed. I smile. It's a side of her I've never seen before. I wish I could

have had that version of her, she looked so effer-
vescent.

I grab a stack of photos and flip through them.
Peering up at the measly photo boards I made, I realize
there's not one photo I brought that features us
appearing happy at the same time. In every picture,
either I'm smiling and she's not, or she's smiling and
I'm not—quite the metaphor for us.

I come across some of us on a vacation at a lake, but
there's something off about my face, I don't look like
myself. Is it because of the huge grin? It leaves me
feeling uneasy. I take two of the photos and slide them
into my purse without anyone noticing. My family
won't mind, and I could use the proof there was a day,
twenty-some years ago, when Mom and I were happy
simultaneously.

———

I'm finally home. Thank God this shitbag of a day is
coming to an end. Micky has insisted on being my
chauffeur since the car was totaled in the accident. I'm
good with using public transportation, I used it often in
college, but eventually, I'll need to get a vehicle. I can't
even think about that yet, I still have to figure out what
to do about Mom's apartment and how I will pay off her
credit cards.

Micky helps me carry the picture boards, at least a

dozen flower arrangements, and a few casseroles into the apartment. No idea where I will put everything. Why don't people give cash instead? The money, you can use. What am I supposed to do with an obscenely large crucifix made of white lilies and a blow mold of Jesus hanging in the center? It's so melancholy—and pretty damn ugly, if I say so myself. I need somewhere to stash it, so I toss it in the extra washroom shower and yank the curtain closed. Problem solved. We get the last potted plant inside and then walk back to her car to say our goodbyes.

When she gets in her car, I hand over two full trays of leftover food from the reception that didn't fit in the refrigerator. She rotates, sets them in the passenger seat and looks back at me with a clenched half smile. "How are you holding up?"

"I'm fine. As good as somebody can be after their mother dies. But at least the funeral is over."

"Are you sure you don't want to come back to the apartment tonight? You didn't have the greatest childhood here." Her eyes shift to the brick building. "It feels weird leaving you. What if I stay with you tonight?"

"Honestly, I think I just need some space tonight. I'm so drained after the last few days." As if confessing it was some kind of a release, my shoulders slump, and I notice how dry my eyes are.

"I'm not surprised, you've been busting your ass putting that service together, and today was *a lot*. Just

9

promise you'll call if you change your mind, or if there's anything you need. Snacks, beer, lasagna, you name it, I'll come running."

"Ha! I think they gave us enough bacon casserole to last six months. Thanks for taking some of the food home for me."

"You bet, babe. Take care of yourself, okay?"

"I will. Love you, Mick."

"Love you more."

"Drive safe," I tell her as I shut her car door.

Micky disappears down the road, and I drag my feet as I walk back inside. I've always hated the way the hallways smell here, like Hamburger Helper and other people. I get to our door, relieved to be in my own space again, but I'm confronted by another scent. Mixed with all the floral aromas from the funeral bouquets is the unmistakable smell of Mom. I never noticed it before, but now that she's gone, it's more potent than ever. How much longer will the apartment smell like this? It's comforting, but it's also a reminder that she's never coming back. It's strange sensing someone in a place, knowing they will never return to it. Though our relationship wasn't great, she was still my mom for the last twenty-two years.

After kicking off my uncomfortable kitten heels, I stand in the entryway. It's so quiet. Needing some background noise, I turn on the television, and The Shopping Channel pops up on the screen. The air is filled with some lady squealing that the *CanTech Portable Cordless Air Inflator with Case and 3 Tips* will "change my life." She actually said that.

I waffle back and forth on whether I should change the channel. Biting my bottom lip, I contemplate my choices. My mother was the last one watching TV, she chose this channel. If I change it, then I'm cutting one more tie to her and her existence here. It sounds ridiculous, I know. But when you have a complicated relationship like ours, every little strand of connection counts. After the host says—for the third time, about not missing out on the new introductory price, the decision has been made for me. *Sorry, Ma, I'm out.*

I find a rerun of *Schitt's Creek* and listen to Alexis bitch about David stealing her yogurt. It's a nice escape. Leaning against the dated pink sofa, I stand watching for a few more minutes—laughing for the first time today. A commercial break hits and I'm thrust back to the present. I need to get out of this dress.

God, it feels good to take my bra off. After pulling on an oversized t-shirt and sweats, I'm a tad lighter after this especially heavy day. I walk into the washroom to scrub the day off my face and notice the black smudges under my eyes. I don't remember crying. I finish washing my makeup off, brush my teeth, then stand and stare at myself in the mirror. Now what the hell do I do?

I walk out to the living room to lock the door for the night. I'm exhausted. Looking at the floor as I walk, my gaze catches on the photos I stole sticking out of my purse. Picking them up, I study them again. Then I take the picture boards and carry them over to our kitchen table. I turn on the overhead pendant light and examine the photos carefully, comparing them to the ones I took from the reception. Something isn't right here. Although similar, the two young girls in the pictures aren't the same.

Why didn't I see this before? Are the pictures I took from the funeral of Mom with some other child? I turn over the photo and "Julianne and Elizabeth" is written in loopy cursive. *Nope, that's my name.* Using the palms of my hands, I rub my eyes and focus, trying to analyze them with fresh eyes. I inspect the image of me running on the beach. Wait . . . where's my birthmark? I have a heart-shaped birthmark on my thigh, but it's not in this photo, and it definitely should be. The hairs on the back of my neck stand on end. I snatch up another photograph, this one a close-up of Mom and me smiling together. That girl has brown eyes.

Mine are gray.

TWO

LONAN

I run my hands over my hair to make sure it isn't sticking up anywhere.

"Hey, Birdie, whatcha doin' up there?"

She sticks her head out of the fort window and smiles at me.

"I'm trying to get this stupid blanket tied up here, but I can't get it over the top of the thing." She emphasizes the last word as she jumps up again, failing to throw it over the beam above.

I smile at her. She looks really pretty today.

"Want some help?"

"Yes, please."

I grip the wood boards nailed into the trunk of the tree like ladder rungs as I climb toward the trap door in the fort's wood floor. The hatch is stiff, but I push it open and hoist myself up.

Bridget is almost seven years old, I'm eight and am a little taller than her but not by much.

"Here," she says as she hands me the blanket and some string.

"What are we hanging a blanket up for?"

"To decorate, it's curtains." She sighs as she looks around. "When I grow up, I'm going to live in this tree fort."

"You can't live here, where would you go to the bathroom?" I grunt as I jump up and throw the rope over the beam.

"I'll have my husband build a bathroom, right"—she crosses the floor and spins around, pointing at an imaginary spot she deems acceptable—"here."

"What husband?" I ask with a laugh, but my face heats a little. I've always liked Birdie. She's funny, she's not afraid of bugs—'cept for ladybugs—her rock collection is awesome, and she's one of the prettiest girls I've ever seen. Especially her eyes, her gray eyes look like this marble I got at the fair last year. Sometimes I wonder if she likes me too, but I'm too afraid to ask. Plus, I wouldn't want Jack to know. He'd probably make fun of us. I can hear him already, *Lonan and Birdie sittin' in a tree . . .*

"I don't know who he is . . . but when I meet him someday, he's going to be the most perfect man in the whole wide world," she says with her arms out wide. "He's going to say nice things to me and build lots of cool stuff for the fort, like a bathroom, a skylight so we can watch the stars, and a garden outside so we can grow vegetables. But only the good vegetables, not the gross ones."

"What about me? What if I want to live here too? This isn't just your fort, you know."

"Do you know how to build things?"

"I can build things. I built a birdhouse with your dad, remember? It's just like that, only bigger."

"Yeah, you're right." She grins. "Okay. You can be my husband."

"Just like that? Cool."

"Well, we have to be boyfriend-girlfriend before we get married. And we have to do nice stuff for each other; like you have to take me out for cotton candy ice cream, and I have to bake you snickerdoodle cookies because they're your favorite."

How does she know snickerdoodles are my favorite? I can do those things; I love those cookies.

"And we have to kiss."

She's looking down at her hands, chipping away at her light pink nail polish. *Uh . . . I don't know how to kiss.* She peers up from her nails and cocks her head to the side. "Do you like-like me, Lonan?

I stare. What if she doesn't like-like me back? I don't know what I'm supposed to say, but I better say something soon, because it looks like she might cry. I open my mouth but close it again. Should I tell her the truth? I've never told a girl I like-like her before. But this is Birdie I'm talking to, I can't lie to her.

"Yeah, Bridg. I like-like you." She looks at me with those gray eyes of hers, and I'm a goner.

"Me too. I mean, I like-like you too."

We can't stop looking at each other. I don't want to make the first move, but I don't think she will either. It's now or never.

"So, uh . . . can I kiss you now?" My voice shakes as I say it, and I hope she didn't notice.

"Yeah, you can kiss me." She blushes.

Wait, now I actually have to do it. Crap, I don't know how to kiss a girl! Am I supposed to turn my head like they do on TV? What if I have bad breath? What did I have for lunch today? Oh yeah, I ate whatever was left in that can of fruit cocktail in the fridge. Sure, it tasted a little like pennies but was fine otherwise. And fruit smells good, right? I wonder if Birdie likes the smell of fruit cocktail . . .

She's blushing, so she must be nervous too. Thank God I'm not the only one.

I close the gap between us until we are standing toe to toe. She smells like grown-up shampoo. I reach down and intertwine our fingers like I've seen Mr. and Mrs. Hayes do, and goose bumps rise on my skin, moving from my arms and onto my shoulders. This feels weird. Good weird.

She leans in and closes her eyes. I want to close my

eyes too, but I'm afraid I'll miss her mouth and kiss her nose or something. That would be awkward.

Holy smokes, I'm having my first kiss. Everybody says you remember your first kiss; I better make it good. At least I picked a cool person. I'm going to kiss Bridget. Bridget, who is smart and funny and brave and kind and pretty. Bridget, who has a nice family. Bridget, who knows my favorite cookies are snickerdoodles. My Bridget.

I lean in, close my eyes, and press my lips to hers. As our lips touch, my heartbeat picks up and my skin feels like it's buzzing. Are all kisses like this? My whole body is warm and fuzzy inside . . . I keep my lips pressed against hers. How long am I supposed to do this for? One Mississippi, two Mississippi, three Mississippi . . . *RRRRIIINNNGGGGGG*!

Fuck. I shoot up in bed at the interruption by my alarm. I'm disoriented realizing I'm no longer eight years old and about to have my first kiss. It's that time of year when I have flashbacks of Bridget in my sleep, it always happens around the anniversary of her disappearance.

Super, my head is already pounding. What time is it? The sun is up, but I am not. The phone dings twice, alerting me that whoever called has left me a voicemail. It's probably my mom, I wonder what she needs money for this time. I'm not ready to deal with her right now.

I fall back and roll over in the soft white sheets of

my four-poster bed, and when I smell a saccharine perfume, I realize I'm not alone. I peek over with my right eye. Goddamn it. Now I have something else to deal with. I hate kicking out a woman—or women—in the morning. I don't remember their names. I'm pretty sure the blonde is Nikki, and the other might be . . . Carly?

I sit up and swipe my hand down my face. I have to stop bringing home puck bunnies from the club. I keep telling myself this will be the last time, then I go out with the team and wake up next to more women. It's real-life *Groundhog Day*.

To some men, this is probably the dream, but I'm over it. It's the same routine every time: hit up the bar, have a few drinks, take home the women, give them a good time, blow my load, rinse and repeat. They're empty fucks. A means to an end. I look over and there's a tied-off condom tossed on the floor. *Classy*. At least I'm good about using protection. Rumor has it that bunnies tend to multiply quickly.

One girl stirs and rolls over, looking up at me. She's cute. She looks up at me through her eyelashes.

"Last night was amazing . . . Lonan Burke." She pops the K at the end and grins. There's something in her teeth. I think she's trying to stroke my ego by using my first and last name, but all I hear is, *I don't actually care about you. I just wanted to bag an athlete.* I give a curt smile back—time to get this over with.

I hop out of bed, making a lot of noise and acting like I'm in a hurry. Thankfully, they get the hint and follow my lead. I'm relieved when they put their clothes back on. While one of them is finishing the ankle strap clasp of her ungodly high stilettos, the other reminds me I have her number and to call when I want to "party" again. Not if, when. I tell her I will.

I won't.

"This yours, Carly?" I ask as I reach down to pick up her purse. She levels a glare at me and snatches it from my hand.

"Kayla," she grits out.

I shrug. Whatever, close enough.

When their Uber arrives, I walk them to the elevator that opens into my entryway and say thanks for a "great" evening. They leave smiling. After a minute, I push the elevator call button again so I can ensure it's empty and provide proof of their departure. I made the mistake of skipping that step once and found some chick trying to sneak back in. They need a code to get to the penthouse, but as long as they're out of the elevator, I'm safe.

I hate this hollow feeling. It's becoming a habit, a toxic cycle that seems to grow bigger by the lay. I'm tired of feeling used whenever I wake up with a woman. It can't always be like this. A few of the married guys on the team seem genuinely happy. When will I settle down? Where would I even find someone who wants me for me?

This is it. I'm done with this lifestyle. I don't want to do this anymore. And when I say it to myself this time, I mean it.

———

I get to the gym by ten and am out of there by noon. Starving, I swing by a local pizza place and pick up whatever they have that's hot. I am well aware I eat like shit, but I cook like shit too, so there's little motivation there. Coach keeps reminding me I need to get a better diet and work with the team nutritionists, but I won't actually heed their advice. When I come off a workout, I just want whatever will replenish my calories and then get on with my day.

I eat two slices on the way back home and burn my tongue because I can't wait the fifteen-minute drive. Like I said, hungry. My cell vibrates, so I fish it out of my pocket and am pleased to see Jack's picture lighting up the screen. It's an old photo he sent me of us playing pond hockey back in our junior high days. I love seeing it pop up every time he calls.

"Hey, man! Good to hear from you," I answer as I hustle inside with my pizza box.

"You too. What're you up to right now, got a minute?"

"For you, always."

"I'm just calling to remind you about the nineteenth. Think you can swing it?"

"Yup, already checked the game schedule, all clear," I assure him.

It's kismet I haven't ever had an away game on October 19 during my whole NHL career. Have I had to take red-eyes to make it back home the morning of? Plenty of times. But I won't ever miss being with the Hayeses on the anniversary of Bridget's disappearance.

"Awesome. Thanks, Burke, I know it's not always easy for you to make it, but it means so much to Mom and Dad that you're a part of it."

"It means a lot to me too. Say, what are you doing this afternoon?"

"I've got a couple of meetings, but I should be wrapping up around four. Why?"

"Do you want to grab a beer after? I'd love to catch up."

"Sure, let me check with Auds to see if she's cool with it. I'll text you."

"Ah, marriage. What's it like having to check in all the time and ask permission to go to the bar?" I only tease to get a rise out of him. Truthfully, I'm thrilled he found Audrey and started a family. She's a great woman and is such a perfect match for Jack, nobody can read him like she can.

"Fucking awesome. What's it like still being a slut?"

he asks. That one hits a little too close to home, at the moment, but I don't give it away and fake my best laugh for conviction.

"Fucking awesome."

———

October 19. For the first few years, the anniversary was awful. It always started as a celebration but ended with fighting, trying to come up with what happened that day. Frustrated rants at the Niagara Falls Tourism Bureau for not having higher quality CCTV recordings. Going through tour bus information and random vacation photos sent to us by people who were at the falls that day—just in case they might have a shot of Bridget in them. Pouring over maps from the New York Water Board, trying to figure out if she could have fallen into the falls, and if so, where her body might be spat out.

It was bleak.

The whole family was put through the wringer, especially when there was no closure. Ken and Lori's marriage was on the rocks, so Jack and I spent a lot of time together. It was his sister but all three of us were tight. We leaned on each other and worked through grief in our own ways. In the fall, when the memories were the hardest, we played hockey for hours. Until our hands and toes froze. It was something to take our minds off her absence and the fact both of our home lives were falling apart, though for different reasons. His parents were distraught and distracted, and my mom was damaged and indignant. And usually drunk.

And then there were the dreams. My memories of her would replay as I slept, always starting up around the anniversary of her disappearance. It's a blessing and a curse. The memories are so vivid they feel real, like she's back. But every time I wake up, it's like losing her all over again. She's a part of me that will always be missing. All of our lives were changed the day she disappeared, split into two timelines: before she was gone and after. Each year got a little easier, until it became more of a celebration of her and less about the loss we still feel.

"I'm home!" I yell when I walk into the house.

Lori Hayes strides into the foyer with a bright smile and hugs me. At six feet two, I have to lean down to reach her short five-foot frame. Losing a daughter almost destroyed her, but she's one of the most nurturing and loving people I've ever met. Ken and Lori took me in to live with them when I was ten and didn't have a safe home life. Without them intervening, I wouldn't be where I am today. They are the most important family I have; nobody means as much to me as they do.

"It's so good to see you," she says into my shoulder.

"Hey, Mom H. Good to be home."

She releases the hug and frames my face with her hands.

"You need to come around more often, kiddo. I miss cooking for you. We still do the big Sunday dinner; I promise to send you home with enough leftovers to last you a couple of days."

Feeding people is her love language.

She drops her hands and turns toward the kitchen. "Maddie is playing outside, but she's been jabbering about you all morning, as usual!"

Jack and Audrey's daughter, Madelyn, is four years old and is everything I would want my daughter to be like someday. She's bright, thoughtful, curious, and creative. Maddie has come to learn about Bridget—or rather Aunt Birdie——with stories from us over the years. We are pretty sure she thinks that "Birdie Day" is a national holiday celebrated by everyone on the planet, and we don't have the heart to tell her otherwise.

"There he is. Congrats on your two assists last Friday!" Ken wraps me up in a big dad, bear hug and claps me on the back.

"Thanks, old man. Speaking of which, I've got some more tickets to give you guys." Contrary to what most people think, players only get two complimentary tickets per game from the league, but I buy eight extra season tickets for the Hayes family and anyone extra they feel like bringing. Seeing them in the crowd means a lot, and they rarely miss a game.

"Aw, this is great. Thank you. You know we'll be there!" he says, waving the envelope as if I don't give him one every year.

Jack is washing a baby bottle at the sink. He looks exhausted.

"Where's Auds?" I ask.

"She's in the den with Liam."

"Are you guys getting any more sleep?" They have a three-month-old, and it sounds like he's got his sleep schedule backward.

"Nah. Babies, man. Never again."

"I heard that," Lori warns.

"I'll take little man later so you guys can grab a nap," I offer.

I love kids. Despite my reputation as a playboy, I've always wanted a big family of my own. The home I had growing up was a far cry from healthy. Being raised by Jack's parents has given me hope for myself—as long as I can get my shit together.

"I'll take you up on that," he says without thinking.

Lori pulls the sliding door open and calls out to the backyard, "Maddie! Lonan is here!"

"Lo-Lo!" she squeals, and I can already hear the swish of her little footsteps as she runs through the layer of crunchy leaves outside. She's panting when she gets in, her cheeks rosy from the chilly autumn air.

"Madaroni and cheese!"

"I've been waiting only forever for you to get here!" she says with her hands on her hips.

"Well, sheesh, I'm sorry I kept you waiting. Did you start the cookies yet?"

"Not yet! Grandma says I get to help measure the chocolate chips and pour in the ingredients."

"Wow, I've never been allowed to measure the chocolate chips."

"Because you eat 'em all!" they say in unison.

I grin and take a moment to let the sense of belonging I get from being here fill my soul. I'm home. I look back to Maddie and ask, "Want to check out the fort?"

"Yes! I need to show you the shutters because the white is falling off, and Dad says you need to paint them again."

I make a mental note to buy more paint next spring.

———

Jack cracks open the garage beer fridge and hands me an IPA and a koozie. We chat about his work, my game schedule, and life in general. As we walk outside, crisp fall leaves and earthy trees take over my senses. The conversation turns to Bridget when we enter the woods.

"Do you remember that time she poured maple syrup in the floor vent?" I ask.

"Oh shit! Yeah, and the whole house smelled like

pancakes whenever the heat kicked on for like three years." He chuckles. "What about when she would insist we play house with her but then she would make herself the"—he air quotes—"family armadillo?"

I snort. "All functioning households need an armadillo. Here we were cooking and cleaning our asses off and Birdie's over in the corner, rolling herself into a ball and doing somersaults."

"I swear she did it just to fuck with us."

Our laughter fades and we walk in silence for a while.

"Do you still have those dreams about her?"

I sigh. "Yeah. Part of me hopes they never go away because it's almost like I get to spend time with her again. The other part wishes I could just leave it in the past."

He nods, and we turn next to the tall ferns, tree fort in view. I've never told Jack about the kiss, not because I wanted to hide it from him, it just never came up.

"Did you know your sister was my first kiss?" I say, sharing my favorite memory.

"What? When?"

"That last summer. It was right up there, actually." I point to the tree fort.

"I always thought she had a crush on you."

My stomach gets queasy, it still hurts when I think about her for too long.

"Yeah. I had a crush on her too."

THREE

Birdie

We're having a much-needed girls' night out. I've been living at my mom's apartment so I can continue working on the bills she was behind on and cleaning out the kitchen along with some of her things. Micky and I haven't seen each other since the funeral, and I'm hoping I can casually bring up the strange photos I found. She's one of the most levelheaded people I know, which is precisely what I need right now.

We became instant friends when she and I were paired up in the dorms during our first semester. It was so much easier living with Micky than living at home. Even with all her sarcastic comments, she exuded positivity, and it was easy to see she embraced all the excitement life offered. At first, I was undersocialized and shy, but she gradually helped me grow out of my shell. She's much more outgoing than I am, and I love that her personality has rubbed off on me over the years. I've also rubbed off on her too. We balance each other out well.

Getting an apartment together gave me my first taste of freedom, and I gobbled it up. I had no one to worry about but myself. She introduced me to nightlife, and every now and then we have a treat-yo'self night where we go out to the clubs and give ourselves permission to do whatever we want without any guilt, whether that be shopping, drinks, or men.

Moving away from home taught me I could be myself, do what I wanted, and feel secure in my decisions because they were just that—*mine*. There was no scorekeeping with Micky; I wasn't emotionally in debt to someone else. Scorekeeping was a constant with Mom, so I thought that's how all relationships were. I've since learned that's just a way to manipulate and feel superior to another person. If one person is up, then the other person only has one place to land: down. The game was rigged from the start. Finding independence gave me satisfaction in the rewards and the consequences of my decisions because it was proof I was in control of my destiny. I was alive!

With my newfound freedom came more attention from men. Our nights out taught me there are many people out there who are willing to offer me kindness and affection with no strings attached. Mom always told me it would be hard to find a man who was interested in me because I was too short, my thighs were too thick, or my clothes weren't flattering enough. I'm learning that's not always true. There are men who find me attractive.

I have had some great boyfriends since moving out, and I found I really enjoy sex. However, some of my sexual proclivities tend to be less vanilla than my partners'. There's nothing wrong with that, it's simply a matter of . . . different strokes. I have come to accept that sexual compatibility is not something to hold out for. I want someone who will bang me like a screen door in a hurricane. Loud, hard, and often. Nothing too crazy, just passionate. I want to *feel* wanted by someone.

It feels good to dress up after living in sweats since Mom died. My ensemble tonight is made up of a flowy burgundy mini dress with ankle boots—a graduation gift from Micky. She, on the other hand, wears pieces that merge rocker with classy, and it always looks edgy and timeless. I admire how creative she is.

We open the door to the cocktail lounge and the warm air wraps around my body, inviting me in. The atmosphere is chic and sophisticated. It's styled like a contemporary arcade, featuring sleek pinball machines, exposed brick, and modern seating areas. It gives off an upscale, retro vibe. I walk by a woman holding a martini topped with a large dollop of cotton candy. *I'm abso-lutely getting one of those before we leave tonight.*

We found a spot at the bar but haven't ordered yet. That's okay, because we're gleefully passing the time by appreciating how attractive the bartender is at the other end. He mixes a drink for another customer as we admire his thick forearms, and rolled-up cuffs put his vivid tattoo sleeve on display. He's scruffy and rugged. His muscles flex as he mixes drinks in a copper cocktail shaker. There's just something about a tatted-up dude in a dress shirt. Neither of us can stop staring.

"Dinner and a show," I mutter.

"Goddamn," Micky drawls in agreement. "I bet that's what he looks like when he jacks off. Think his dick is as big as that cocktail shaker?"

I chuckle.

"Don't laugh, that man might be the one to end your dry spell so you can get your rocks off. I mean, look at him."

"Get my rocks off? Do people even say that anymore?"

"Shut up, you know what I mean. You still want me to order for you?"

Usually, Micky orders since she's the mixologist extraordinaire. *Mixologist is such a douchey word.* Her dream is to someday open a patisserie cocktail lounge mashup. It's so perfect for her. Most of the time, her drinks are better than the ones we get when we go out.

But then we would miss out on being able to appreciate fine specimens like this one.

"Sure, surprise me."

The bartender saunters toward us.

"What can I make for you ladies?"

There's a twinkle in her eye. *Shit, here we go.*

"We'll both have a Woody Creek martini, shaken hard—extra dirty."

She leans over to amplify her cleavage. *Rhinoceroses are less horny.*

"Coming right up," he says as he winks at her.

When he turns his back to grab the vodka, I rotate ninety degrees and judge her with a raised eyebrow.

"What?"

I scoff a laugh and shake my head, she absolutely knows what. The bartender makes our martinis and sets them in front of us.

"On the house."

We thank him, and he goes back to helping some of the other patrons at the bar.

"Nice work, killer. Cheers."

"To getting our rocks off!" she says.

I smile.

"To getting our rocks off."

———

We chat about school and work for a while. I graduated from the chef program early last spring and have been teaching private cooking lessons at clients' homes while I look for a restaurant opening. I ask about Micky's plans for her culinary practical—she graduates this coming spring—and I love listening to all her creative ideas for her patisserie program exam. Each student must complete a practical exam and serve their dishes to some of the top executive chefs in the area. Coming up with a menu is stressful, so I help her work through some of her plans. After we finish strategizing her petit fours, there's a lull in the conversation.

"Hey, so, I wanted to talk to you about something that happened at the funeral."

"If this is about me telling people your mom holds the world record for opening the most soda cans in under a minute . . ."

"It's not—what? Don't even tell me."

"Okay, I won't," she agrees as she takes a sip.

"I wanted to talk to you about some weird pictures I found."

I open my purse and pull out the two photographs to show her.

"Look at these and tell me what you see."

"Oh my God, is that you as a little kid?" she fawns. "You're so adorable!"

I shake my head, exasperated.

"No, Micky. Look!"

She peruses the photo for a few seconds.

"I'm not sure what I'm supposed to be looking for," she replies, glancing back and forth between the two. I pull out my phone and use the screen as a light to better view the images.

"See the leg? There's no birthmark there. I'm supposed to have one right there." I jab a finger into my thigh to further prove my point.

"Okay, and? These pictures are like twenty years old, cameras probably didn't pick up on details like that back then."

I huff and grab the other close-up picture and slap it down on the bar.

"What about this one?"

"Am I still supposed to be searching for a birthmark?"

"Look at the eyes."

"Okay . . ."

"Do you see it?" I ask wringing my hands.

"See what, babe? I'm sorry, you're going to have to spell it out for me."

"These eyes are brown." I point at the photo, then to my eyes, "Mine are gray, see?"

I'm trying not to act frantic, but these pictures have been bothering me for the last few days, and I can't hold it in anymore.

She pauses. "I see that. So, what are you saying?

You think you have a twin or something? Maybe it's someone else."

"I don't know. But see?" I flip the photo over. "*Julianne & Elizabeth*. It says it's me and Mom."

"It's a little weird, I guess. Where did you get this picture? Who took the photo? Maybe they know." She shrugs.

"I have no idea who took it, I just found it on the table and took it home because there was something off about it. It wasn't until I got home that I realized the eyes were a different color." I go on, "Besides, what am I supposed to do? Call up some relative I barely know and be like, 'Oh, hey, remember me? I stole your photos and now think I might have a body-snatcher situation on my hands. Can you tell me if I'm crazy or not?' That sounds ludicrous."

Micky is silent. I stare at her, waiting for her to say something or assure me I'm not, in fact, crazy.

"Have you ever thought maybe Julianne could be related to your birth parents? It kind of makes sense. I mean, she didn't adopt you from an agency, right? Your biological family must have known Julianne in some way to choose her to raise you."

Whoa. That never occurred to me. How have I not put that together before?

"I've got it!" she announces. "You should take one of those genetic genealogy test things! I took one last year. It gives you the names of other people you're

35

related to that also took the genetic test. Maybe there's a sibling or cousin or something."

"But I don't have a biological *sister,* and even if I did, why would she have a photo with my adoptive mom?"

"Exactly. Because maybe Julianne is a relative."

While bizarre, what she's saying adds up.

"I wouldn't forget having a twin, though. Shit, am I losing my mind?"

Micky takes a deep breath.

"Honestly, B"—she glances down at her martini on the bar top and twirls the stem between her fingers— "please don't take this the wrong way, but I think you've been under an incredible amount of stress, and you're starting to deal with a lot of issues and feelings that're coming up surrounding your mom's death. You've experienced a huge loss. Do you think it's possible you might be searching for something that isn't really there?" She winces.

Then she adds, "You know I love you, and I'm not saying that you're wrong, you very well may be on to something, but this is a little out-there. Don't you think?" She puts her arm around my back and lays her head on my shoulder.

I sigh and pick up my photos, reluctantly stuffing them back in my purse.

"Yeah, you're probably right. I just can't shake my gut feeling that something is weird about this."

She sits back up. "Then, by all means, you need to go after it and get answers. What do you need me to do? I will support you any way that I can."

I pause, wondering if I'm just looking for something that's not really there.

"What's the name of that genetic test again?"

FOUR

Birdie

Six weeks later . . .

"Ughhh!" I have to develop a new lesson plan and menu for my clients. I hate coming up with menus. There are too many options and not enough structure. I have a problematic client I wish I had never met. She wants me to draw up *another* twelve-course chef's menu—the first two she turned down—for a home dinner party. Twelve courses at a dinner party are ridiculous. Even as a chef, I think it's pretentious. I should refer her to someone else, but I'm cursed with being a people pleaser.

I crumple up the paper and chuck it against the wall. I'll just serve them a sack of dicks—they can take it or leave it. Twelve courses of bagged-up schlong.

"Chow down, motherfuckers!" I shout to the empty room.

I'm surrounded by so many crumpled balls of notepad paper it looks like a hailstorm ripped through here. Yelling at imaginary people is my cue to take a break and step away. It's much nicer outside. The fresh air helps to clear my head and shake off the anxiety. Lately, my brain has been all over the place. Micky was right when she suggested I might be going through an especially rough time in the grieving process. Clearly, my lack of sleep must have manifested into strange delusions about my family. Thankfully, I'm getting more rest these days.

My phone dings with a new email from Stellar Genetics. They have my results. I follow the link they give me to access the breakdown of my ancestry. It says most of my family originated from Europe. Wow, I'm almost 50 percent Irish. Looks like St. Patrick's Day is about to get real crunk.

I click the tab marked *Relatives*. This was a bad idea.

Ken Hayes - Paternal parent / 100%
Lori Hayes - Maternal parent / 100%
Jack Hayes - Full sibling / 100%

Nope, not dealing with that right now.

I close the website and stuff my phone back in my

pocket, pretending I never even saw their names. The few memories I have of my old childhood are all happy ones. But clearly, there was more going on than my naive six-year-old brain could understand. Being sent away broke me in a way they will never know. I tortured myself in my youth, trying to understand why they did it. Was it because I got car sick and threw up in the new family van when we went on vacation? Did I ask for too many presents on Christmas? My adoptive mom said I cried all the time when I was little; maybe I was too much to handle. She also liked to remind me I was lucky to be adopted and not in the foster care system. I'll be honest, there were many days where I would have gladly taken my chances. I was told over and over my birth parents cared enough to choose a good mom like Julianne—but did they really? Or maybe they knew the same Julianne everyone else at the funeral knew too.

Every few months, I would think about trying to find my older brother, Jack, but nothing good will come from that discovery. They either sent him away too and he's as damaged as I am, or he was chosen over me. Neither result in a happy ending, so why poke at an open wound?

———

I'm working in Mom's bedroom to clean out some items in her closet. She had a lot of shoes. None fit me, though, so they will need to be donated along with her clothes. I don't want any of her things, they taunt me—a constant reminder they were chosen over me time and time again. I set aside a few items for women's shelters, but the rest of the stuff can find a new home at a donation drop-off. Next come her purses, but before I begin, I need to clear a much bigger area. I drag the heavy plastic garbage bags of clothes out of the walk-in closet and into the bedroom.

Even on my tiptoes, I can barely reach the purses on the high wire shelving that wraps around the small space. I have to jump for most, but the ones with shoulder straps hanging down are within reach. There's got to be at least fifty purses here. As I go through the contents, the small closet fills with the scent of old lipstick and leather. Most are empty. She kept them in mint condition, each has been carefully cared for over the years—because that's what you do when you love something.

As I run my fingers over a beaded purse with complex stitching, I reach inside and pull out a small stack of papers. I'm about to set it down to go through later—along with the other random things I've found—when I spot my name on the paper. It's my birth certificate . . . *but it's not.* It says the birth mother's name is Julianne Fournier. What is this stuff? Two hospital bracelets fall from between the papers. One is teeny with my name on it. The other has her name. None of this makes sense. More documents with my name are paperclipped: hospital discharge papers and medical history. There's no way these are mine. This Elizabeth had her tonsils removed. I don't have to look in the mirror to know mine are still there.

Who is this other child? My heart races and dizziness sets in. Or . . . am *I* the other child? If these papers belong to another Elizabeth Fournier, then who the fuck am I?

There's one place I can look.

My fingers fly across my screen and open the Stellar Genetics website again. I click on my relative matches and look over their names. Ken and Lori Hayes. Those are the names that *should* be listed on my birth certificate. They're the ones who abandoned me. My hands are sweaty as I look over their names. Am I ready to go down this rabbit hole? I'm not, but the mystery will eat me alive, so I have to. I enter their names into the Google search bar. The very first result is a website, BringHomeBridget.com. Shit, that's my old name . . . How could I forget? My finger hovers over the link before clicking it.

Staring back at me is a full-screen photo of myself as a child. I drop my phone, and it clatters to the floor. Scrambling to pick it up, I read as fast as my eyes allow.

Name: Bridget Lynn Hayes
Birthdate: 02–14–1994
Missing since: 10–19–2000
Last known location: Niagara Falls, NY
Hair: Brown
Eyes: Gray
Height / Weight at disappearance: 43 inches / 45 pounds

Bridget Hayes, age 6, was last seen on October 19, 2000, while on vacation in Niagara Falls, New York with her family. Members of her family last remember seeing Bridget at approximately 1:30 p.m. near the Observation Tower Visitor Center. She was wearing a tan and orange sweater with blue denim jeans and a light pink coat. She also may be going by the nickname "Birdie." The Hayes family resides in Chanhassen, Minnesota. The second picture shows Bridget's age-progressed to 29 years.

If you have any information regarding her whereabouts or disappearance, or if you believe you were at Niagara Falls around that time, please contact Tips@BringHomeBridget.com

That missing girl is . . . all the information and clues leading me to this moment slam into me. The strange pictures from the funeral. The lack of family nearby. The reason I was never allowed to go on trips. Why I couldn't talk about my family. The strained relationship with my "mom"— Julianne was not my mother, and that's the last time I'll use that word to talk about her.

And I'm two years older? According to this, I'm almost thirty! And it looks like I'm from the United States. I always assumed my biological family was in Canada somewhere. I suppose at age six I wouldn't know the difference. If I'm from the United States, do I have citizenship? I click the link for more pictures of the missing girl and scroll through various photos of me.

My fingers halt as a family portrait of the four of us pops up. That was my family. My hands shake and my stomach tightens—my real mom and dad. I tuck my knees to my chest and stare at the photo for what feels like hours. More memories come to me. Being tucked in at night, running errands together, playing with my brother, Jack, and another boy, but I don't remember his name. It's a part of my mind I've had locked up for a long time, but looking at these photos is triggering these little flashbacks of my old life, frozen in time.

What am I supposed to do now? Was I abducted? This is crazy, right? How could she have gotten away with it for so long? There's a part of me that wants to stuff the papers back in the purse and walk away. It feels very *red pill-blue pill*. I've just had a bomb dropped on me, and now I need to figure out what to do. I need to get the hell out of here.

———

I can't sleep. I lie in bed and toss and turn. I know the choice I have to make, ignoring this isn't even an option. A cruel thought pops into my head: what if this was all staged? If they wanted to send me away, they could have made it look like an abduction or disappearance. It removes any blame or judgment from friends and family. It would allow them to ship me off to Julianne and still look like doting parents that miss their child. For all I know, they told people I fell into Niagara Falls. There's a chance this website was made to make it *appear* like people are looking for me, but in reality, no one is searching and they don't want me to be found.

Okay. Hypothetically, if Julianne was a "kidnapper," why would she steal a kid to simply raise them? What was her motive? It's not like she enjoyed children. Besides, aren't kidnappers usually murderers and pedophiles? She wasn't either of those, she just had mood swings and a temper. Was there a ransom and my parents chose not to pay it? Or maybe they couldn't afford to take care of me and then Julianne was stuck with me? But then where is the *real* Elizabeth Fournier? I Google her name but find nothing but my Facebook page. Everything I search leads back to me. None of this is adding up.

Should I email Lori and Ken? What if I show up at their house and they slam the door in my face? I couldn't handle being rejected twice by my biological family. Or they could be mad I didn't find them sooner.

I go back to my internet sleuthing. I find a few archived newspaper articles from the early 2000s about me being a possible victim of an abductor, two more articles covering anniversaries of my disappearance. If this is all a show, they're damn good at selling tickets.

I log into my bank account. Just over five thousand dollars. How much is that in USD? I do the conversion and check airline prices. It's enough to get me there and back, with a few nights at a hotel, and still leave me with enough to cover rent for the next month or so. I could go and do some reconnaissance. Now that I have their full names, it isn't hard to find their address and know where they work. They still live on Briar Lane.

Maybe they have regrets? I think I'm a nice enough person, perhaps they would want to have coffee, and I could get answers to why they chose not to keep me. I do the calculations in my head, everything seems to pan out. And if they are looking for me, it's only a matter of time before they locate me. As soon as they check their Stellar Genetics account, they'll see they have a new match. I'd rather have the upper hand and find them first. Wait—am I really doing this? Is this actually happening? Things like this don't happen in real life!

One more thought passes through my mind before I fall asleep: I need to find Julianne's journals.

FIVE

Birdie

I've flipped this apartment upside down. They aren't here, which only leaves one place for them to be. The journals must be in the storage space in the basement. I went down there once, and it was like a pack rat's paradise. But I want those journals. She scribbled something in them every day, they must hold some answers to what went down. Fuck it, I'm calling Micky.

———

"So, I brought some snacks and two bottles of wine. You know, better to be safe than sober."

"Ever the Girl Guide . . ."

"What's a Girl Guide?"

"Canada Girl Scouts."

She ignores my reply as she sets the bag on the countertop. When she faces me again, her eyebrows shoot up and she digs her hands into her hair.

"God! I still can't believe this! You were right the whole time! If you hadn't followed your gut—I mean, thank God you didn't listen to me! This is the craziest story ever. You're probably famous."

"Hoo-ray," I deadpan, swinging my finger in a circle. This is not the kind of famous anybody wants to be.

"Tell me again why you won't just email them?"

"I feel like I'd be showing my hand. Like it was me crawling back to them. If I can find them before they find me, I can control the situation more. I know, it's stupid, but I just couldn't handle more disappointment."

"If you did email, what would you write?"

"*Sup, fam. It's ya girl, Anastasia,*" I say, exaggerating my voice.

I find two clean glasses and pour the wine. Generously.

"Oh, she's a party girl," Micky says, observing the volume in the wineglass. "Okay. So, these journals . . ."

"I gotta find 'em. They must be in this building somewhere, and they aren't in the apartment. That only leaves basement storage. Julianne was always writing in them. There's got to be at least a dozen or so. I've turned this apartment upside down and can't find anything. But I don't want to dig through the storage space on my own."

"Julianne, huh?" She picked up on me not calling her mom.

"Yeah. Julianne feels more appropriate."

"Hell yeah." She smiles and clinks her glass to mine. "Well, come on, Nancy Drew, where's the flashlight?"

———

When I push open the heavy metal door to the basement, it smells of old cardboard and damp concrete. Flickering fluorescent lights illuminate the rows and rows of what appear to be eight-foot cubes made up of 2x4s and chicken wire. It's fucking creepy down here.

Our footsteps echo as we walk through the aisles.

". . . 23 . . . 24 . . . 25 . . . 26. Here we are."

It's packed full, the spindly wire walls are practically bursting. I knew it was bad, but this is some next-level shit.

Micky blows out a surprised whistle. "So, when were you going to tell me that Julianne was single-handedly keeping The Shopping Channel alive?"

"Right? I had no idea it had gotten this out of control."

"It's okay. That's why I'm here. You ready for this?"

I take another gulp of my wine—thankful I brought it with me—and set it down outside the chicken wire door marked with a big 26 above it. I put my key into the flimsy lock and drag the door open with a loud screech, careful not to disturb the pile of haphazardly stacked boxes on the other side.

"Lovely," I comment as I take in how big of a job this is.

"What should I be looking for?"

"Books that have writing in them."

She stares at me for a moment before saying dryly, "Oh, thank God you said that—I've never seen a journal before!"

"You asked!"

"I was hoping you had some clue as to which of these boxes they might be in." She holds her arm out and swishes it around like she's showing off fabulous prizes on a game show.

"Yeah, this is more of a start-at-the-top-and-work-our-way-down situation."

She nods.

"To the hunt," she toasts, raising her glass.

"To the hunt."

———

"I want you to know this is the worst scavenger hunt I've ever been on," Micky declares, lifting another box.

It's been two hours, and we've barely made it through half of the boxes. The little walkway outside the wired-off "room" is filling up. There is so much junk in here. I can donate most of it, though, nobody needs three Flowbee haircutting systems. Shit, nobody needs one Flowbee haircutting system.

These shouldn't be donated. They should be incinerated.

"I've reached the Christmas decorations. Think they could be in here?" she asks.

"Maybe? But I doubt it."

She pops off the big plastic lid and pushes around the contents of the container.

"Nope, just a big box full of nutcrackers," she confirms.

"Name of your sex tape," I mumble, closing another box and pushing it aside.

"Pfft, I wish. How about Halloween decorations?"

"You can give it a shot bu—wait! We didn't have Halloween decorations. Julianne thought it was a stupid holiday for kids."

"Wow, that woman must have been a riot at parties." She grunts as she pries the lid open on the corner. "Oh, shit . . . Jackpot."

Ripping off the rest of the lid, she tosses it onto the pile of unopened boxes. She hauls it out of the storage space so the shadows no longer obstruct it.

"These have to be them."

I crouch down and pull the hardback books from the box. There's one for every year since 1976. I pull out everything from 1992 to the most recent year and set them aside. I can't carry more than twenty journals anyhow.

"I'm going to take this box up."

"Sounds good. You know what this means, right? You have to go."

"I know."

We pack up all the other boxes sitting in the walkway and pile them back into the tiny space. There has to be some service that can come and clean this stuff out for me. It takes forty minutes to pack everything back in there like some horrid game of *Tetris*.

April 7, 2000

All Elizabeth ever talks about is how pretty Miss Tiffany is. Is that woman even qualified to teach? She isn't very intelligent. I could do a better job myself. The few times I've met that woman, she was nothing special. She was plain, borderline homely. She's a preschool teacher. That's enough to tell you she made poor choices in life. I live in luxury, and she's wiping noses all day. I have made so many sacrifices in my life for Elizabeth. How does she repay me? By giving her teacher all the attention. If this Tiffany only knew what an ungrateful, difficult child she had in her classroom everyday, maybe she wouldn't spoil her so much.

August 9, 2000

She knew how much I hated that, but she wouldn't stop. I snapped. Motherhood is nothing like what they make it seem like in magazines. Children are rude and irresponsible. Untidy, even now, I'm cleaning up this mess that she caused. On top of that, she was clumsy and got hurt all the time. I must have told her to look where she was going twenty times a day, but it wasn't enough. I did everything I could. Miss Tiffany called and asked why she won't be returning to school. I told her I could do a better job of schooling that child. At least I'll never have to hear about how pretty Miss Tiffany is anymore.

"Pretzels or cookies?" The flight attendant pulls me from my thoughts.

"Huh? Oh, um, pretzels, please."

"Anything to drink?" she asks, handing me two packs of pretzels.

"Ginger ale?"

She fills a plastic cup with ice and opens the tab on the can, and it releases a satisfying hiss. The bubbly drink glugs into the cup, and she hands it to me.

"Thank you," I give an appreciative smile, and she nods, moving on to the person sitting next to me.

I take a sip and set the cup back on my tray with shaky hands. My first plane ride and I'm crossing into the United States to Minneapolis to meet my biological family. The only thing keeping my mind off the nerves is reading these journals. I've been tearing through them page-by-page. But after the last one, the hair on the back of my neck stood up. I feel sick—I have to turn these in to somebody. I would have done it before I left, but I didn't realize just how nefarious their contents were. I am scared to keep reading, but I need to find out what happened. Most pages are filled with narcissistic ramblings, but I've dog-eared the pages I think will be helpful to the police.

My life is spiraling out of control. One minute I'm planning a funeral for my "mom" and the next I'm finding out I am likely a missing person. After the last forty-eight hours, I knew I had to get out of Vancouver for a few days. Everything I thought I knew was a lie, it feels like I'm stuck in an alternate universe. Normally, I'm not impulsive, but what's the point of playing it safe? It's never done me any good. I've decided that whatever happens, happens. Might as well live on the edge a little.

August 11, 2000

I've decided to landscape the backyard. There will be a new patio, just like the one featured in this month's home decor digest. Francine is going to be so jealous. The workers have been leveling out the dirt all morning, and they need to hurry up and pour the slab. I have no idea what is taking so long. In the meantime, I've just bought the most beautiful collectible on The Shopping Channel. It reminds me of Elizabeth. She's my little angel.

After traveling for five hours, my nerves are shot. I tried everything to distract myself from thinking about what's to come. I can't stomach another journal entry right now. I think she murdered a child. It sounds wild, but based on her writing, I'm lucky to be alive. Regardless of how this trip goes, I need to turn these in to the authorities. How could I have been so naïve all this time? My life has never felt more out of control, like one of those nightmares where you know you're dreaming but you can't wake up. I want to wake up.

When the plane lands, I stop in the airport washroom. I need a minute to gather myself. The landing was jarring, and the anxiety has my mind racing. Thinking is near impossible with all the toilets flushing, hand dryers whirring, and the clickety-clack of suitcases being rolled over tile. I give myself one last look in the mirror, gather my jacket and carry-on, and head out. I can do this.

Nothing I do can prepare me for what's to come tomorrow when I see my former family. Nothing tells you how to react in these moments, and the anticipation has been pure torture, like waiting for a daunting punishment. But I'm here for answers.

———

Wow. I let out a whistle after entering my posh hotel suite. They accidentally booked the room I had reserved to someone else, so now I get to stay in a significantly upgraded room. I've never stayed in a hotel like this before, but I am guessing this is one of the nice ones—nothing like the Rosebud Motel. I'm grateful I decided to stay someplace a little classy, I'll gladly accept the extra pampering right now. And if things go belly-up tomorrow, I want a comfortable, safe space to return to.

Letting go of my suitcase, it tips over behind me as I walk into the bedroom. This place might be bigger than my apartment. I open my arms wide and trust-fall onto the fluffy duvet cloud that is my king-size bed. *This* is living. This bad boy is massive. How many times can I barrel roll across the bed before falling off? I lie on the edge, tuck my arms in, and roll to the other side, over and over until I fall off the other side—*thump.* Five times. Shedding my travel clothes, I climb into the bed, a nap is calling my name.

Five whole-ass hours later, my eyes open from one of the most restful sleeps I've had in over a month. It ran right through lunch and dinner. My stomach is growling, and the minibar is not an option because there's no way in hell you'll catch me paying twelve dollars for a pack of peanut M&Ms.

After a quick shower, a little primping, and some fresh clothes, I'm feeling confident enough to ask for a table for one. Why is there shame around eating by yourself at a restaurant? But if I'm visiting the city, it would be doing a disservice to myself to not indulge at least a little. And it's a hotel, I'm sure businesspeople dine alone here all the time.

I order a smaller entrée, being mindful of the budget I have set for myself. I've got a bit left over, so I can spend it at the bar afterward. If there's ever been a time to self-medicate with a drink, it's now. I find myself oddly paranoid I'll accidentally run into a family member. The chances are slim, there's nothing to worry about. Still, my birth parents are only thirty minutes away—and Jack is twenty minutes outside the city. I internet stalked him too. He has a family now. I wonder if he thinks I was abducted too? Would they tell him they gave me away?

My thoughts are suspended when the hottest guy I've ever seen passes by my table. *Hold up.* This man is more attractive than any one person should be allowed. He's handsome as hell with his trimmed beard and thick locks begging me to dig my fingers into them. He walked in from the attached bar, wearing the most bright and genuine smile. It's confident and sexy. Some men think they have to look broody to convey strength, but this guy shows no hesitance to express enthusiasm as he speaks with the restaurant host.

Before long, he heads back into the bar, I keep my head down as he walks by, I don't trust myself not to blush at seeing him up close. I finish my meal, which was delicious, and pay the bill. I'm almost positive I've seen the guy from the bar look over at me. A drink sounds lovely, and I'm more than ready to let go of all the stress I've carried the last few days. For now, I'm going to forget about the journals, the genetic test, the website, everything. Tomorrow will be hard. Most likely the hardest day of my life. So, for tonight, I'm going to live in the moment and let myself enjoy one last night of normalcy before my world collapses around me. I might even ask that guy if he wants to come up to my room later. After the week I've had, what's the worst that could happen? He says no? Big fucking deal. I'll move on to the next hottest guy. Even if he rejects me, it will still be the least of my worries.

I grab my clutch purse and move into the dimly lit space. It's more cocktail lounge than bar. Dividing the room is a long fire table that matches the one behind the bartenders. Private upholstered sofas and booths wrap around some of the back corners, and the rest of the room is peppered with high-top tables. It's dark and seductive, the kind of place Micky would love.

My eyes are pulled to the back where some women whoop and toss back shots of clear alcohol. If the hot pink penis tiara is any indication, I'd say their bachelorette party is in full swing. Little celebrations seem to be happening all over. The deeper I go toward the bar, the more I notice people are here to party. This is the perfect environment to help take my mind off the present.

In the corner, is a booth seating a jacked group of men, which is where the guy with the gorgeous smile is sitting. He's still here. Various beautiful women are draped on their arms, they look like supermodels. The women are flirting their little hearts out, and honestly, good for them, Lord knows I'd be doing the same if I was in their shoes.

First, I'll get a drink to take the edge off. I'm naturally on the shy side, so some liquid confidence will help build up the courage to meet someone. Generally, I wait for men to buy me a drink, but tonight, I'm willing to go outside of my comfort zone if it means I can bag a man as fine as that one. Most people are at high-top tables and booths, but the bar top is not packed, so that's where I find my seat.

SIX

LONAN

We wrapped up two back-to-back games in Anaheim and San Jose. We won both, but not by much—which is bullshit. We can play better than we did, considering how poorly Anaheim has been skating this season. Back-to-backs already suck, but when you factor in all the traveling, hotels, and press boxes, the fatigue piles up quickly.

Even our star wingers, Sully and Banks, were skating like shit. Passes weren't connecting, and we looked sloppy. And it takes a lot for me to admit Banks's puck-handling skills in the first place. Personally, I think he's an absolute tool. We call him Banks because his last name is Teller and he comes from money. Serious money. There's nothing wrong with having rich parents, but he's a trust-fund baby with a bad attitude. Last night he got in a fight with some local

San Jose fan that called him a "cake eater." Naturally, he threatened to beat the guy with his money clip and then he had a make-out session with the man's wife for good measure. He practically needs a babysitter when we go out nowadays. One of these times, he will piss off the wrong person and it will bite him in the ass.

Sully, on the other hand, is our golden boy. I've got no issue shouting his praises. He's the poster child for hockey captain. Nordic, blond hair, tall, chiseled jaw, and nice as hell. He always plays good cop. It's what makes him a strong leader on the team. He's got a great rapport with the refs, the coaches, the staff, and his teammates. However, outside of studying the game, he doesn't do much else. We all agree he could use a better work-life balance. He lives for this team and is fiercely protective of it. Whenever a fight breaks out, he's one of the first ones to have your back. On paper, he doesn't seem like the most riveting man, but looks can be deceiving. There's a tough side to Sullivan. But he's one of those secretly dangerous types—the kind of person with a presence other men don't want to fuck with. I've never seen him lose control, and I want it to stay that way.

We've been taxiing around the tarmac for the last forty-five minutes. I stand to stretch and crack my neck. Everyone is getting cabin fever—pun intended. My teammates with wives want to get home, and everybody else wants to party.

"Who's up for a beer after we get off this goddamn merry-go-round?" Jonesy groans.

A few people cheer.

"Burke, you in?"

"I dunno, this trip was brutal. I'm pretty beat," I answer truthfully.

"What the fuck, man? You never come out with us anymore."

"It's the bunnies—I need a break. Same old shit every time. It's not exciting anymore. I'm bored."

"Oh, fuck, he's turning into Conway."

Barrett Conway was one of the biggest sluts on the team until a few years ago. He still goes out, but it's rare he takes anybody home. He met some puck bunny a few years ago and got hung up on her. Then she dipped out, and I guess it fucked with him or something. I don't know what went down. Sometimes I think he goes out with us just in case she shows up again. It sounds pathetic, and he'd never admit it, but every time he's scanning the room, it's obvious he's looking for someone specific.

"I'm not turning into Conway."

"Please. You wish, asshole," he says, turning around in his seat.

I laugh. "It's nothing on you, bud. I'm just saying the difference between you and me is that you fell for your bunny, and I'm trying to get away from all mine."

"I didn't fall for her, but she was cool. Just wish I

would have gotten her number. I think she said she had family in Phoenix. Maybe she moved. Would have been nice to have a little pussy on the side when we play Arizona." He smiles, his big white shit-eating grin. "And at least I still go out. You've just been sitting at home for the last couple of months."

Next, Bishop pipes up, "Burke, you gotta get your dick wet. Jonesy said he's tired of giving you handjobs in the locker room." He shouts the last part toward the front of the plane.

"Jonesy wishes." I chuckle.

Jones whips around in his seat. "Yeah, man, my fucking hands are tired." He mimes like he's got arthritis. "Why don't you do us all a favor and find someone else to cover for me tonight, eh?"

Conway chuckles but levels his gaze with mine. "Look, whatever you do, get her number."

"Yeah, yeah."

I should go home after we get off the plane. Pick up a couple burgers, watch a movie, jerk off, and call it a night. But the last time I went out for a beer was when I met up with Jack over a month ago. I can still go out tonight with the guys and *not* take a girl home, I suppose. However . . . it has been a long time since I got laid.

———

By the time I get back to my place and change out of my travel clothes, I'm ready to let loose. Fuck it. I've been celibate for almost eight weeks—that's long enough. Two months ago, that would have seemed like a lifetime. I throw on jeans and a black Henley and call it good. I'm not going to work too hard, but if it happens, I'm not going to say no either.

I don't know why the boys wanted to come to this hotel bar tonight. We always go to Top Shelf. They know us there, we have our own section, and it's closer to my condo. Whatever, a change of scenery might do the body good. While pulling into a parking spot, Banks hands his keys to his Porsche to the valet. I roll my eyes. Hope the other guys are up for watching him tonight, because I'm off the clock. The rest of the team better be here, so I don't have to make small talk with him the whole time. He's a douchebag and cocky as hell. I get the feeling he thinks he's more important than our other players, but I'm probably "projecting my insecurities," as my therapist would say.

I press the lock button on the key fob as I shove my keys into my pocket. Inside the bar, the guys have taken over the corner booth—generally, the corner spots are the only ones that fit us and our large group. It's a nice cocktail lounge but very different from the hockey bar where we're regulars. I get the allure of this place. It's no surprise everyone who came out tonight is single.

These bars offer the perfect environment for picking up women.

After I slide into the oversized booth, it doesn't take long for the server to come over and take drink orders. We order a few rounds of beers and relax after the long flight, and just as I suspected, the bunnies start hopping over, one of them climbing right into my lap.

Usually, I would happily let her sit here, but tonight I find the lack of respect for my personal space annoying. I slide her off to sit next to me instead. She introduces herself as Shoshanna. She's hot, but it's not doing anything for me. *Why am I not into this?* Shit, maybe I am turning into Conway.

Opposite the entry doors is the hotel restaurant. I still haven't eaten anything since the plane. As soon as I see the dining area, the smell of food registers in my brain. I need food. I scoot Shoshanna out of the booth so I can get something to eat. I walk into the connected restaurant and place an order for a burger with one of the seating hosts and then I place a to-go order for a few hours from now. Nothing better than going home with a bag of food after having a couple of beers. Besides, my fridge is practically empty at home. I really should go grocery shopping more often.

As I turn to head back into the bar, my gaze catches on something that looks even better than a burger. *Damn.* There's a hot-as-hell brunette, and she's eating alone. She looks familiar, but I can't place it. Shit, have

I slept with her before and don't remember? Nah, there's no way I would forget a woman that looks like that. Besides, she doesn't look like a groupie. My feet almost stop me at her table, but she doesn't lift her head, so I keep moving.

I order another beer when I get back to my table and kick myself for not asking that woman to join me. Before long, my burger arrives, along with a few orders of fried appetizers for the table—I'm not that big of an asshole that I'd order food for myself and no one else. I scarf my entire meal down in a matter of minutes. Now I'm ready to for fun. Perhaps I was hangry earlier. Though I'm not any more attracted to Shoshanna on a full stomach than when I had an empty one.

A bunch of the guys have their hands full, so to speak. Shoshanna hasn't given up, and she's putting on the heat now. She invites her friend over because they "do everything together" and says neither of them have ever had a threesome. I have to choke back a laugh. She's practically a goddamn three-musketeer. I know this because 1) She's a shit liar, and 2) When I was taking a piss, Strassburg, our goalie, told me he took both her and another girl home during preseason.

The conversation with these two women is dull. They keep steering it back to going back to my place, and it's clear that they only want a hit and run. I should be into it—typically, this horse and pony show would work for me, but it's just not cutting it tonight. Am I tired? I don't want to bring down the vibe if the other guys are enjoying themselves. Finishing my beer, I throw down some cash. I turn my head to peek into the restaurant to see if that woman is still there, but her table is now empty. *That sucks.*

As I reach for my jacket, she walks in. That's what I'm talking about. Now, *her,* I'm interested in. I need to shoot my shot before some other asshole beats me to it, so I head to the bar where she's taken a seat.

"What can I get started for you?" the bartender asks her.

"Do you have any specials going on?"

Damn. She has this sexy raspy voice that is going to haunt me for the rest of my life if I don't talk to her. I imagine her using it to say my name.

"Depends on what you like?" he replies.

Here's my chance.

"Make her a Bootlegger," I interject.

"You got it, Burke," the tender answers. Shit, I hope he didn't just give away my identity. Maybe I'll get lucky and she'll just think I know the bartender because we're friends, and not because I'm a defenseman for the Minnesota Lakes. If I can get a shot at having a normal conversation with her, that would be ideal. I am so tired of fake flattery.

"You from around here or just visiting?" I ask.

"Just visiting. This is my first time in Minnesota. What about you?" she asks.

Please, please, please, don't let this one know who I am. Not this one.

"Local."

Even sitting on a barstool, I tower over her.

"Nice. So, what is in a Bootlegger?" she asks, tapping the bar top.

"Honestly, I don't know everything in it," I say. "But it's the official drink of Minnesota, so it's sort of a requirement when you cross the state line. Imagine if lemonade and a mojito had a baby."

"So, is that your job? You're the local that's been assigned to ensure I consume the Bootlegger upon arrival?"

"Something like that." I smile.

And with that, the bartender sets the drink in front of her. It looks a little fruity and tropical. December generally isn't Bootlegger season, but they are tasty year-round.

"This is the state drink of Minnesota? I would have expected something a little more . . . Canadian."

"Hand to God," I say, holding up my right hand. While I do that, I check her left hand. *No ring.*

She takes a sip, and her eyebrows pop up.

"Damn."

"Right?" I smile, pleased that she likes it. So far, so good.

Behind me, the guys are calling for me. Can't they see I'm working on something? *Worst wingmen ever.*

"I, um, I think your buddies are trying to get your attention." She nods in their direction.

"Yup, they are." But I pay them no mind and don't take my gaze off her. She's even more stunning up close. Full pouty lips, huge gray eyes—there's something familiar about her eyes but I can't place it. They are hauntingly beautiful. Beyond that, she's petite and curvy. Great smile too. I try to focus on her sparkling eyes and smile, but my brain wants to spend more time checking out her body.

"What do you do for a living?" I nonchalantly move my barstool a little closer to hers and a faint blush spreads to her cheeks. She's confident but has a touch of wariness that is so refreshing.

"I'm a chef, I teach mostly private classes. You?"

"Interesting. That actually works really well for me because I suck at cooking."

I don't answer her question, but hope she doesn't notice.

"That's impossible. Nobody sucks at cooking. If you can read, you can cook. What's the best thing you can make?"

"Peanut butter and jelly sandwich."

She covers her mouth with faux shock. "Oh my God, I didn't realize you were illiterate. I'm so sorry."

Add sense of humor to her list of attributes. I suck my teeth at her flirty insult. "Pretty good, Gray. Pretty good."

"Gray?"

"Eyes." I point to my eyes, then to hers. "You have pretty eyes."

That time, she definitely blushes, and I have to bite my bottom lip to keep from kissing hers.

"Wow. I wasn't aware we were in nickname territory already. Does that mean I get to give you one?" she asks.

"Of course. Whatcha got?"

"Oh, I'm going to need a little bit of time. Choosing a nickname is an enormous responsibility." She tries to look stern by hardening her features.

"That's true. I'm glad you're taking it so seriously. You don't think I was too hasty coming up with yours, do you?"

She takes another sip of her drink and gazes up thoughtfully. "No, it's brilliant, actually. I mean, it's giving you a lot to play around with. I'll be disappointed if you don't work it into some cheap Fifty Shades references before the end of the night."

"Oh, I might be able to do you one better if you play your cards right." I wink and take a drink of my beer.

Jonesy yells out something about handjobs, and I roll my eyes. This time, I look in his direction with an expression that, I hope, conveys *fuck off very much* as obviously as I intend it to. The drunk hollering doesn't cease, so I hold up my index finger behind me.

"Is that so?" she replies.

"I mean . . ." I shrug. "How about I give you my number, and you can text me if you decide you want to find out."

"Sure."

She hands her phone over for me to add myself as a contact. I send myself a text message to make sure I have her number. *Conway would be so proud.*

"I've got to get back to my table, but I hope I hear from you later."

"It was nice chatting."

She says it so sweetly I wonder if I've misread the room. Doesn't matter. I'm laying it out there. It's up to her to decide what to do with it.

"You too." I wink, and it earns me a sexy smile that eases the hesitation from a second ago.

When I get back to my table with the boys, I make sure the server knows to add her drink to my tab. She stays to finish her cocktail, but the next time I glance up, she's gone. A heavy dose of disappointment settles in the pit of my stomach. Flirting with her tonight was energizing and fun. For the last couple years, any banter with a woman was such a chore. But tonight, it was as if she and I existed in this little bubble together. She awakened something that's been dormant for a long time. Passion? That can't be it.

I want this girl. Bad. At least I've got her number. I could always text. I'll reach out tomorrow and see if she wants to grab coffee or dinner. I know she's on vacation, but I travel enough that my odds of seeing her again aren't beyond reason. I open my text messages so I can save her as a contact. I didn't ask for her name for fear she would ask for mine, which is why I saved myself in her phone as Hot Guy From The Bar. Under *Contact Name*, I type *Gray*.

"Your date leave?" Conway asks.

"Yeah. But I'm really fucking glad I got her number." I waggle my phone in my hand.

He smiles as if he's relieved someone else finally grasps what he's been trying to explain to us for the last couple of years. None of us could understand a woman, much less a bunny, holding that kind of space, but I'm understanding some of his behavior lately.

"When you meet someone that makes you feel something again, it hits different," he says.

It really does.

Less than ten minutes later, my phone vibrates.

> Gray: Hot Guy From The Bar, eh?

A smile explodes onto my face. *There's my girl.*

> Me: I wanted to make sure you knew it was me. 😊

74

Gray: Actually . . . you've been re-saved as PB&J. 😬

> Me: Lol perfect. Likely the only time I'll be remembered for my culinary skills.

> Me: Did you already go home? I was hoping I could at least say goodnight.

Gray: I'm staying at the hotel. Wanna come up?

Gray: You don't have to say goodnight.

For once, I didn't see that coming.

> Me: You think you can handle the 50 Shades of PB&J?

Gray: PenisBalls&Jizz?

What the fuck? And yes, please.

> Me: You're disgusting.

> Me: Wanna get married?

Gray: Room 804

Fuck, this girl is cool. And what's better, I'm fairly positive she doesn't know who I am. I've hit the lottery! It's a completely organic hookup with no pretenses. I check myself in the bathroom and grab a few mints from the restaurant before I head up to her room. It's so unusual for me to feel nervous. In the elevator, I select her floor, lighting up the beautiful round eight button. This feels like an early Christmas present, though I didn't do anything to deserve it this year. I step off the elevator and start down her hallway.

I told myself I would stop sleeping around and find something more stable. But what's more stable than actually liking who you fuck? Baby steps are still steps. I don't even care if we just hang out and talk all night. I'll have a good time either way. When was the last time I said that about a woman? I can't remember.

804. Here we go. I reach out to knock but stop half an inch short of the door. This is unlike my typical hotel hookups—if that's even what this is. Do I know how to *just* hang out with a woman I'm attracted to? If she makes a move on me, there's going to be nothing to hold me back. I open my wallet and check for a condom. All set.

I knock twice.

When she opens the door, I already know I'm done for. She's in thin pajama pants and a white shirt that is nearly see-through. No bra. I'm putting my money on hookup rather than hangout.

"Well, look who it is," she purrs, opening the door wider for me.

"Hey." It comes out deeper than I intend. My sex voice is activated the second I see her peaked nipples through her shirt.

"Nice PJs." I bite my lip. *So nice.*

"Thanks. Hope you don't mind that I changed."

"Not at all." I enter her hotel room and am instantly impressed with its size. "This is a big suite for one person."

"Isn't it! I got a free upgrade because they booked my room to someone else." She runs over to the doorway of what I assume is the main bedroom and points inside.

"You can roll over five times before falling off the bed—I checked. Well, you're probably more in the three-to-four-rolls range. Do you want a water?"

I can't help but chuckle at how adorable her nervous rambling is. This is wonderfully different. If I was with the women from downstairs, they would already have my dick in their mouth.

Pussy is everywhere, chemistry isn't.

"Sure, I'll take some water. Thanks."

She pads over to the fridge and hands me one, then opens another for herself. When I take a drink, it mixes with the peppermint I finished on the way up and makes my mouth minty cold all over.

"Do you want to watch a movie?" she suggests.

"Wow! Buy me a drink first?"

"What do you think the water was for?"

I like this one. "Clever girl."

She smiles and heads toward the bedroom. "I thought you might want to Netflix and chill."

"Don't get me wrong—I would Netflix and chill you so hard. But right now, all my focus is wrapped up in finding out how many times I can roll on the bed without falling off."

"If I didn't know any better, I'd say you were making fun of me."

"I would *never*."

I kick my shoes off and lie down on the edge of her bed. As I roll, I count out loud.

"One . . . two . . . three . . ." I catch myself before hitting the floor and situate myself with my back against her headboard. "Looks like I'm a three. Gotta say, this is the most unusual way a girl has gotten me in her bed before."

"I find it has about a 73 percent success rate." She gestures her hands up and down, palms up.

"Come here." I crook my finger at her.

She kneels on the bed and crawls over to straddle my thighs. Her hips flare out from her waist. She's curvy and soft and so damn hot. I gaze over every inch of her, taking my time. Sliding my hands around to her ass, I scoot her up on me so she's better aligned with my cock. The pulse point on her delicate neck quickens.

"I want to kiss you." I can't take much more of this ridiculous see-through shirt.

Her lips curl into a sexy little smile, and she leans in. The scent of fresh oranges and springtime surrounds me, and my greed surges. Our lips brush—

there's an instant connection. I squeeze her hips while moving my lips with hers. The tension is filling the room, and the pull between us is drawn more taut with each kiss.

All my blood is rushing south, and it's hard to rein it in. When she nips at my lower lip, I quit trying to pace us slower. I move one of my hands up to her neck, my thumb pressing against her chin and drawing her mouth open, granting me access. As her hips roll, I trace her pouty bottom lip with my tongue before swiping it against hers. It's slow and deliberate. She lets out a small whimper. *How many other sounds can she make?* I can't help but smile against her lips.

"How far are we going tonight?" I need her consent before I take this any further.

"Far," she pants, pulling her shirt off. *Fuck.*

"Damn it, Gray." I flip her over on her back and suck one of her nipples into my mouth. She runs her fingers through my hair, and it only amps up the energy between us. I slip my fingers under her waistband and peel off her loose cotton pants. She didn't even tie the drawstring.

"No panties? You're just full of surprises."

She giggles.

My lips caress her stomach and slowly work their way down. I grip the insides of her thighs and spread them. *That's a pussy I could fall in love with.* I flatten my tongue and lick her from her core all the way up; I can't help but smile at how good she tastes. *Where did this girl come from?*

She squirms and moans and gives me the sexiest noises from her smoky voice. She sounds even better than I imagined she would. She gasps when I add a finger.

"Fuck, you're wet."

"I need more."

Of course, she does. She's perfect.

"I wanna feel you shake tonight."

I add another finger, latch onto her clit with my mouth and suck. She arches her back and curses. She's dripping and sweet, and it's all for me. Music plays in the living room, but this dark bedroom is filled with the sound of her sweet moans and my fingers pumping into her wetness.

"I'm close," she warns.

Her legs tremble, and she clenches around my middle and ring fingers. She tries to squeeze her thighs together, but I push back and hold them open.

"I know, baby. You're doing so good, almost there."

"Shit," she says before clamping around my fingers. I suck her clit between my lips while my fingers curl inside her. She grips my hair and grinds against me as she climaxes. Watching her come was the best foreplay I've had in a long damn time. I slowly stroke her down from her orgasm.

"Why are you so good at that?" she asks on a breath.

I smile and take her mouth in mine again, dipping my tongue inside so she can taste how sweet she is. When I do, her hands move to my cheeks and she takes me deeper. I don't think I've ever kissed a woman as much as I have tonight.

Opening my wallet, I pull out the condom. After shucking my pants, I watch her as I roll it on.

"Get on all fours."

A smile lights up her face, and she sits up on her knees to turn around for me. *Obedient.* I need to see more of her. I turn on one of the small desk lights in the corner and dim it down before sliding my palm up her back to her neck.

"So pretty."

She grinds her ass into me when I line up behind her. I reach around and slap her wet clit while I slowly slide inside.

"Oh my God," she mewls.

"You're so fucking tight. Give me a second." I give a slow exhale and slide my hand back down to her ass.

I need to relax and let her body adjust to my size before I begin to thrust, but she beats me to the punch. Her back arches and her shoulders drop down. *Damn.* She rocks against my erection, and it's almost too much.

I slap her ass, and she jumps.

"You're not supposed to start until I say so." It comes out like a growl; she's sparked something inside me.

"I can't help it," she whines. "You feel . . . so . . . good." She punctuates each word by sliding up and down my length.

Tell me about it. Her ass is perfect. I grab her hips and pull her into me. Hard. She exhales. "This is better than good."

I control her movements, and seeing her tight body bent over before me, is a vision I will hold on to for a long time. Her little gasps and moans are stoking the fire within me, slowly building to an inferno. She picks up her momentum to match mine. Her cries grow louder, and her body tenses up as it did before. It takes everything in me not to pound into her without mercy.

"Give it to me harder," she breathes, barely above a whisper.

I'm happy to oblige, as soon as she shows me a little confidence.

"Nuh-uh. If you want something, you need to ask for it."

"Harder," she says softly.

"Come on. Tell me what you want, baby."

"I know you can hear me. I want you to fuck me harder!"

I chuckle and slam into her, plunging deeper with each long stroke, just like she asked.

"God, you're something else, you know that? You are suuuch a good girl when you use your words."

That unleashes something in her. A sob escapes her

lips, her pussy locks up on me, and she turns feral. I lift my arms and she takes over. Jesus, there's no way I can last with her like this.

"Shit, Gray, slow down. I'm gonna come." My hand connects with her ass again, and it does nothing to curb her movements.

"Come with me," she pants.

What?

I've never come *with* anybody before. I hesitate, but when she grinds against my cock again, that's all the convincing I need. I wrap her hair around my fist and pull back, exposing her neck for my hand. "You ready to come for me?"

"Yes!"

I thrust into her repeatedly, and she shudders as her willpower fades.

"Show me how you come for me."

I release her hair and neck, grip her hip with one hand, and reach around to slap her clit again. She's clenching around me. Right before I come, her hips buck, and that coil inside me snaps. The sound of her pleasure ricochets off the walls—there's no way the neighboring guests aren't hearing this. I don't care. My thrusts become uncoordinated, and I drive into her over and over as I fall over the edge right alongside her, gasping and panting. We come together.

While catching our breaths, her cunt still twitches around me. That was some damn good sex.

"Holy shit."

She laughs—we're both riding a post-sex high.

"Who are you?" I laugh with her.

"I'm Gray," she says. "And you're PB and J."

"I may have chosen the wrong nickname. You're anything but gray."

With that, she turns around and kisses me.

———

By the time I leave her hotel room, it's well after midnight. I forgot my to-go burgers, but that's okay. Tonight was the most fun I've had with a woman in a long time. And not just because the sex was phenomenal, the girl fucks like a vixen. She's funny, sweet, and didn't once mention hockey. I want to see her again—another first for me. The only thing I have is her phone number. I'll text her tomorrow and see if she wants to meet up again before she heads back to wherever she came from. Might be nice to grab dinner together and show her some of Minneapolis.

I stand in front of the large floor-to-ceiling windows in my high-rise and look out over the skyline. Until tonight, I didn't realize how lonely I've been. My condo is fully furnished, yet it feels so empty. Sure, there have been parties and pretty girls here—there have been lots of girls—but it's never felt warm and inviting.

I'm beat, back in my bedroom, I try to add some

coziness to the room as I brush my teeth. I pick up the remote for the fireplace and turn it on. It does nothing to help. Even with the ambiance of warm flames, it still feels like a frigid, sterile space. It's not going to be fixed by some cinnamon and spice candle either. It's probably something unobtainable, like family or love, that turns houses into homes.

October 15, 2000

This has been the most stressful week of my life! Everyone is breathing down my neck. Elizabeth has gotten us into a situation that I need to get us out of. Quickly. She always was such a problem child, if she would have just shown an ounce of obedience I wouldn't be in this mess. I need a vacation. I hear the falls are beautiful this time of year.

SEVEN

Birdie

Last night was incredible. That was the best sex I've ever had. With one of the best-looking men I've ever seen. He's texted me to see if I want to get together tonight, but as much fun as that would be, I'll probably never see him again. I have to do what I came to do.

The driveway to my parents' house is longer than I anticipated. I don't remember the house being set back that far. I'm unable to simply park outside and spy on them. I'm being such a stalker, but this feels like the safest option. I don't have to give up my cards and wait for the shoe to drop. It's my choice.

I've been parked on the street for over an hour. I'm tempted to pull into the driveway to see if they are even home. If I pretended to ask for directions, would they recognize me? Deep down, I think I've known this trip would result in some kind of confrontation, but I'm not ready to admit it to myself. This is, hands down, the scariest thing I've ever done. I'm terrified.

Something traumatic happened when I was six years old, but my mind has either suppressed that memory, or I've truly forgotten. For as long as I can remember, I was told that Julianne was my mom because my biological parents didn't want me. After being told you're unwanted so many times, you stop questioning it. I assumed that was a part of life. Some kids were adopted, and I was one of those kids. But as I look at it through the lens of an adult, it makes less and less sense.

What parents give up a child six years in? How much bullshit have I been fed? The more I read these journals, the more I despise Julianne. She was a horrible person. It's an odd feeling, hoping I've been abducted because the alternative is worse.

I haven't let myself have hope over my birth parents in . . . I don't even know how long. I gave up a long time ago. Could it be that there's still a family out there that wants me back? My life has been spent wanting to be wanted.

The lonely thoughts are interrupted when a car cuts through the trees, pulling out of the driveway. I duck down and peer over the wheel to see which direction they go. Thankfully, they turn onto the road in the same direction I'm facing. I wait for the car to pass and then I follow.

Keeping a safe distance behind, I realize I have no idea who I'm following. It could be my mom, my dad, or a goddamn housecleaning crew. I get a little closer. Based on the rear silhouette, the driver is a woman. Probably my mom. I white-knuckle the steering wheel and my thumbs tap in a quick staccato. What am I doing? Do I think I'm some fucking PI? This whole thing is a terrible idea. I shake my head, throwing out the self-doubt and negativity. This is about finding answers. My mouth forms an O, and I blow out a deep breath. *You got this, Birdie.*

I follow the driver into a Target parking lot and sit up as tall as I can to watch where she parks. I find a spot one row away but keep my eye on the car. I can't yet make out her face, but I've seen the pictures of her on the website, and those photos brought back a few of my own memories, or at least made them a lot less fuzzy. The woman steps out of the car, and my hands shake. I don't know if I can do this. *No, I have to do this!* This is my only chance, this is why I'm here. *You don't need to say anything, you can see if it's her and leave*, I promise myself, but I know it's bullshit. After I walk in there, I won't be leaving the same as I was.

I grab my purse, jump out of the car, and lock my door. My pace quickens as I try to keep up with her. After I clear the doors, the loud snap of a shopping cart being pulled from the stack gets my attention, and I see her profile before she walks away from me. It's Mom.

My heart is racing, it's pounding. My hands tremble, and a cold sweat has broken out on my skin. My throat is tight, and I try to slow my breathing, but it's as if I've forgotten how to breathe. I can't get in enough oxygen. She turns down the aisle for office supplies and my feet are tempted to just keep on walking by, but I don't let myself.

I stand by the shelves on the endcap, trying to gain enough courage to take the last two steps. She's alone in the aisle, looking at Sharpies, like it's any other Wednesday. My mom is right there. She's right there! That's the mother I've wanted for twenty-two years, and here she is. Looking at markers. *Look at me, Mom. Please, just look.*

My emotions take over—I can't do this any longer. I need to know. I need my mom.

I shake away the tremors from my hands and take the last steps. At first, I just stand next to her but then her perfume hits me, and I'm thrown back into my childhood all over again. Every hug she ever gave me, when she tucked me in at night, buckled me into the car, every time she was close enough for her smell to surround me and make me feel safe. Without thinking, I just say it.

"Mom?"

She turns toward me, and I almost startle with how much she's aged.

"Huh? No, sorry, I'm"—her eyes narrow—"Birdie?"

Her voice.

"Yeah."

"No . . ." She slowly shakes her head, and her chin wobbles.

"Yeah, it's me. Have you . . ." I clear my throat and tilt my head back to wipe my eyes. "Have you been looking for me?" My lungs freeze and my face twists with emotion. It's like ugly crying before the tears hit.

Her eyes widen in recognition. "Oh my God. Birdie!"

She slams into me and wraps her arms around my body with remarkable strength. She has my arms pinned to my sides. Her hold transforms into a hug that only she could give. *Her hug*—the specific way she hugs— the closeness, her perfume, the way her voice sounds when she's pressed against me, her earrings, the tiny scar on her temple. All the little details I forgot about are right here. I've missed this so much. Why did she leave me?

I tell myself she couldn't fake this reaction, but I am pulling to dissociate from the moment. I screw my eyes tight and fight it. She's trembling as much as I am, her knees give out, and her body goes weak. I lunge out to grab her, and our wet winter boots squeak as we drop to the floor together. Collapsed in front of the Post-it notes and staples, we find each other again. Holding each other and crying, I don't know how long we sit there.

"Ma'am have you fallen? Do you need help?"

"We're fine," we say at the same time. Our accents aren't the same, but our inflection is. Holy shit. *This is the bond.*

"Birdie, my god. Oh my God, Birdie. I love you so much." She pushes the tears and hair from my face, and her eyes dart back and forth between mine. Her hand covers her mouth in shock.

"I can't believe—Are you hurt? Where did you come from? Where have you been?"

"I'm fine. I live in Vancouver. Do you want to—"

"Vancouver? Wait, Ken! I have to call your dad. I need to call Jack. Oh my God. Vancouver? How did you get to Vancou—? How did you get here? Are you okay? Oh my God, Birdie."

"Mom."

She smiles wistfully, like she's been waiting to hear those words for a long time.

"Yeah?"

"Do you still have more shopping to do? We can finish getting what you need and then go talk or—"

"Jesus Christ! What? No!" She laughs and sniffles. "You're here! What on earth could I need?"

She smiles, covers her mouth with her hand, and stares at me in awe. "Oh my God. I can't believe you're here. You're really here." I feel something shaking and realize it's her hands on me. Her grip hasn't loosened once.

"I can't believe I'm here either." I sniffle.

"Let's go home. I want to take you home. Will you come to the house with me?"

"I have a rental car; I can follow you."

"Sweetheart, it's your car, or my car. I'm not leaving you. I've spent twenty-two years away from my baby. I'm not letting you go."

"Your car is fine."

I stand and help her to her feet. People are staring at us, as our reunion attracted some attention. My hand is clutched in hers. When we make it outside the doors, I inhale the cold air. *This is real.* She only let's go to reach into her purse and pull out her cell phone. She taps the screen a couple of times, then holds it up to her ear. Her hand finds mine again.

"Ken—" She chokes. "I have Birdie."

There's silence.

"Ken! Did you hear me? I have Birdie! She's alive, she's here!"

"Lor—"

"I know. I swear to God, Ken. I know how it sounds, but I'm on my way back. Can you call Jack and have him meet us at home? We have to tell Lonan too. And we need to call Tim, we have a lot to figure out."

I grin. Lonan! That's the other boy I couldn't remember. He was Jack's best friend. I haven't heard that name in a long time, pretty sure I had a crush on him growing up. That'll be a blast from the past, I'm sure. I don't remember Tim, though. I'll have to ask who that is.

She holds her phone to her shoulder. "He's crying," she whispers, smiling. We walk across the parking lot.

"Okay, honey, I'm going to hang up now, I have to drive home. *We* are coming home!" She laughs. Then she hangs up the phone and turns to me. "Are you hurt? Do we need to stop at the hospital?"

"No, I'm fine. I'm fine."

"Are you sure?"

"Yeah, really, I'm okay."

She points at a row of cars. "I'm over here."

I don't tell her I know where's she parked because I followed her. Vehicles slowly circle the parking lot looking for a good spot, the petrichor smell of wet asphalt hangs in the air, and red carts rattle as shoppers bring purchases back to their cars. We are surrounded by the most mundane scenery, but I connected with my mom today, and I'm going home. It's surreal to have the most overwhelming, emotional experience of my life while surrounded by people running errands.

"Who's Tim?" I ask.

"What? Oh!"

"He's the detective, well, chief of police now."

"You're on a first name basis?"

She stops and looks at me like she's confused by my question.

"Birdie, we have been searching for you for twenty-two years. We are on a first name basis with the entire department. And the local FBI agents. And a few at headquarters too."

We move again. "Are you okay coming home with me? I should be asking you this before deciding, I'm sorry. I'm not used to seeing you all grown up."

"Yeah. I just . . . I have a lot of questions."

"Me too, sweetheart."

We get closer to her car, she unlocks the door, and we climb in. Her scent permeates the car's interior, and after putting on my seatbelt, I cozy into the soft leather and exhale. I did it.

My mom drives a white Volvo, it's very clean. She starts the car and the radio plays, and she's listening to the same station I had on in my car. I turn my head to glance at her again, and she's beaming as she continues to wipe away stray tears. It's been so long, it's hard for me to not stare. She keeps looking at me too. We're on our way home. Together.

"How did you know it was me?"

"I just knew." She smiles.

EIGHT

LONAN

At thirty-one, I'm certainly on the older side of the sport. I've been doing blue-line shuffles and wall-retrieval drills for the last hour, and my knees are feeling it. This is one of the most demanding sports out there. These days, my joints practically pop and click just from ripping ass. Although we're generally smaller than football players, the hits we take are more brutal. My body aches, and I already know I'll need to up my physical therapy. We're having a decent year, but every game counts, so we all need to be playing at our best. The pressure to succeed can be overwhelming, and we have a lot of work to do if we want a shot at playoffs in the spring.

Another half hour of individualized drills with the defense coaches and I'll be able to go home. We wrap up on the ice and head back to the locker room. I yank off my gear, hit the showers, and go over everything my trainers say I need to improve upon. The older I get, the harder it is for me to play better than the year before. But my conditioning plan is primarily minor tweaks.

While zipping up my bag, I grab my jacket and dig my phone out of my pocket to check for messages. I'm supposed to be getting a call to schedule a sports massage. When I unlock my phone, there are seven missed calls from Jack. Blood drains from my face.

What happened?

I call him back. While the phone rings, my mind strays to the worst possibilities. Is someone hurt? Did something happen to Lori or Ken? Was there a car accident? Is it Audrey? Are Maddie and Liam okay? I break into a sprint to get to my car as quickly as I can, knowing I might need to meet him at a hospital.

No answer. I call again.

Finally, he answers.

"Dude! Where have you been?" he yells so loud I have to jerk the phone away from my ear.

"The fuck, man? Is everybody okay? I've got seven missed calls from you. What the hell is going on?"

"I've got some news, Burke," he chokes out.

Oh my God, somebody died.

He was trying to get ahold of me, and I didn't have my phone on me. I'll never forgive myself for this. When I reach my car and start it, my phone connects to the Bluetooth. His voice plays on the car speakers, but during the connection, I missed the last thing he said.

"What? What is it? Do I need to meet you somewhere?"

"Are you sitting down?"

"Damn it, Jack! Yes. What happened? You're freaking me out—"

"It's Birdie."

My heart drops. *Please don't say they found her body, don't say they found her body.* A wave of nausea hits me, and I grab the handle, ready to open the door.

"She's here!"

I pick up on the inflection in his voice. He's . . . ecstatic. *It can't be.*

"A-alive?"

I squeeze my eyes shut and brace for the worst.

"Alive."

My eyes fly back open, and I'm stunned into silence.

"We're still making sure everything's legit. I'm on my way over to Mom and Dad's right now to see her. Dad said she's been living in Vancouver. Police want to do a paternity test—I'll let you know as soon as I know for sure."

NINE

Birdie

Mom and I spend a lot of the drive stealing glances at each other. And a lot of time is spent trying to convince her I'm okay. I'm not hurt, I haven't been locked up in a kidnapper's basement for twenty years. Well, not the basement. They must have so many questions; I have just as many, so I doubt I can give them enough answers.

I explain what hotel I'm staying at, and she invites me to stay with them instead and tells me I'm welcome to use one of the bedrooms to rest in if I find myself needing a break. I want to finish meeting everyone and get a read on the situation before I commit to anything and cancel my reservation. At some point I'll have to go back, all my things are still in the room. For now, I want to get to know the family I've spent decades away from.

I appreciate her being so cognizant of the time it might take me to process everything. It's a lot.

We pull into the long driveway, and now that we pass through the pine trees, I get a clear view of the house for the first time since *before*—it's huge. It seemed massive when I was a child, but even as an adult, it still looks impressive. Now that I see the outside, I can remember the inside layout. And all the trees are so much taller than they were the last time I was here . . . Getting out of the car, I keep my jacket held tightly against my chest.

My dad bursts through the front door as fast an older man can. He moves a lot slower now. They're so much older, and the time I've lost makes me feel sick. "Oh, Bridget."

Bridget. It's been forever since I've heard my real name.

He coughs, trying to cut off a cry. "I can't believe this. How? Are you hurt?" I chuckle at the constant barrage about my condition. He's engulfed me in the best dad-style bear hug. He still uses the same aftershave.

"Hi, Dad." I lean into him and let him hold me . . . My dad. I never thought I would have a dad again.

"I-I didn't believe her." His voice shakes trying to stay strong, but it only makes me squeeze out more tears. Mom strides around the car and rubs his back as he hugs me.

"Oh, Bridget, honey." The old man wipes his face. "I love you so much. We love you so much. We have missed you so much. Where did you come from?"

"Vancouver!" my mom answers. She's riding a high.

"How the hell did you make it all the way to Vancouver? Are you okay? Bridget . . . were you? Did someone hurt you?"

"No, I swear, I'm fine. Really."

"She's had a long trip, Ken. Let's get inside."

My jaw drops slightly when we walk through the extra-wide door, but I do my best to hide my surprise. Growing up in a tiny apartment makes this place look like a palace, probably due to the high-vaulted wood ceilings above. It has that smell of home, the one you can only smell after you've been gone a long time on vacation, or living in Vancouver with a sociopath for three-quarters of your life. Either way, it's a significant upgrade from the previous one my "home" used to be. The door closes behind me, and my eyes stay glued to the exposed wooden beams and catwalk above. My dad offers to take my coat, I shut my gaping mouth, smile and nod. I look back to the catwalk for a moment—I remember Jack and me running back and forth across that thing so many times. Wow.

"I'm not sure if you remember any of this . . ." He gestures to the house.

"I do, actually. My room was up there, on the left,

right? I have a memory of running with Jack and throwing my stuffed animals over the side."

He stares at me as if I'm a figment of his imagination. "I can't believe this is happening."

"Are you hungry? When did you last eat?" Mom asks.

"I'm good, I had breakfast this morning, my appetite is still settling from nerves."

"If you're sure. But you can always help yourself to whatever you can find, I mean it, anything—this is your home too."

I thank her and give a tight smile.

"We have so many questions," she says, dropping her arms.

"We both do," I say.

My dad speaks up. "If there's anything you don't want to talk about, we don't want to pressure you. I don't know what you've been through all these years. This is on your terms. But I did have to call Tim at the police station and let him know. We have all been looking for you."

My chest is tight, and I divert my gaze. *I wasn't unwanted.*

They look at me, heads tilted and brows squished together like they're confused by my silence.

"Bridget. You're our child. We *never* stopped looking for you."

The front door opens and slams shut, followed by

heavy footsteps. Wow, there's Jack, all grown up. He's taller than my dad. My brother stops and stares at me.

"Birdie?"

"Jack Rabbit." I forgot all about his nickname until the words came out of my mouth.

"Holy shit." He crashes into me with a hug. We hold on to each other for what is probably minutes. "I missed you so much, B," he says into my hair. He's already falling back into his big-brother role flawlessly.

"Missed you too."

We all sit down, and I explain the little I know about what I suspect happened. I tell them about Julianne. The journals. How she told me I was adopted. Hearing that was hard on them. Mom and Dad are especially crushed, they are heartbroken I grew up thinking they didn't want me.

I'm livid. Being mad at Julianne doesn't even scratch the surface of my feelings toward her. But I'm also angry I let her manipulate me for so long without questioning anything. I was so stupid. Julianne did so much damage. It's not something I'll be able to easily erase. Even though my parents have told me I was never unwanted, it doesn't mean the years of programming haven't made me believe it. I've spent the majority of my life hearing it, and I can't take away the deep emotional wounds that go with those messages.

Jack is on a laptop trying to run information about Julianne and dig up anything he can on her based on what I told them. I show them the Stellar Genetics page with the DNA match. Apparently, the whole reason they all joined was in case I ever did so they could find me. I don't like to think about what would have happened if I'd never taken that test. They all feel guilty they haven't been keeping up on the updates, but I don't blame them. After I joined, I easily got twenty emails a day telling me that a new *eighth cousin, four times removed* had matched to me. It's annoying as hell; I turned off the notifications same as them.

They have questions about what happened that day, but I don't remember. I have no recollection of even going to Niagara Falls. There are no memories of me going missing. If that's what the police want to know, they are out of luck.

"There's no pressure to try and remember anything," Mom reminds me.

I can't count the number of differences between our lifestyles. They seem so dependent on one another, so connected. In contrast, my independence has been a large part of my life. I'm pulling back and struggling to reconcile that we are not only related but that I'm a missing piece of their puzzle too. And what does this mean going forward? Going back to Vancouver doesn't seem like an option for my future.

TEN

LONAN

Jack: It's her.

October 19, 2000

Visiting Niagara Falls was the best decision. Sometimes life throws you opportunities and you have to be ballsy enough to take them. Most people aren't smart enough to do what is necessary.

But I'm not like most people.

ELEVEN

Birdie

The truth is out. I was abducted. I'm at the police station doing something called a "return home interview," and they have been asking me questions all morning. I immediately hand over the journals and explain I've dog-eared pages I think are relevant, and I gave them the address of Julianne's old apartment in case they wanted to investigate more. I'm told there's been a new lead on an old murder case in which Julianne Fournier is a suspect, apparently Vancouver and Toronto detectives have been working the case for the last few months. That's reassuring. One of the men leave to grab evidence bags for the journals, and I'm left alone with Tim Rollins, the main detective on my case.

"So, if I was taken, wouldn't there have been some kind of AMBER alert for me?"

"There was, Niagara Falls had one sent out within the hour, but that was in 2000. Unfortunately, we didn't have the technology to broadcast it as successfully as we do today."

"What about in Canada, though? I mean, Niagara Falls is close enough to the border, why wouldn't they do it there?"

"They didn't have an AMBER alert system until two years later. Once she took you over the border, she was in the clear. Even if she had been stopped, she would have claimed you as Elizabeth, and she'd have all the documentation to back it up. Hell, even the photos are convincing. Your resemblance to her daughter was remarkable. Unless there was a DNA test, nobody would have thought the wiser."

"And I never told anyone, so nobody thought to do it."

"Birdie, I'm going to level with you for a minute, human to human. You are the victim here; you were only six. God knows what would have happened to you if you would have tried to report her, it would have blown her cover, and she would have done anything to protect it. Off the record, if she did kill Elizabeth, she wouldn't hesitate in killing you too. Your silence might have been what kept you alive."

The other detective returns, and Tim sits back in his chair and nods to me to make sure I understand what he's saying. I do. But it's still a hard pill to swallow.

They stand and bag up the evidence as I say goodbye to it. They're the last things I have of Julianne's, and a giant weight has been lifted when I let go of them. She's not my problem anymore. I hope every single person who spoke at her funeral discovers how vile and deplorable she really is. I want every thread of her reputation to fray and burn.

Despite the smorgasbord of pamphlets in front of me, regarding trauma and how to find support systems, I just want to leave this all behind. For now, I will box it up and hide it away in the deepest, darkest part of my brain. I don't want to spend any more time thinking about her. I've wasted too much time, and I need to start living my life again.

The air smells like stale coffee and copy paper, the phones are ringing behind the big metal door, and one of the fluorescent lights in the far corner of the room flicker just enough to make me want to toss this chair up there and smash it.

"Do you have any more questions?"

"Not right now." *Please, say I can leave.*

"Understandable."

He sits back down, and I groan internally. My ass is numb from this hard plastic chair. This is why people break when they're being interrogated. It's not the cross-examination, it's the goddamn chairs.

"This is still an open investigation, we want to rule out that there isn't a group of people working together, or that it's not part of a trafficking ring. Details of the case are best kept to yourself right now."

"Okay," I answer. "So, does this mean I can leave?"

"Yeah, we should be all done here. We've got your phone number and will call the Hayeses and you with the formal paternity test results within the next couple days. Here's another card with our contact information." He hands over the fifth business card of the day. "Please call us if you have any questions or remember anything at all, even if you think it might not be important."

"I will. Thanks."

"Oh, and we will do our best to keep this under wraps, but be prepared for the media to get ahold of you. It's very likely this is going to explode when the story hits. Try and keep a low profile in the meantime."

Shit. I didn't think about the media and how sensationalized this might become. Though, I also didn't think I would end up being a missing person, and yet here we are. I've seen enough television specials about kidnapping victims returning, it's a big deal. I just struggle to see myself as one of those people. I don't have cases like theirs. Julianne didn't show signs of being a murderer, she was just a mean old bitch.

"Thanks for the heads-up."

My chair squeaks as I push it back to stand and shake their hands. Talking about Julianne makes me anxious, I need to get the hell out of here.

———

"Are you sure I can't make you some lunch, Bridget?" Mom asks.

It takes me a second to respond, the *Bridget* thing is something I'm still getting used to.

"Oh. Um, no, thank you." I try not to sound too surprised, but she must pick up on it.

"Do you go by Bridget?"

"Honestly, I forgot I was Bridget until I found the website. I've always gone by Birdie. It's funny. I never liked the name Elizabeth—it's a fine name, but didn't seem to fit me. Probably a reason, eh?"

"Jack was the one who actually nicknamed you Birdie. When he was little, he had a hard time saying Bridget. His Bridg always sounded like bird. Before we knew it, you were Birdie."

"I don't mind, Bridget," I tell her, "but it will probably take some getting used to, and all of my documentation is under Elizabeth. My passport, my driver's license . . ."

"About that." She and my dad share a glance before she moves her gaze back to me. "There's something called the Presumption of Death Act in the United States."

This sounds ominous.

"After you were missing for so many years, you were declared legally dead. I'm so sorry, honey. I promise we never gave up looking for you. We were struggling to keep things going, and the counselors thought it might bring us closure."

"I can't imagine the position you were in." I understand why they would have done it.

It hits me this wasn't just devastating on a parental level, their marriage and everyday life were deeply uprooted too. This family, which looks so put together, was in shambles when I disappeared. I feel awful. And now I'm supposed to pack up my things and leave them a second time?

"So, I'm dead?"

"Basically," Jack answers, leaning back in his chair.

I turn to him. "Can I be made *undead*?"

"Nope. We gotta kill you now. Needs to match the paperwork."

I like him. Mom's head whirls from me to him.

"Jesus Christ, Jack. She literally just got here." She searches my face for indignation, but I only laugh. We share some of the same snark.

She lets her head fall back. "Well, they still share the same offbeat sense of humor."

Seems I'm not the only one that notices.

Ken rolls his eyes. "Great, just what we needed."

So. I'm dead. Interesting. What do I do with that information? Am I supposed to be claiming Bridget as my real identity now? It sounds like a logistic nightmare. Who do I talk to about that? I have no idea how this stuff works in the United States, but I assume it's not as simple as flipping a toggle switch from dead to alive.

"Am I supposed to be claiming Bridget or Elizabeth as my identity?"

"You were born here, so you have United States Citizenship. You have an identity and a social security number, they just are listed as deceased for the time being."

"Is this like a social insurance number in Canada?"

"I would assume so. You will need it to get a job, credit cards, and bank loans. Buy insurance, purchase a house, a car . . ."

Oh okay, so I'm fucked is what you're saying?

"Once Tim sends over his police report, we plan to file a motion with the Social Security Administration to reverse it, but it's a slow process. It can take a while."

———

I decided to stay at my parents' house. Last night, my dad drove me back to my hotel to gather my belongings, and I canceled my reservation. I'm sure the hotel was relieved to free up one of their nicest rooms.

We just finished lunch, and so far everything is going really well. I'm surprised at how comfortable it feels to be here. I've loved catching up and meeting Jack's family. His wife, Audrey, is incredibly sweet. I have a niece named Maddie that might be the cutest little girl I've ever seen, and a baby nephew, Liam, that I was able to hold for a couple hours yesterday while he napped.

I'm walking out of the washroom when I hear a muffled argument coming from outside, so I creep toward it until I see Jack on the front porch, he's talking to someone on the phone. His back is to the window, so he doesn't see me. Still, I withdraw into the corner to stay hidden. I can't make out what he's saying, but I hear "Birdie" a few times. Pretty sure he's too old to call actual birds "birdies." He better not be leaking my story to a morning show or some shit.

"Hey, hon"—*busted*—"would you mind running upstairs and letting me know if there are any sheets on the guest bed?" Mom and I both know this is a fool's errand meant to divert my attention. I'm not about to cause any problems, though.

"Sure thing!"

When I reach the top of the stairs, I duck around one of the walls off the catwalk. Pretty sure I did this when I was little and wanted to stay up past my bedtime. God, the memories that are coming back . . . it's wild.

Mom steps outside, and if I peek around the corner, it's easy to see them talking on the porch from this vantage point. *What are they saying?* This looks so shady, eavesdropping on people. But after stalking them from my car and following Mom to the store the other day, it doesn't seem so bad. When she turns to open the front door, I Pink Panther my ass into the guest bedroom and check that there are sheets on the bed before casually walking downstairs.

"Yup, they're on the bed." I pause. This is awkward. "Is everything okay? Maybe it's best if I go back to the hotel for the night. If me being here is causing stress, I don't want to—"

She side-eyes me. "What? Why? Because of that?" She points toward the front door where Jack is still on the phone. "No, honey, that's nothing. We *all* want you here with us." She sounds assertive enough.

"As long as it's not a problem."

She leans in to give me a hug. I get a lot of hugs around here.

"Oh, I almost forgot"—she brightens up—"Lonan is going to be stopping by for supper. He's a part of the family. Do you remember him? The three of you kids used to be thick as thieves. He's been dying to see you again. I told him it was okay, is that all right with you?"

"I remember some. And yeah, that's fine. It will be good to see him again."

TWELVE

LONAN

O pening my car door, the smell of cold fresh snow and wood smoke from the chimney hangs heavy in the air. I gather my nerves and a bouquet of magenta peonies—it felt strange to show up empty-handed—and walk toward the house.

Jack has been acting fucking weird since Bridget came home. It's like he's gatekeeping her. He says they are trying to keep it "*just family*" right now. Well, then what the fuck does that make me? He wasn't the only person to lose her. Since when am I not family? I lived with them for half my life. Lori must have heard us argue on the phone earlier today because she snatched it up and invited me for dinner herself. I can't figure out what the hell his problem is, but it doesn't matter now, he's not my focus tonight.

I pause on the porch, taking a minute to prepare

myself. She's probably not how I remember her. She will undoubtedly look different and may have a different personality, and she might not be the sparkly ray of sunshine from before. After being taken, she's most likely withdrawn or timid. Reuniting with everyone has to be stressful. Every part of me wants to bust into the front door and hug her, but Mom H already told me she doesn't remember much of me.

I force myself to turn the door handle and push it open. The sounds of people laughing, fire crackling, and some light Christmas carols fill the space. Doesn't matter how big this house is, it has always felt cozy.

"I'm home!" I holler.

As usual, Lori hurries around the corner and gives me a giant squeeze.

"Finally, all my babies are home under one roof!"

She's positively glowing, I've never seen her so happy. She looks down at the flowers and pats my arm.

"She's in the kitchen, I'll send her out here so you can introduce yourself without an audience. Are you ready?"

"Been ready," I lie.

My heart is pumping with adrenaline, the only time I feel like this is when I'm on the ice. I don't know what to do with myself. A wrinkle in the brown paper holding the peonies keeps my fingers occupied while I shift from one foot to the other. A woman appears from the other room, and I freeze. So does she.

No way.

"Gray?"

I rub my hand over my face. This is why she looked familiar—it was her eyes. There's only one person on earth with those eyes. But damn. She's grown up. *A lot.* Shit, what have I done?

"Oh my God." She steps back, her mouth agape. "Um . . ."

"I don't know what to do right now," I admit.

"Me either. Can we just, like, forget whatever happened the other night?"

"Not a chance."

Is she kidding? I'll still be thinking about that night on my death bed.

"Excuse me?" She narrows her eyes at me.

"You heard me."

She hasn't stopped blushing since our eyes met.

It takes me a minute to get over the fact this isn't just Gray—this is Bridget. Emotions fog my vision. I have to look away for a second to compose myself, and when my gaze returns, I shake my head and drop it in disbelief. No doubt, it's her. If I had taken longer to look at her that night, maybe if I hadn't taken her from behind, would I have seen the resemblance? I don't know. But the woman in front of me is Bridget—*and she's a fucking smokeshow.*

Somehow, her silver doe eyes are even more

bewitching than before. High cheekbones and full, pouty lips. Her hair is the same chestnut color from when we were young. But her body . . . she's still petite, but those sexy-as-sin curves are anything but small, and I got to know them well the other night. That innocent crush I had as a kid is not so innocent anymore, especially now that I've been in her bed. I can taste her and still feel the way she came around my cock if I think about it long enough.

I can't believe she's standing in front of me right now. She's alive and breathing—and every one of her breaths steal one of mine.

"Let's start over," she says.

I vehemently disagree. But I'll let her think that's what's happening.

"Hi . . . I'm Birdie." She holds her hand up in a shy wave.

Say it again.

"I know."

"It's Lonan, right?"

"I've also gone by PB and J."

She attempts to hide her smile by biting her lip and rolls her eyes at my refusal to drop the one-night stand. *One night my ass.*

My smile is permanent. They will bury me with this stupid ass grin on my face. God, Bridget. My fingers itch to touch her again, but I resist. It's a pretty big ask of myself, considering I've already done it.

"Did you bring me flowers, Lonan?" She nudges the conversation forward.

I'm suddenly aware I've been standing in front of her grinning like an idiot for the last sixty seconds. She's already got the drop on me, and she knows it too.

I clear my throat. "I did. Last time I checked, magenta was your favorite color," I explain, handing over the peonies. "It's been a while though." Dumb joke.

She takes them from me, looks down at the bouquet, and chuckles. "These are really nice, thank you."

Tilting her head to the side, she studies my face, and it reminds me of the day in the fort when she asked if I *like-liked* her. What is she thinking? Does she remember that? Or, more likely, has she realized who I actually am? If she follows hockey, like most people in Vancouver do, she's seen my face. Which means she sees #14, defenseman for the Minnesota Lakes, and the team's resident fuckboy. Not her childhood friend with whom she shared her first kiss—the same guy she gave hope to two nights ago after blowing his mind with incredible chemistry and even better sex. I had sex with Bridget. Why do I keep struggling to realize she and Gray are the same person?

It's hard to reconcile that the sweet little girl I grew up with is the same sexy woman that, less than forty-eight hours ago, had me coming harder than I ever had before. My brain tries to resist merging the innocent memories with the sinful ones.

I've barely said two sentences to her when Jack marches in to the living room shooting daggers at me with his stare. "Hey, we're gonna start eating, are you guys coming?" He's focusing on me, not her.

I cut my eyes at him before returning my gaze to his sister.

"Yup," I answer, not taking my eyes off her. "You hungry?"

Her face flushes a little from my choice of words and it's like an aphrodisiac. *Goddamn it, have a shred of self-control.*

The temptation shuts down when little Maddie sprints over and grabs a handful of Bridget's sweater.

"Aunt Birdie! Want to help me set the table? You can sit next to me!"

"Sure!" She laughs, looking down and brushing the hair out of her niece's adorable face.

"Hey, Madaroni, not gonna say hi to your favorite uncle?"

"Hi," she says and then grabs Bridget's hand and whisks her into the kitchen.

Looks like Bridget is already the new favorite.

"I don't blame ya, kid," I mutter.

———

In the kitchen, I watch from the corner of my eye as Bridget and Maddie set the table. The second she puts her wineglass down at a place setting, I position my drink directly across from hers. Jack must notice because he pulls his chair out more aggressively than usual when he sits next to Bridget. *The fuck is this dude's problem tonight? Does he know?*

Hot dish is not the traditional Christmas Eve-Eve meal, but besides cotton candy ice cream, it was her favorite dinner. I frown at how desperately Lori and Ken want to recreate home for her. Who wouldn't? My stomach drops when I find out she only plans to stay a week. I have no idea what her life is like back in Vancouver, but I assume after last night there's no boyfriend in the picture—not that it would stop me from pursuing her.

I gaze across the table, and she's nodding at something Ken brought up. She's beautiful. Most of our first meeting was spent in dim lighting, but seeing her sans shadows gives me a chance to admire the little details.

Having been with a lot of women is not something I'm proud of, but it has built up my confidence enough that I can be assertive without trying. With Bridget, it's a different story, especially after our night together. I already care about her, but now sexual attraction has been mixed into the sentimental history we have. The result is a desire unlike any I've experienced before, which makes that assertiveness not as easy. I have to work for it—it's unnatural for me.

When I stretch my legs, my foot grazes hers under the table, and we make eye contact. A grin pulls at my lips and I look back down to my food and return to eating. But I'm not moving my foot. I've been dying to touch her all night. If this harmless brush of skin is the best I can do, I'm taking it. I glance back up when, to my surprise, she doesn't move away either. *Interesting.*

I caress her ankle, keeping my eyes locked on hers, I don't give a shit who notices. If I want to look, I'm going to. I can tell she's trying to suppress a smile. Jack finishes the last of his beer in one gulp, sets his napkin next to his plate, and shoves away from the table. *Loudly.*

"Mind helping me grab some more wine bottles from the cellar?"

Guess we're doing this now.

"You bet, bud."

Following him downstairs, we step into the wine cellar, and I shut the door behind us. We both know we're not here to pick out wine.

"Maybe a cabernet?" I feign ignorance.

"Don't," he warns.

"Don't what?" I bite out.

"You can't mess with her, Burke. She's not one of your girls you take home after the bar, fuck, and then kick out the next morning."

She kicked me out, thank you very much.

"Whoa! Who says I'm messing with her?" I wouldn't call it *messing*, more like reacquainting. Light flirting at best.

He levels me with a stern glare, it hits the mark. I put my hands up. "Okay, I get it. I get it. I'll try and rein it in, but it's hard. I mean, have you *seen* her?"

"Hey, asshole, she's my *sister*."

I fucked my best friend's sister. He's already become overly protective of her. Imagine if he knew I slept with her. He'd go ballistic.

"Okay, but you know I wouldn't do that to her, right?"

"No, I don't know that. You've never had a serious relationship. You chew women up and spit them out."

"Bridget is different."

"First of all, she prefers Birdie. Second, she *just* came home! You think you can sleep with her since she's going to be going back to Vancouver in a week?"

"Jesus! All I want to do is get to know her again."

"Bullshit. I see the way you look at her. You want to do more than that. Get to know her? You want to take her out on some dates? Wine and dine her?"

I let my mind wander and picture what that might look like. Taking her to fancy restaurants, bringing her to games, seeing her in the WAGs box, hanging out and doing nothing—and other times, doing everything.

"Wait—do you still . . ." He narrows his eyes.

I shrug. I don't *still* have a crush on her, this crush began two nights ago when she made me rethink my view on relationships and want something more than sex.

"Yeah, let's run through that. You take her out a few nights, pull all your usual Lonan Burke bullshit, and she catches feelings. Then you sleep with her—"

"Hold up a sec—" I wave both my hands in rebuttal.

"I'm not done yet," he continues, "You take her home and once you get what you want, you stop returning her calls, and you drop her. Just like you do with *alllll* the other ones, except she's not like the other ones. This is Birdie. This is my sister. If you hurt or humiliate her, she'll be on the next flight to BC, and she might never come back. Burke, your actions affect all of us, I can't let you do that."

I stand there waiting for him to finish. Is that truly what he thinks of me? I should have been more honest regarding my past relationships because he has it backward.

"Now it's your turn to listen."

We're already crowded in the small cellar, but I step closer, invading his space even more. "I know that my relationship history is sketchy, at best. And sure, hookups aren't uncommon for me. I own that shit. But those women you're talking about—they seek me out. They only want to take home a hockey player for the bragging rights. They want to use *me*, not the other way around."

He crosses his arms and sarcastically laughs. He won't even look at me.

"My first year in the NHL, women threw themselves at me constantly. I followed along like a good teammate and did what everyone else did to fit in, but I didn't see it for what it was back then. My dumbass even asked a couple of them out because I thought they actually were interested in *me*." I scoff. "After enough times, it becomes a matter of simply going through the motions. Women always want something from me. Hell, my own mother won't talk to me unless I'm wiring money into her checking account. This family is the closest thing I have to the real thing. So, fuck me for trying to connect with someone I actually care about."

He's silent for a minute, but I stare him square in the eye. He needs to know I'm serious.

"I didn't—"

"It's fine. I never corrected you in the past, I should have." If I don't tell him what I'm thinking, my thoughts will eat me alive, so I keep going. "I promise you, if anything develops between us, she will hurt me long before I hurt her." Though, I hope it never comes to that.

"You know she doesn't live here, right? She hasn't said anything about moving here yet, she's got a whole life in Vancouver. She's going back, man." His resolve is crumbling.

"We'll see." I have a suspicion he's only taking down the cockblock because he wants to see if I can be the one to get her to stay, but I'm so desperate I'd probably take a trade to Vancouver if I had to.

We're at a stalemate. I'm ending this conversation before he gets in my face again.

I pull a couple random bottles from the shelves and pass one to him.

"We can't go back empty-handed."

THIRTEEN

Birdie

Never would have thought I'd spend this year's Christmas Eve with my real family. We're cleaning up from dinner, and I'm washing dishes while Audrey dries. Everyone is chatting in the kitchen except for Lonan, he's occupying Maddie with some floor hockey game in the living room. I can hear her giggling from here. He showed up this morning with fresh cinnamon bread. At first, I was surprised to see him again, but it sounds like he spends every holiday with my family.

Not only is he stupid hot but he's really sweet with my niece and nephew. There's this spark between us I'm struggling to ignore. Every time our eyes meet, he looks at me like we have unfinished business, and it sends a flush of warmth through me. Unfortunately, I have no business entertaining anything more than friendship. He plays for the Lakes. Maybe someday we could meet up when he plays in Vancouver. If that's where I'm living.

I have a lot of shit to work through, but when he's around, the only thing I can think about is the night we spent together. He's intimidating in the most exhilarating way, and I find my focus narrowing in on the threat of him. The rush of endorphins have me feeling guilty. I remind myself he's an NHL player, and it's simply a matter of being starstruck. Who wouldn't feel flutters in their vagina while looking at him?

Funny, I was so worried about running into my parents or Jack at the hotel in Minneapolis, meanwhile I was fucking his best friend the whole time. *Small world, eh?* What am I going to do now? I'm torn between wanting to never see him again and dragging him upstairs for a repeat of him between my thighs. I'll never be able to look him in the eye without picturing his dick or the sound of him growling *good girl* in my ear.

"*Birdie?*"

Audrey is looking at me with raised eyebrows. Shit, I wasn't paying attention. *What were we talking about?*

"Sorry," I fluster. "What was that?"

"Pajamarades. Has anybody warned you about it yet?"

"Pajamarades?"

"It's a Christmastime tradition, it's just charades

while wearing pajamas. However, it's my duty as your sister-in-law to warn you what's about to go down."

I laugh. I like Audrey. If we had met in Vancouver, I'm sure we would have become close friends. "Lay it on me."

"Those nice people in there, the ones that look like they are out of a Hallmark movie"—*Thank God, it's not just me*—"they are ruthless. It doesn't matter if it's your first Pajamarades or your twentieth, the Hayeses take no prisoners. It's like a sporting event, they become completely unhinged."

"Got any advice for a first-timer?"

"Yeah, pour yourself a tall glass of wine and just yell along with the rest of them. You're going for eighties Tom Hanks freakout. But if you hit The Burbs, you've gone too far."

———

After dishes, I was instructed to put on my pajamas for Pajamarades. My most Christmas-y pair are a red silk button-down set. I'm relieved I brought more than just boy shorts and camisoles. As I take the stairs back down, I can feel his gaze on me. I'm not looking back this time, there's nothing between us, tonight is about family. This entire trip is about family. Besides, I need to rally my energy. My body is still tired from sledding with Maddie this afternoon. But I'd be lying if I said that some of the aches weren't due to Lonan's monster penis. I go to the kitchen and pour my large glass of wine to prepare for the shitshow.

Maddie comes bouncing into the kitchen in fuzzy penguin footie pajamas. "Aunt Birdie! Lonan says I'm supposed to ask you to be on his team, but not to tell you that he said to be on his team."

From the other room, Lonan yells, "Miss Maddie, your ability to follow instructions leaves much to be desired!"

He's not helping.

"How about I join your team, Mads?"

"I'm on Lonan's team!"

Great.

"Of course you are."

"She said yes!" Maddie squeals as she runs back into the living room.

Wine glugs into my stemless wineglass. After, I join Maddie, Lonan, and Audrey in the living room. He's relaxed with one of his arms stretched over the back of the sofa. I feign a scolding expression and mouth, *The child? Really?*

He smiles back at me and mouths, *Nice PJs.*

Those were his exact words when he came to my hotel room, the pink of my cheeks could probably be seen from space. I sit next to Audrey to avoid being sucked into his orbit.

She clinks our glasses. "Nice pour."

The rest of the family make their way to the sitting area, and before I know it, the room is filled with a cacophony of movie titles and hysterical flailing gestures. Audrey was right, these people are on the edge of their seats, yelling and pointing like a bunch of Wall Street floor traders. It's insanity, and I love every second of it.

Lonan is up next, watching him act out movie titles in those flannel pants is borderline indecent, his thighs are built like tree trunks, and every time he extends his legs dramatically, the merchandise goes on full display if the lighting hits it just right. It's distracting. Attempting to focus on the task at hand, I follow Audrey's advice and throw out random movie titles in hopes that one of them sticks.

"*Braveheart*!"

"*The Godfather*!"

"*Alien*!"

"*Pulp Fiction*!"

He points at me and touches his nose. Sonofabitch, it *was Pulp Fiction*.

Every seat is taken in the living room, the fire is blazing, and with each glance in his direction, the room seems to get warmer—this wine is not helping to control my ogling. Probably time to switch to water, but after the last few days I've had—taking my first plane ride, meeting my biological family, being interrogated at the police station, and fucking my childhood crush, I deserve this big-girl sized glass of wine.

The only thing that sounds better than wine is a good night's rest—or getting put in my place by Brown Eyes over there. I could use a solid eight to ten hours before tomorrow's Christmas festivities. Christmases with Julianne consisted of the two of us at the apartment, it was low-key and quiet. The contradictory chaos of the Hayes house is a welcome one. I'm enjoying the lively commotion while everyone is laughing and so happy to be with one another. A true Merry Christmas. It's another Hallmark qualifier, but I'm embracing it with the rest of them. Sitting back and watching it unfold fills me with happiness too.

Lonan takes off his sweatshirt, and when he pulls his fully tatted left arm out, a silent curse leaves my lips. He's definitely nailed the bad-boy-next-door look.

I, too, want to nail the bad boy next door. Again.

I swallow and try to look away, but as he peels the heavy layer away, the shirt underneath clings to it, exposing a delicious wall of abdominal muscles. *Oh, holy night.* He pulls the shirt down, and my gaze returns to his face. He gives me a cocky half smile and winks, letting me know I've been caught. It sends equal amounts of thrill and embarrassment through me.

Dear God, it's me, Birdie. Why the fuck are you punishing me like this?

My cheeks heat, and I'm seriously considering

flinging myself into the fireplace. The last gulp of wine is my only cover, it's the perfect opportunity to step away from the game and get that drink of water from the kitchen.

I'm washing my wineglass in the sink when Lonan's deep voice catches me by surprise, and I flinch.

"So, what do you think of your first Pajamarades?" I keep my back to him so he doesn't see the lingering blush on my face.

"Oh, um . . ." I rinse off the soap. *Focus, Birdie.* "It's a lot of fun! Maddie is so funny when she gets up there and starts giggling." I laugh, drying my glass, thinking about her adorable fish lips when she acted out Finding Nemo a few moments ago. I let it derail my thoughts from him.

I'm forced to face Lonan when I slide the now-clean wineglass back into the rack under the kitchen island. Then I open and close cabinet doors in search of a tall glass to fill with water. My mouth is as dry as a desert, and I'm hyperaware of my every move.

"God, I know. She's such a cute kid," he says as he twists off the cap off a new beer.

Jesus, where the hell are the glasses?

As if the Lord himself is answering my plea, Lonan, without turning around, reaches behind him and opens a cupboard door. And lo and behold, there they are. He doesn't hand me one. *No, that would be too easy.* Instead, he positions himself in front of them, watching me with a wicked gleam in his eye. I walk toward the glasses, but his feet remain firmly planted, blocking me from the shelf. I stand there like a petulant child, my heartbeat racing, letting the anticipation of whatever game he's playing build and build. He studies me over the lip of his beer as he slowly takes a swig. Why is he doing this? His throat bobs as he swallows, and it's strangely erotic.

We continue to stare at each other until I break the silence. "Could you hand me a glass?"

He takes another drink.

"What's the magic word?"

I reach out. "Please?"

He grabs a glass and holds it out to me. *"That's a good girl."*

The muscles in my core tighten, and I pray my face doesn't show any tells. I snatch my hand back and steel my demeanor, thankful he can't hear the pulse that's ringing in my ears. The room is filling with sexual energy again.

"I'm going to call it a night," I say, turning on my heel.

"Just like that? I thought you wanted a drink."

"I'm not thirsty," I respond. Hoping he picks up on the double meaning.

"Wait, wait, wait," he backpedals, "I'm sorry. I didn't mean to make it weird."

He sets his beer on the counter and stalks toward

me. His hands are stuffed in his pockets, and he averts his gaze to the floor.

"I, ah . . . I haven't had a chance to tell you I'm really happy you're home." When his gaze lifts to meet mine, his eyes are glassy. My shoulders relax at his candidness.

"Thanks," I say cautiously. "It's been a pretty surreal experience, to say the least."

"In a couple days, I'll be traveling for a game, but I'd like to stay in contact. I'm in Vancouver and Seattle several times a year, if you're up for it, I'd like to see you when I'm in town. That is, if you decide not to move here."

I smile and nod. I point behind me. "Well, I'm going to go say good night to everyone."

"Can I say good night?"

If it were anyone else, I'd say he was being suave, but his eyes are still shining, and I oddly want to console him. "Sure."

He takes two steps, until he's right in front of me. He smells incredible, masculine and earthy, like cedarwood and spice. Instead of holding out his arms in a hug, he takes my hand, and as soon as his fingers grasp mine, I'm transported back to a tree house. And Lonan is with me. We were standing like we are now. The memory slams into me. "Oh my God."

"Are you okay? What's wrong?"

"I kissed you."

"We did a lot more than kiss," he says with a smirk.

"No, I mean as a kid. We kissed in a tree house."

His glossy eyes shine more now. He scrubs his hands down his face while he blows out a breath, trying to gain some composure.

"Yeah, i-in a tree house, I remember it," I repeat.

Stepping forward and grasping my hand again, he pulls me into his hard chest and wraps me up in a giant hug. He doesn't let go, just holds me tight against him and presses a kiss to the top of my head. It's a simple gesture, but the way he does it feels packed with so much more than nostalgia.

———

After waking from a night of deep, heavy sleep, I turn over to lie on my back. Thinking over everything that's happened the last few days, it's becoming easier to accept that this is my life now. My world has been shaken up, and I'm still feeling the aftershocks. My brain is exhausted, the new memories and flashbacks have been draining. Warm blankets wrapped around me keep me drowsy, in that hazy space between sleep and consciousness. Slumber sounds like such a sweet escape from the decisions that need to be made.

This year's Christmas was wonderful. We spent the day together doing family things and relaxing. I caught up my family with what I've been up to, my job, friends, what I want to do with my career. Lonan and I stayed up late eating ice cream and talking. He's so down-to-earth, and we share the same sense of humor. It's hard to deny the attraction we have for each other, but I'm trying to hold a boundary.

For Christmas, he gave me his #14 BURKE hockey jersey. We spent most of the time watching Maddie open her gifts and laughing at all her overdramatic faces of surprise. She's like a little ball of animated cheeriness. I love being Aunt Birdie.

Last night, before I went to sleep, Lonan gave me another hug, and instead of more flashbacks, this time, I only felt fireworks. The timing sucks; my life is too complicated right now to handle something more, especially with a man my parents consider a son.

When they discuss the possibility of moving me to Minnesota, it sounds like an opportunity. I am still thinking it over. It's a huge decision. The majority of my life has been spent in British Columbia. But I've graduated and don't have a firm job in place. My apartment lease with Micky will be up in the next few months, so I'll be looking for a new place.

Is it crazy to look here?

It all feels like fate. I'm on the precipice of starting my life in Vancouver, but why not start it here instead?

Still, that means a lot of work for me. I need to move out, finish getting rid of Julianne's things. I can confidently say there is nothing of hers I plan on keeping, the last thing I want is to be surrounded by mementos of her. The childhood trauma she's left me with is a big enough souvenir. In fact, leaving Vancouver and Julianne behind would be a new beginning. The more I reflect on the situation, the clearer the answer becomes. It's not why should I move to Minnesota, but rather why wouldn't I?

My best friend, Micky, is from Seattle, she said she always planned to go back to the States after university since she's visiting on a school visa. The other reason to stay is to fix that mess at the social security office. I need to do that, regardless. Until then, I've been given the okay to continue with my Canadian identity—which comes with its own set of problems. It's a big adjustment, but even with the new challenges I'll have to face . . . my gut says to stay.

———

Lonan left about an hour ago, and strangely, I already miss him. We are getting to know each other well, and right now, he's my closest friend here. Another reason I can't ruin this by sleeping with him.

After much thought, I've decided I'm going to make the move. It's a chance to take my life back, this place is a part of me. I'll always wonder what could have been if I don't. My parents are sitting in the living room, murmuring. I suspect they are discussing me, so I join them.

"So, first . . . I can't tell you how much this means to me. Thank you so much for your generosity. I'm over-whelmed with all the kindness." Their faces drop, and I realize they think I'm turning down the offer, so I blurt out, "I'd like to give it a shot."

I've never seen two people more relieved.

November 23, 2000

She's giving me a migraine with all this damn crying. She says she wants to go home but I'm not going back to Ontario.

There is no going back.

Vancouver is where we are starting our new life. Besides, when I went to open a new bank account, one of the bankers couldn't keep his eyes off me. Yes, this is going to be a fresh start for us.

FOURTEEN

Birdie

Three weeks later . . .

My plane has just landed at the Minneapolis-St. Paul airport. The whine of the turbines slowing is comforting instead of frightening this time. Two huge checked bags with my clothes are—hopefully—making their way over to baggage claim. I've shipped the remaining items to myself at my new residence, the Hayeses' house. It didn't take me long to decide what to do with Julianne's things. Everything was either donated or sold. I couldn't apply for a B-2 visa because I needed to prove I didn't plan to abandon my Canadian residence, which is basically the whole plan. I've got three months in the States before my passport visit expires. It's a race to see whether I'm resurrected by social security or given the boot first. I'm living two lives simultaneously.

The only things coming with me to Minnesota are my laptop, the collection of recipes I've developed over the years, my chef knives, my *toys*, toiletries, a few bits of memorabilia, and of course, my clothes.

There's no way I can handle being around Lonan Burke without being able to jill off. The tension in the room doubles when he's around. I was too embarrassed to bring my sex paraphernalia through airport security with me, so hopefully they aren't lost in shipping. I've labeled the box as "*TOOLS.*" Technically, it's not a lie.

Micky and I said our goodbyes this morning when she drove me to the airport. She promises to visit during her spring break, and I'm already counting down the days. I'm looking forward to seeing my family again. We FaceTimed several times while I was gone. I need to get to the house and unload my things, because I'm told we are heading to the Lakes game tonight to watch Lonan play.

I'm looking forward to seeing him too.

———

Every player on the ice is getting chippy, every check seems to hit harder than the one before it, and more than once there's been a few double-takes I expected to lead to a fight. Tensions are high in the third period with only five minutes left. The game is tied 2–2, but a lot of hockey can happen in five minutes. We are sitting in Lonan's seats, and I'm wearing the jersey he gave me for Christmas. It still has the faint smell of him on it.

His talent is unbelievable. He scored the last goal when he joined in the offensive rush, and he's been turning over the puck and applying pressure to Buffalo's forwards all night. I'm still getting to know Lonan, but I love seeing this competitive side of him, he's aggressive, quick, and so reactive.

He subs out, and I watch him on the bench to see how he's doing. Sweat is dripping off his face. His cheeks are flush, and he leans over, resting his elbows on his knees. He rinses his mouth with water and spits it out. Kinda gross. But kinda hot. He's focused. After a minute, he stands, ready to take another shift. He jumps the boards and is already back in position before the other defenseman's ass hits the bench.

Before long, he's surrounded by the opposing team, he sends a rim pass up the boards to Conway, their right winger, and there's a breakaway. He passes it to their center, it bounces back and forth as they rush the Buffalo goalie, and with two minutes left in the game, Conway sends it in.

The entire arena erupts into madness before the goal horn blows. If they can hold it down until the end, we won't go into overtime. Puck battles fill up the remaining minutes, but no goals are made. When the buzzer sounds at the end, we throw our hands in the air and high-five the other season ticket holders around us.

Lori cups her mouth and yells over the celebration happening around us, "He's got to hit the bike and finish up some stuff, but he'll meet us at the bar in forty-five!"

"The bike?"

"Stationary bike."

I nod like it's the most obvious thing in the world, but I'm new to behind-the-scenes hockey. Previously, I've only watched hockey when Vancouver was playing, cheering for a rival feels like I'm betraying the Canucks, but how can I not when he's on the ice?

I haven't seen Lonan in almost a month, so when we get to the bar, I take a minute to run to the restroom and clean up. I add another swipe of mascara and some lip gloss. A few women enter behind me, dressed to kill, wearing tight skirts and stilettos. They chat about the hockey players, and it sounds like they know the routine. One woman mentions number fourteen, and I book it out of there. Beautiful women come with the territory, I'm not an idiot, but there's no reason to torture myself by listening to them talk about Lonan for any longer than I have to. Ignorance is bliss.

I settle into the booth with my parents, and they have a beer waiting for me. A big gulp of bubbly ale calms my nerves. Why am I so nervous? This is Lonan, Lonan from when we were kids. Nothing more, nothing less. He's just a friend. Act normal. Tonight, I'm here to have fun, enjoy a drink or two, congratulate Lonan on his win, and go home. *Alone.*

A loud commotion comes from the entry doors, and about half the team walks in. When our eyes meet, he gives me one of his incredible smiles, and it's contagious. A couple of fans step up to get autographs. Then one of the girls from the restroom intercepts him, and my heart sinks a little. She reaches up and places her arms around his neck as if she knows him well. His shoulders tense. He politely removes her hands from his body and continues making his way over to me.

Standing outside the booth to greet him, he wraps me in a giant hug, pressing his body against mine. His woodsy cologne envelopes my senses, and I close my eyes, breathing him in. He smells so good. My body reacts to him without thinking, all of my previous mantras have been tossed out the window. Why does he have to be so damn attractive?

He leans his head down to my ear and whispers, "How does it feel to be home?"

Chills rise up my neck, and I step back to distance myself, tucking a lock of hair behind my ear—just *friends.*

"It's good! Scary, but good," pops out of my mouth. I don't want him to know how petrified I am of the unknown.

His eyes bore into mine, it's like he can see right through my mask and read my thoughts. Everything tells me to look away but then he'll know I lied. *Break the tension.*

"Congratulations on your goal and win! I loved watching you out there!"

"Thanks." He continues to search my eyes, then leans down so I can hear him over the loud sports bar and says, "You only feel scared because you're doing something really brave. It's going to be okay. If you ever need anything, just ask."

I avert my eyes, concentrating on my hands to avoid his intense gaze. Moving to a new place and trying to live an old forgotten life is, well, it's fucking nuts. Putting all my trust into people I have no reason to is irresponsible. So far, all my decisions have been made by following my gut instinct. I hope like hell it's not leading me down the wrong path.

I can't deal with these thoughts right now. My hands shake, and my anxiety rises to the surface, but I swallow it back down and paste on a smile—time to have a drink or twelve.

"Are you thirsty? I ordered a beer for you," I tell him as I slide back into the booth across from my parents.

"Sounds good." He drops the subject but gives me a hard look that says we're not done talking about this. It's been a busy day, now isn't the time to hash through my emotions.

We enjoy another round of beers and talk about the

game. Hearing Lonan's passion for hockey is fascinating to witness firsthand, especially after watching him play tonight.

The bar is much louder now and my parents drop cues they are about to head out. I reach for my purse and coat, but Lonan rests his hand on my thigh, stopping me, his handprint brands me, the warmth seeping into my jeans and spreading across my skin.

"If you want, I can take her home afterward," he offers.

Shit.

"Sure, if Birdie's okay with that?" They look to me for an answer.

"Yeah, it would be nice to catch up a little."

"Okay, we'll see you at home." Ken nods and then focuses on Lonan. "Take care of her."

"Yes, sir."

We share a curious glance, and I wonder if he's thinking about the night we met in the hotel bar. I sure am.

LONAN

We've joined the other players in the team's usual spot, a sizable high-back sectional with lower drink tables in front. For a hockey bar, it's a bit unusual. Our seating is more reminiscent of a nightclub VIP area, and I'm pretty sure they set it up this way so it's easier for us to entertain women and get drinks. Whatever gets us to show up. I've officially introduced her to the team as Gray. They remember her from the hotel bar and know she moved from Vancouver. That's it. They don't know there's a whole fuck ton more to that story. So far, we've been able to keep her return under wraps from the press while we try to navigate getting her set up in Minnesota. I'm sure it's only a matter of time before the media gets ahold of the story.

I'm acutely aware of her closeness along my side. My thighs open to touch hers. Again, she doesn't move away. It's comforting and helps me come down from all the adrenaline during the game.

I don't know what we are, but after staying up late and talking with her on Christmas night, I want more. She's easy to talk to, funny, intelligent, and has the kindest heart. Despite everything, she remains bubbly and cheerful with everyone she meets. The nurturing manner in which she plays with Maddie makes me want things I've never considered before. Those are the parts of her I remember. But she also has a darkness about her —I can see it in her eyes. It's something I see reflected in myself, and that part is new.

She's been through a lot, and it could be that we've both experienced the effects of neglect, or it may be the shared trauma in her disappearance. She brushed off my comment about being brave awfully quickly tonight, and I'd like to know what that's about. Our lives changed after she went missing, but I can't dwell on the past tonight. I shake off the bad memories and focus on her sitting beside me.

The only thing that matters now is that she's here and establishing her life in Minnesota. Near me. We have so much time to make up for, and I plan on doing just that. I peer down at her while she laughs at one of Sully's jokes. She has one of those infectious, genuine laughs.

Jonesy orders a round of shots. Then Conway buys another round. She's taken each one, and the servers make sure our drinks are never empty. Did she have drinks before I got here too? I'm more aware of how close she is. But instead of feeling like I want to pull away, I want to lean in. It's the first time a woman's touch feels like giving instead of taking.

There are a few bunnies hanging on some of the guys' arms. They're pretty, but none could ever compare to how stunning this girl is, especially when she's wearing my number. My chin drops to my chest to hide my sly smile, imagining her wearing nothing else. Except maybe my fingers wrapped around her throat like a collar. I already know she looks great on all fours.

I blink away the memory and try to concentrate on the current conversation happening at the table. As reality comes into focus, I notice the way Banks is looking at her, and I don't like it.

"So, Gray, you have a boyfriend back in Vancouver?" *This fucking guy.*

"No, I didn't have much time for boyfriends last year."

I bore my gaze into him and slowly shake my head, signaling to back down. It's an unspoken rule, you don't hit on a teammate's date. Granted, she's not technically my date, but I've prefaced her as a close friend—that should be enough for him to get the message.

"Good news for me, then, huh?" He winks at her. His cheap comment drags Sully's gaze away from one of the bunnies; he's picking up on this bullshit too. I put my arm around her and sit up, ready to tell him to get fucked.

She chuckles and nods to the women trying to get Banks' attention from a few tables away. "Looks like you have your hands full as it is." Then she meets my gaze. "Hey, I haven't had anything to eat since the plane, what do you think about getting some food?"

Hell yes.

"Yeah, I'm starving."

I grab one of the menus off the table and open it up.

"What are you hungry for, baby?"

I don't mean to call her that, but I'm not taking it back. It's only a matter of time. Hard to tell if the flush in her cheeks is from that or the drinks she'd had tonight. She doesn't seem to notice and sips her beer while reading through the menu. Her eyes light up and she points to the appetizers.

"Let's get nachos!"

"That's my girl." I give her side a squeeze.

That time it's on purpose. Making her blush has become my new favorite hobby. Besides, I want to know where we stand and make my intentions clear without scaring her away. Toeing the line while she's a little tipsy allows me to do some mental recon while she's not so guarded. Some of the guys are already filtering out, mostly the married players hurrying home to their wives. Banks walks off to chat up more groupies.

I pull her closer, even though we're essentially sitting by ourselves now.

"So, no boyfriend, huh?"

"Oh, I see how it is."

"How is it?" I chuckle.

"Shots!" Jonesy yells when a tray of them shows up again. These guys need to ease up a little on the liquor. I place our food order with the server after she drops off the shots. Then give Jonesy a pregnant blink, he gets the message and turns his attention away from us. *Finally.*

Bridget picks up her shot and tries to hand me one, but I shake my head.

Her brow furrows. "Why not?"

"I'm driving."

"Welp, more for me!" She takes her shot, then

prepares to toss back mine, but I snatch her wrist and carefully peel the glass from her fingers, setting it back down.

"You're too small for that much alcohol. Boyfriend. Go."

"You're kind of a flirt, huh? The thing at the house, asking if I have a boyfriend . . ."

"This isn't flirting, Gray. It's just talking."

"Oh. Yeah. I know." Her shoulders droop.

I lean back, smile, and bite my lip, then take a chance by grabbing her hips and pulling her onto my lap. I open my legs so she's straddling my thigh. Her hair is piled into a messy updo, and her sweet scent is like a drug. With one hand, I reach around her stomach and haul her back so she's pressed to my front. Her breaths come in quicker, and feeling her like this is exhilarating. Then I grasp her neck and pull her ear to my lips.

"If I was flirting, I'd tell you how turned on I am seeing you in my number and how pretty you look straddling me like this. Do you remember what happened the last time you were on my lap?"

Goose bumps spread across her skin under my fingers.

"Mmhmm." Her voice is tight.

"All I did was ask if you have a boyfriend. So?"

"No boyfriend."

Sweet relief.

"Good."

Her chest rises and falls. Is she feeling trapped or aroused? I hope both. Her thumb strokes the arm I have wrapped around her. I don't take for granted how well we fit together.

"You are *so* a flirt," she says matter-of-factly, making me laugh.

"Do you want to tell me why you're drinking so much tonight? Does it have anything to do with you feeling anxious about the move?"

"Something like that."

"What else?"

She says nothing for a while, but I refuse to fill the silence. The only way to make her talk more is by me speaking less.

"I shouldn't be sitting here."

I can feel the sting of rejection coming. How is it that it seems like every other woman in the bar would throw themselves at me, but the one I want is holding me at an arm's length?

"Then move. I'm not keeping you here."

She doesn't.

She turns her head to the side so I can only see her profile. "I get that this is your life, and you're probably used to the attention from a lot of women, but it blurs lines for me. I need my friendship to be enough for you right now."

Ouch. I wish she could understand she's not just

some other woman to me. There's something between us, and there's no way she doesn't feel it too.

"You're enough for me. In any capacity." I lean forward to bring my lips to the shell of her ear. "Just because I get a lot of attention, doesn't mean I give mine away as freely."

Our food shows up shortly after, and she sheepishly slides off my lap, leaving me with the unfortunate loss of her body heat. My gaze remains fixed on her.

"I love bar food," she mumbles between bites. I take that as a sign that we're done talking about us. That's fine. I'm willing to give her time to realize this is going to happen. I've waited this long, what's a little longer? Her friendship is enough for me. For now. The conversation goes quiet, and she's chipping at her nail polish. I can tell she's getting in her head, so I drop the subject and move on to something I know she likes talking about: food.

"What's your favorite food?"

"Ever?"

"Yeah, ever."

"Oh my God, I could never choose."

"All right, your favorite at this moment—besides these bomb-ass nachos."

"Maybe Dungeness crab? There is so much incredible seafood in Vancouver. Oysters, salmon, and sushi . . . I'm going to miss that for sure."

"What!? You're telling me lutefisk in some church

basement isn't better than fresh seafood from the Deep Bay? Outrageous."

"Crazy, right?" She giggles, happily munching on nachos and the extra jalapeños in a dish on the side.

"What's your favorite food?"

"Honestly? Snickerdoodles. The ones you and your mom used to make. Fuck, they were so good."

"It's a cookie!"

"So?"

"You can't choose a cookie, it's not even a—" *Hiccup.* "Meal."

"I like what I like. And I like your snickerdoodles."

"That's what all the boys say," she says, waggling her eyebrows.

"Give me names," I tease.

"This creep named Lonan. Plays hockey, obsessed with me, about yay tall." She holds her hand at the top of my head.

"Oh, yeah. I know that guy. Hear he's got a big dick, though."

"You're incorrigible." She nudges my shoulder with a smile on her lips.

We chat for a while about everyday things. It's so easy. No pressure, no hidden agenda—it's real. Is this what trust feels like with a partner? We haven't had a lot of one-on-one time, but whenever we're together, I can take down my defenses and open up. It's a weight off my shoulders.

On her way back from the bathroom, she stumbles. It's time I get this girl home.

"Okay, I think we've had enough fun for the night," I say, taking her arm.

When I'm not looking, she grabs the old shot off the table and downs it. *Damn it.*

"Bridget," I scold under my breath.

"Food waste is a serious problem. There are sober Russians in Russia who would love that vodka!" *Pretty sure it was tequila.*

I stand up and grab her by the waist, pulling her against me.

"Okay, World Hunger, let's go." She's loaded enough for the both of us.

I pick up our coats, and she takes my arm. As we make it toward the exit, she leans into me, molding perfectly to my side. I look forward to the day she's this close with me sober.

———

"I didn't know you could drink so much."

"You'd be surprised at how much I can swallow." She giggles. *Yeah. She's drunk.*

Regardless of her sobriety, her comment conjures the image of her on her knees, those big gray eyes looking up at me while I slide down her throat. My cock swells, and I vow to make her pay for that smart mouth if I ever get the chance again.

For now, I just grin and shake my head at her.

Most of the drive home is spent listening to the radio, interrupted by her occasional hiccup. There's no pressure to say anything. I keep stealing glances of her from the corner of my eye. Her lush, pouty lips are silhouetted by the streetlights. She's so goddamn beautiful.

When we arrive, I walk her to the front door.

"Shhhh!" she stage-whispers, "My mom and dad are sleeping so we have to be quiet."

Then she pushes the oversized door open and stumbles inside.

"How much did you have?"

"No," she says, nodding her head. *That answers that.*

"Why don't you go upstairs, get ready for bed, and I'll bring you something to drink?"

She snaps her fingers and holds up her arm to point at me. "I'll take a Tom Collins. Up."

Drunk Bridget likes the jokes.

"You'll take a water." I smack her butt and point for her to go upstairs. *God, that ass.*

She spins around. "Hey! Don't tease me if you can't please me." Then she snorts at her own rhyme. "I'm a poet and didn't know it."

You have no idea who you're playing with, Princess.

I can't wait to teach her my bark will always be followed by a bite.

"Go."

My voice comes out much darker than intended but it gets her moving.

As I stand in front of the fridge, filling a glass of water, my mind flashes back to us standing here on Christmas Eve. I relax my jaw to keep from clenching it. The way she looked when I called her a good girl gives me a rush. She tried to play it off like she didn't notice, but I saw her blown-out pupils and the way her lips parted. I know exactly how it affects her. Thinking about Bridget earning more praises from my lips makes my dick twitch. *The fuck is wrong with me?*

When I climb the stairs and turn the corner to her room, I almost drop the glass. She's standing there in a baggy crop top and boyshorts with a frothy toothbrush hanging out of her mouth. I try to keep my eyes above sea level, but she's got the most grabbable ass I've ever seen, and it only brings back more memories from the hotel. I want to sink my teeth in it.

She looks at me and raises her chin. "Sup." Then goes back to brushing her teeth again. She's oblivious to what this is doing to me. She wouldn't be standing there so carelessly if she knew the thoughts running through my head. Her head tilts back to keep from drooling toothpaste, and she pads back into the attached bathroom. I curse under my breath and definitely don't peek around the door to check out her ass as she leans down to spit into the sink.

When she walks out, my gaze settles on her thighs and then I notice it: the birthmark. Peeking out is a sexy sideways heart-shaped birthmark on the inside of her thigh. How did I miss this the other night? I have to remind myself this isn't a dream, not only because she's currently climbing under the covers looking hot as fuck but because that mark reminds me it's her. It's hard to believe I've been given a second chance to have someone as wonderful as her back in my life again.

Before she closes her eyes, I make her drink the entire glass of water and then refill it again before setting it on her nightstand. By the time I get back, she's sleeping. I carefully untangle her hair from the messy bun and study her face again. I let myself stare at her for as long as I want, taking her in and getting my fill. When it's time for me to go, I run my fingers through her soft chestnut hair and lean down to whisper, "Good night," pressing a kiss to the top of her head.

"Night, Lonan," she says on a breath, her eyes still closed.

I need to go home and clear my head—both of them.

March 3, 2001

All of our neighbors keep fawning over Birdie. I'm so tired of hearing about it. As if I don't know what she looks like. But not one person has commented on my new designer coat. Well, I'm certainly not going to let them fill her head up with false compliments. If that's what she thinks, she's got another thing coming. Elizabeth needs someone to keep her humble, and who better to do it than her mother? It's only fair I prepare her for life.

FIFTEEN

Birdie

I t's Hayes family dinner night, it happens every Sunday. Tonight, I get to cook, it feels like forever since I've been able to make any food for myself, or others, and it's long overdue. Cooking gives me a sense of control that I've been fiercely craving since moving here; without it, my life is unbalanced. Cooking grounds me.

Fresh seafood is hard to come by, so instead, I found a great cut of meat for Beef Wellington with fingerling garlic potatoes. I'm in my element.

My family has been doing everything for me, giving me a place to live and being patient with my state of mind after "coming home." I'm caught between feeling thankful and suffocated. But in this moment, I'm happy. I'm cooking, and everyone is in good spirits.

Mom, Dad, and I are hanging out in the kitchen,

enjoying a few glasses of wine, and I'm listening to stories of Lonan and Jack, when they were young hellions. Fleetwood Mac is playing softly on the stereo in the other room. I drizzle olive oil over the potatoes and take in a deep, satisfied breath.

"So, then what happened?" I ask.

"After we saw their arms, we about died!" Dad laughs.

Jack walks into the room. "Oh god, please tell me we're not telling her the tattoo story."

"You should have seen them, Birdie—they were hideous! I love my boys, but neither one of them is an artist. On their eighteenth birthdays, we took each of them to a tattoo parlor so they could cover them up," Lori adds. "Luckily, they had three years to figure out what they wanted to get."

Audrey laughs, she's heard this story before.

I turn to Jack. "Sooo, what did you get?"

He rolls up his sleeve to show a tattoo of five trees in a row. It's a tad faded but it still looks crisp on the edges.

"When we would go up north in the summer, Lonan and I would take out the boat and spend a lot of time out on the lake fishing. There were these five trees along the lakeshore, one for each of us—that included Lonan. It seemed fitting." He points to the fifth tree in the line. "This one is yours. We always gave you the smallest tree because you were the smallest."

I admire it a little longer. "I like it."

"What do you like?" Lonan calls from the entryway; I didn't even hear him come in.

"His tattoo. I got to hear all about the prison tats."

"Oh, yeah. That was awesome," he says, walking into the kitchen with a bottle of wine and a small bakery box. "Uncle Lo! Did you bring me anything?"

Maddie leaps into his arms, and with impressive reflexes, he sets down the bottle of wine in time to catch her.

"Madelyn Bridget, we don't ask for gifts. Sorry, L," Audrey smooths out Maddie's hair while she perches in Lonan's arms. He's a natural with her.

"Of course I brought you something!"

He sets her down and hands off the bakery box, and she runs off to the dining room table, popping the cardboard flaps and digging into a colorful cupcake.

"Her middle name is Bridget?"

The namesake pulls at my heart. That little girl was given my name.

"It was never a question," Jack says. "It's fitting too; she reminds me of you when you were little." Then he smiles. "But you were more of a pest."

"Dude, I just got back, and you're already giving me shit?"

"How long are you going to milk that abducted-child card, huh?"

I drop my mouth in faux shock, and he mirrors my expression before we bust out laughing.

"Rude."

"Mom!" Lonan says, taking a beer from the fridge, "What on earth are you making? It smells delicious!"

I bite down on my lower lip to hide my grin. Not just because my ego has been stroked but also because their special relationship makes me happy. Mom nods toward me.

"Birdie's cooking tonight," she hollers back and gives me a knowing smile.

"Really." It's more like a statement as he sizes me up.

I've added rosemary, sage, thyme, and garlic to the potatoes and am now adding the last bit of salt and pepper. I pour them onto a hot sheet pan and pop them into the oven.

"Yup. Food should be ready in twenty."

He leans his hip against the countertop. "Can I help?"

My gaze falls to his chest; that shirt stretched across his broad chest is doing something to me. I want to drag my nails across it.

I clear my throat. "You can set the table."

"Yes, ma'am."

Mom is watching us carefully.

"Hey, let's let Birdie finish cooking. Who wants to play a quick round of UNO?" she suggests.

I squint at her and shake my head disapprovingly. She has a sneaky side, I suspect she's playing matchmaker, considering we're alone again.

"So, what tattoo did you get?"

"Which one? I have a lot of them."

I noticed.

"The one you got on your eighteenth birthday to cover up Jack's handiwork."

"Oh." He pulls his arm out of his sleeve, and I fight for my life to not stare at his abs. "This one."

It's an artistic blackbird, shaded with black ink, except for the small bird-shaped hole in the center where Lonan's flesh shows through. My fingers brush over it, his jaw flexes, and a chill passes over his inked skin. It's beautiful. He doesn't take his eyes off me, and his throat bobs on a hard swallow. I take my time admiring all his other tattoos. The blackbird is my favorite.

When I step away, he returns to the dining table, setting a plate down in front of each chair. "How are things going with the living arrangement?"

"Good. I love it here."

Peering at me as if I'm being given a lie-detector test, he offers a hesitant nod and shoves his hands in his pockets. I failed. Usually, the silence between us isn't bothersome, but this one feels awkward.

"Really, it's fine. I can't complain. But sometimes it's hard being around people all the time. I'm just used to my independence, is all. This was a big move, and I'm not totally sure I'm ready for it."

There. That should be an acceptable answer. What's the point of trying to explain something he could never understand? It makes me look selfish that I want to pull back and protect myself from the kindest, most-loving people I've ever met. I struggle to understand my own state of mind, much less try to break it down for a rational person.

"Do they know how you feel?"

I try to respond, but my mouth opens and closes like a fish out of water. *Of course, they don't know. That would break their hearts. I didn't even want to tell you.*

Relief floods me when my phone rings. It could say spam across the screen and I would still answer. I'll renew my car's extended warranty if it gets me out of an uncomfortable conversation. So I'm even more excited when I see its Micky.

"Sorry, I have to take this," I say, swiping the call to answer. I walk down the hall, away from everyone, and hide out in the dark laundry room. I need a quick vent session with my best friend, and I don't want anyone to see me.

"You just saved my ass!"

"Told you I'm psychic. I could sense you were in need of my services. Why are you whispering?"

"Remember that Lonan guy I told you about?"

"Yeah, the hockey hottie that gives you a snail trail?"

"Those weren't the words I used."

"I Googled him and took some liberties. Cause *dayum*. Number Fourteen can get it."

I close my eyes and a smile tugs at the corners of my lips.

"I miss you so much, Mick." My voice catches.

"Oh, babe. I miss you too. What's going on?"

I stumble through everything I've been feeling lately in a hushed voice. It's like a floodgate of emotion and all the shit I've been trying to repress bursts through the levy. Thankfully, she understands me and my babbling. I tell her about the social security fiasco. That I'm unable to find a job anytime soon, and that my life is stuck in limbo. That I can't shake my attraction to Lonan. That I feel smothered here. Micky doesn't say a word; she simply listens.

"And another thing!" I whisper-yell, "I can't even let myself feel bad about any of these things, because then I'm an ungrateful asshole! All I've ever wanted is a family that loves me, and now that I have one, I just want to escape. Why am I like this? I feel so guilty all the time, and that pisses me off too."

She waits to speak, making sure I've gotten out everything I wanted to say. Even though we are separated by thousands of miles and a phone call, she gets me. I choke out a sob and quickly wipe away the frustration trying to spill from my eyes. Gah! I don't have time for this right now. I'm sure somebody will come looking for me any minute when they realize I'm no longer in the kitchen.

"Feel better?"

"A little." I shudder.

"Okay, now take a deep breath. In for four seconds, hold for four, out for four."

I do as she says, and it helps. I roll my shoulders, trying to send that soothing breath to the areas of my body holding tension.

"Listen, all of those feelings are valid. It would be weird if you didn't feel this way. And why are you adding guilt on top of those emotions? You're going through enough as it is. Sometimes you just need space from people. There's nothing wrong with that. You're an introvert; you're *supposed* to feel that way." She pauses. "That said, if at some point you need a break and want to come back here for a bit, I would love to have you. Although, from where I sit, it looks like I'd be better off moving in with you and getting to know the rest of that hockey team . . ."

I chuckle and roll my eyes, dabbing the tears away with the cuff of my sleeve.

"When are you coming here?"

Something shifts in the hallway. Is somebody out there?

"Shit, can I call you later? I'm in the middle of a Beef Wellington, and I have to pull it out to rest."

"You're making a Wells? Promise to cook me one when I visit?"

"Promise you'll help me?"

"I'll sous—I mean it this time. I miss our little cooking duo. I'm getting takeout tonight. There's this new sushi place that literally opened a block away. It's amazing."

"I'm moving back," I say matter-of-factly.

She laughs. "Don't even think about it. You can do this. And, hey, send me a cross section of the Wellington!"

"Obviously. Chat later, eh?"

"Love you!" she singsongs.

"Love you more!"

I end the call, shove my phone into my back pocket, and walk straight into a wall of muscle in the dark. It's Lonan, I've already memorized his cologne. *Where the fuck did he come from?*

"You scared the shit out of me! What are you doing back here?"

"I should ask you the same question."

"I was on the phone. Were you eavesdropping on me?"

Even in the dark, I can make out the silhouette of his tight shoulders. He braces his arms against the wall, boxing me between them.

"I'm getting a roll of paper towels from the closet. Your timer went off, by the way. I took out the food and set it on the counter."

"T-thank you."

"You know you can always come to me if you need to chat or vent or whatever, right?"

Yeah, but it feels weird talking to you about my parents, who seem to be your parents as much as they are mine.

"Uh-huh." I slip under one of his arms and scurry into the kitchen to return my focus to cooking. He doesn't follow me.

As promised, I shoot off a picture to Micky of the cross section, and she sends me back an animated *O-face* GIF. She's not wrong. This is one slutty-looking Beef Wellington.

When we sit to eat, Lonan compliments the meal but still seems reserved. He's been acting odd since finding me in the hallway. Talking to Micky was just what I needed. Maybe Mom and Dad are right and I should find a therapist. But I don't want to hash out everything with Julianne. I don't need to. I just need to move on from everything that's happened. Leave the past in the past, focus on the future. Life has been confusing as of late, but cooking and chats with my bestie have brought back a sense of normalcy. I'm fine. Everything will be fine.

That thought was doomed as soon as it crossed my

mind, because the next thing I know, the doorbell rings. Mom furrows her brow and exchanges a curious glance with my dad. He shrugs in response. Then wipes his mouth with his napkin, dropping it next to his plate as he walks toward the front door.

"Lori . . ." She hurries to his side, and I can hear her gasp from here.

"Story's out," he calls from the front window.

The rest of us shove out of our chairs and try to get a peek at the activity happening outside. Two news vans are parked in the driveway, and they appear to be doing camera and sound checks. Are they here for me?

Lonan is the only one who hasn't moved from his chair. He looks a little rigid, but that might just be his muscles. Mostly he's busy staring at the table in front of him. He takes a long pull from his beer and goes back to eating. This kind of excitement is nothing out of the ordinary for him. On the other hand, Mom flies into action, crossing the house and lowering the blinds and curtains as she makes her way from one side to the other.

"I'll get the windows on the back side," Audrey says, heading toward the rear patio doors.

What a nightmare. I guess we knew it would happen eventually, but damn. This sucks.

"I don't have to go out there, do I?" I know they wouldn't make me, but I have to ask.

"Of course not, but we should probably figure out

some kind of strategy here. They look like they're prepared to camp out. Who knows how many more are on their way."

"Jack, pull Lonan's car into the third stall. If they run his plate, it will turn into a circus," Dad instructs, still peeking out the side of the window.

Shit, I didn't even think about how this would involve Lonan. Jack braves the press and runs outside. The press are peppering him with questions, but he keeps his head down like he's done it a thousand times before and quickly pulls the car into the garage. I stand around, being 100 percent unhelpful, twisting my wrists, and trying to come to terms with the new challenge added onto the pile. What's one more chainsaw to juggle?

SIXTEEN

LONAN

I pull Ken and Lori aside and offer a possible solution for Bridget's privacy. All I care about is her not fleeing back to Vancouver—which is why I called the news stations to leak her story. All it took was an anonymous tip that Bridget Hayes has been found alive and is back home with her parents.

She was right, I was eavesdropping on her phone call earlier. It wasn't my intention, I really was getting a new roll of paper towels, but my ears pricked up when I heard some of her conversation. I didn't hear everything, but what I caught spooked me.

I'm moving back.

Promise you'll help me?

When are you coming?

Her words keep replaying in my mind. That was all it took to know I had to act fast. It's collateral damage.

She wants to go home, but with the media involved, she's forced to lay low here. At least for the next few weeks—and I have the perfect solution.

Was it a dick move? Absolutely. But ask me if I care.

————

She's snuck off to do dishes. Unfortunately, I get the sense she feels like a burden for bringing the press to her parents' door, and that's on me. I'll convince her she has no reason to feel like this is her fault. She's constantly setting impossible expectations of herself.

"Hey, Birdie, can we talk for a minute?" Ken asks her.

"Sure." She walks into the living room, her arms wrapped around herself as if she's trying not to take up space. "What's up?"

"Have a seat, honey," Lori coaxes.

She sits, watching her parents faces with a forced grin that doesn't reach her eyes.

"The choice is up to you, Birdie, but I have an offer for you," I begin.

Her gaze meets mine, then bounces between the three of us. She probably thinks we're staging some kind of intervention.

"Okay . . ."

"I need a personal chef to work with the Lakes team

nutritionists and get me on a better diet. The coaches have been riding my ass for the last couple of years to eat better."

Silence. She stares at me. Shit, did I offend her?

"I'm not following. I can't work until I have a social back in order."

"I'd pay you in cash."

"You want me to cook for you?"

"I also need a house sitter." *Great fucking follow-up, asshole.* I'm sure she's champing at the bit now.

"A house sitter," she repeats.

"You don't need to clean. I already have a service that comes by a couple of times a month. I just need someone to turn the lights on every now and then and keep it occupied while I'm traveling during the season."

There's no reaction from her, nothing to clue me in to what she's thinking. So I keep going.

"Being a personal chef should work to fill the gap in your resume while we wait for the social security stuff to straighten out. It will also allow you to build up some savings, since you'll have room and board covered."

"I'm confused. I'd live at your condo too? Does this have something to do with the press? Am I being kicked out?"

"No!" Lori and Ken say in unison.

"You don't have to move into the condo, but you staying there would offer privacy from the press until everything dies down. I already have protocols set up for my security, and I'd have them apply to you as well. The media will be much better controlled over there."

She looks like she's considering it, so I continue, "As long as they don't get a look at you when we leave, they won't know what you look like. You're still using your old name on your documentation and social media, so as long as you're away from this house, you'll be free to move around the city unnoticed. And you'll have some independence." I hope that last part piques her interest. "It's only thirty minutes from here, so if you decide you want to come back, you can."

She nods and looks down at her hands, picking at her fingernail polish, an old habit.

"Can I sleep on it?"

"Take as much time as you need."

"Honey, we love you. We don't care where you live as long as we get to see you enough. We have no problem coming to you for a while. This will always be your home, even if you're not sleeping here."

———

I'm anxious. I got home three hours ago, but I'm restless and can't sleep after what went down tonight. I've essentially forced her to move in with me, placed her between a rock and a hard place. But I can't bring myself to regret it either. It's better than her going back to Canada. And sure, she should get more independence and not be dogged by reporters, but the selfish part of me can't wait to have her all to myself. Her family will come here to visit, but they won't be here all the time.

After throwing out my proposition, I couldn't get a read on her. She can be so hot and cold. There's no way of knowing how she'll respond. Rolling onto my back, I let out a deep exhale and stare at the ceiling. It's in her hands now. She'll let me know what she decides. I roll onto my side and adjust my pillow, unable to get comfortable. This bed feels empty and lonely.

My phone dings and I snag it from the nightstand, fumbling to unlock it.

> Bridget: Do I have to cook for all your hookups too?

Holy shit, she's in.

> Me: I mean, if you're hungry, go for it 😵‍💫

> Me: Is that a yes??

> Bridget: Yes. To the job.

The reflection in the floor-to-ceiling windows shows my fist pump lit up by the glowing phone screen.

> Me: When do you want to start?

> Bridget: Soon. The news vans aren't moving. Does Wednesday work?

Bridget: It would be nice to drop some things off earlier though. Maybe get a kitchen tour?

Me: Hell yeah.

Me: Leaving for a game tomorrow, but I'll be back Tues afternoon.

Me: I'll pick you up and we can take some boxes over.

Bridget: Thanks, Lonan, really. For all of this.

Me: Just trying to take care of what's mine 🩶

Bridget: I'm yours, huh?

Me: My house and my diet, conceited.

Bridget: Jerk. You just earned yourself a week of kale.

I wince at her message. She's right about that. I don't deserve her gratitude, this whole thing was orchestrated by me. But she guessed another thing right—she's mine.

SEVENTEEN

LONAN

She's really moving in. Ken and Lori meet us in the underground garage of the Elevate Tower, and I grab a cart so we can take her things up in one go. While I'm doing that, I let her say her goodbyes. It's not really goodbye since she won't be far away from them and they still plan on getting together. Though Sunday dinners will probably be hosted here for a while. I won't always be able to make those due to my game schedule. They open the trunk and unload her things onto the cart. When they pull out of the garage, it's a bizarre feeling having her here without them.

"Where's the rest of your stuff?"

She looks around her to make sure she's not missing anything. "This is it."

"Five boxes and a couple of suitcases? That's it?" I

observe her belongings. Each box is labeled with its contents next to the shipping labels.

"I left most of my things with Micky when we lived together; I didn't need them anymore."

"You and Micky still close?"

"She's my best friend. In fact, I've been meaning to talk to you about that. She was planning on visiting at some point. Maybe during her spring break. Would it be okay if she stayed with me? If I'm still living here, I mean."

"Of course. This is your condo too."

She rolls her eyes as she heads toward the main elevator.

"Actually, we're taking this one," I say, walking around the backside of the brick elevator shaft. I swipe my keycard and push the cart into the elevator, keeping my hand on top of the box to make sure it doesn't fall. "This one takes you to my condo. 1-0-0-5-1-4-9 is the code you'll need to enter."

"You have a private elevator?"

"I'll program the number into your phone but try and memorize it."

The front desk and homeowner's association have already added her as a resident. I've explained they need to apply my same security measures to her, as well. However, I didn't tell them why. They assume she's my girlfriend. I haven't corrected them.

"Why do I need to remember the code, won't you be with me?"

"Not always. I'll be traveling a lot, and I'm not going to keep you inside like a pet. You are free to come and go as you please. I want you to be independent here. Go explore, feel free to do whatever you want."

I need to get her a car. The more room she has to fly, the less she'll feel like she's in a cage.

"I don't know where I would go."

"That's okay, I'll show you around the neighborhood. I've got a few different vehicles, so feel free to take whichever is available."

She nods, and her shoulders are less tense than they were ten minutes ago. When we reach the top floor, my stomach clinches. I hope she doesn't find my home as unwelcoming as I do. The elevator doors open to the penthouse foyer, and I become hyperaware of every piece of furniture, every windowpane, every floorboard. Does she like it?

"Holy shit," she whispers under her breath. She drops the suitcases and slips her shoes off, moving down the hall toward the floor-to-ceiling windows that wrap around the main level.

I roll the cart into the entry hall and grab the two rolling suitcases she's abandoned.

"Holy fuck. Your kitchen . . ." she shrieks.

That makes me smile, and I kick off my shoes next to hers.

"Why didn't you tell me it was so big? I would have agreed to move in a lot sooner!"

"That's what all the girls say," I say, stealing her joke. "Will it work for you, chef?"

"Yes. Yes, this will do nicely." Her fingertips glide over the marble countertops, and she examines the eight-burner stove.

I shake off the image of grabbing her curvy hips and setting her bare ass on the cold stone island. It's going to be hard living in such close quarters. Literally. At least the hot water bill will be lower—I predict many cold showers in my future.

"Feel free to look around; I'm going to drop these boxes off in your bedroom."

"Mmhmm . . ." She's distracted by the built-in coffee system.

I stack the five boxes to carry them into her new space. Her bed has been fitted with all new luxury bedding, and I had the front desk bring fresh flowers for the nightstand before I left. The soft aroma of calla lilies hits me as I turn into her bedroom. Unfortunately, the wider box in the middle of the stack catches the door-frame, and the top three boxes tumble onto the floor. *Damn it.*

I survey the mess. The box labeled *TOOLS* took the brunt of the fall, laying on its side, the contents spilling out. I kneel to clean up the mess.

Hold up.

"Oh, Little Bird."

There are at least five vibrators and a few pieces of lingerie scattered about that I pray to never unsee. I quickly gather the items and shove them back into the cardboard box. This is going to be fun. I bring in the rest of her suitcases, join her in the kitchen, and lean my hip against the counter, enjoying the view of her bent over to look into one of the lower base cabinets.

She slides a stack of mixing bowls aside I didn't even realize were in there.

"I don't see a juicer anywhere, so we'll probably need to pick one up." She's taking inventory. "And how do you only have one fry pan? It barely even looks used. Please tell me you utilize this gorgeous kitchen."

"I utilize this gorgeous kitchen," I parrot, obviously lying.

"You're breaking my heart right now," she whines. She stands up straight. "I need to go grocery shopping because you have zero food in the fridge. Also, I'm going to need a few more tools in this kitchen if I'm going to meal prep."

It's too easy.

"Huh. Maybe we should check your box back there labeled 'tools'?" I motion my thumb behind me and cock my head to the side.

She freezes and slowly turns around. "Don't open that box."

We stare at each other in silence before her eyes get big.

"Oh my God." Her face pales.

"The box fell over. I put everything back."

"You touched my sex toys!?" she screeches.

I furrow my eyebrows and play dumb. "Toys? I thought you said they were *tools*?"

Slack-jawed, she faces the windows with a palm across her forehead and mutters, "This isn't happening right now."

I take three strides, stand in front of her, and tuck a strand of hair behind her ear.

"Everybody masturbates, Princess. I did this morning. But don't worry, I'll keep your little secret just for me." I give her a wink. Her nervousness is so refreshing. I follow the blush down her neck to her open neckline.

"I'm begging you to ignore everything you saw."

I scoff. "Absolutely not. Come on, let's go buy some pots."

"Pans," she corrects.

"And that big juicer you want so bad."

"You have to stop." She laughs.

Good, she's starting to relax.

"Get your purse. You're driving."

As much as I love seeing her flustered, I don't want her wrapped up in her brain overthinking our arrangement. Driving forces her to focus on something else and gives her a little practice in the Land Rover. She needs to get acclimated to driving something bigger than she's used to—that's a fine double entendre.

Pulling into the Williams-Sonoma, she has her list in hand. Such an organized little thing. We get to the cookware section, and I can't take my eyes off her. She's unapologetically giddy. It intrigues me when she reaches for some of the less expensive brands, and I suggest we upgrade. Without looking at me, her inspection of the pans continues, "No, you're just paying for the label. These are actually better."

Well, I'll be damned. I love that she knows what she wants.

She carefully selects her pans, a juicer, and some meal prep containers she says I'll be able to take with me to practice. I don't have the heart to tell her that the team usually buys us lunch when we go out. She's weaving between the aisles, breaking down why specific cookware is better than others, and how they need to be cleaned and maintained. Her eyes sparkle when she speaks, and a lot of what she's saying is going way over my head, but I am thoroughly entertained by her enthusiasm.

When she stops at an aisle for baking, she gives a double-take to one of the stand mixers.

"Which one is best?"

She walks up to one of the demo models. "This one, but we don't need it. I'm guessing your diet will be more protein-based." She keeps checking out a matte silver one on the end. Her smile grows.

"Micky and I had a patisserie class together in college. Neither of us could make a macaron to save our lives, so we stayed up all night. We must have had hundreds of macarons that were either deflated, hollow, or porous. Or burned! Anyway, finally, around four in the morning, we got the hang of it. God, we ate so many shit macarons that night. It was years before I had any desire to eat one again." She laughs.

"Do you like baking?"

"Sometimes, but I only bake for fun."

"Are you sure you don't want one?"

"No, no, no. I mean, yes, I'm sure. I was just being nostalgic. Ready to go?"

"Yup, let's check out."

I feign disinterest but sneak a photo of the barcode. After the way I gave her shit about the sex toys, she deserves a little something special.

July 20, 2003

It's bad enough I have to spend all day schooling her, but she's constantly outgrowing her clothes. And the meals. My God, I feed her twice a day, and somehow it's still not enough for her. Figures I end up with the most spoiled child of all time. How much does she really expect from me? Home economics will be starting immediately. Lucky for her, I'm a fabulous cook so she'll be far ahead of her peers at the public school. Finally, she will be pulling her weight around here. At least she's a quick study.

EIGHTEEN

Birdie

I spent the last three hours at the grocery store and am worn out. So much time was wasted trying to convert measurements from metric to the imperial system. Why do they think Canada abandoned it in the '70s? The rest of the world gets it. Waiting on you, America! The weights and measurements here are arbitrary and make zero sense. Good thing I picked up a measuring scale the other day, because I'm not dealing with that dry measuring cup bullshit.

The fridge was practically bare, besides half a case of beer and a few bottles of hot sauce. He likes it spicy, which is no surprise, considering the mouth on him. But even when he's not being flirty, the timbre of his voice makes me weak in the knees. The crush I had on him as a child has been gone for a long time, but it's obviously never strayed too far. Only this time, my filthy fantasies have obliterated any trace of the old puppy love. *This bitch wants a bone!* Especially because I know what the bone looks like. I just haven't had it in my mouth yet. Okay, that's enough, this metaphor is getting gross. The odds of that encounter still astound me. And while he's sexy, charismatic, and charming, there's more to him than that. It goes deeper than he likes to let on.

He's away at dryland training—why isn't that a spectator sport? I got a preview of his workout in his home gym—*two very exuberant thumbs-up.* I scheduled a meeting with his nutritionist to review his diet and devise a menu that will work with his training and game day schedules.

Since I also need to eat, I bought a couple of items for myself, but it will be easiest if we share the same meal plan. I'm ensuring I have enough to get us through the next week or two.

I pull into the parking garage, find the elevator code, and type it in. It's my first time entering his condo by myself. Thankfully, I have my trusty cart helping me bring up all the groceries. I walk into the entry, neatly kick off my shoes, and carry the paper bags—that I can barely see over—to the kitchen. I set them down with a humph and then it catches my eye.

The stand mixer. Holy shit, he bought me a stand mixer!

There's a note attached that reads, *All yours. Go wild.* I try not and look too far into that. Then I see that there's also a pack of AA batteries leaning up against the side with another note that says, *For your toolbox.* Cheeky bastard. I admire the machine again and turn it on and off, exploring the different attachments. I bounce on my tiptoes and giggle. This was way too nice of a gift, but I'm too selfish to demand he take it back. I need to come up with something to make him as a thank you.

Me: OMG! 😎

Lonan: You like it?

Me: Of course, thank you so much. This was a really big gift.

Lonan: How was your first time driving around the cities?

Me: It was good! And I found almost everything I needed at the store. Now we aren't going to starve! Cool, huh?

Lonan: Glad we won't starve. But if it came down to it, I already had plans to eat you first, so . . . 😉

Me: Wow. Shameless.

Lonan: Lol

Lonan: Got a couple meetings to finish up, but should be home around 3.

Me: See you then 🙂

I put away the groceries as quickly as I can and get started on marinating the chicken for dinner tonight. Once that's done, the baking begins.

While mixing ingredients, I can't help but imagine what it would be like to live here, not just as a guest. It's a foolish delusion, but I let myself have it. It's a fun fantasy I can entertain while admiring the view of the Minneapolis skyline and Lake Bde Maka Ska blanketed in snow. It's beautiful.

I'm pulling the first batch of cookies from the oven when I hear the telltale ding of the elevator. I attempt to suppress my reaction to him coming home but like Pavlov's dogs, I salivate as soon as I hear the bell. When he emerges from the hall, I'm greeted with one of his panty-melting smiles, and the butterflies become frenzied. Maybe some handcrafted orgasms tonight will help douse the flames I feel right now.

"Oh my God, are these—"

"Snickerdoodles. They're still hot, so be careful."

He plucks one from the cooling rack and shoves the whole thing into his mouth.

"Fuuuck, they're the same as before. You have no idea how much I missed these. You never forgot the recipe?"

"I asked Mom." I smile.

"You did promise these to me when we were kids. Took you long enough to pay up," he says with his mouth full.

"How much of that do you remember?"

He swallows. "All of it." His smile returns. "Remember asking me to be your husband?" he teases.

"I did not." I roll my eyes, placing some cooled cookies into a container.

"You absolutely did! We made a pact that we would live in the fort when we grew up. I was going to build all your ridiculous additions onto the tree house, and in exchange, you would bake these snickerdoodle cookies."

"They were not ridiculous."

"You baked the cookies. Darling, is this your proposal to me?"

His voice dropped an octave. I know we're joking around, but I still feel it low in my belly. Very low. *Just friendship, remember? Don't complicate your arrangement already.*

I laugh. "How do you remember so much?"

"You don't forget a first kiss like that. You had some moves."

"Pretty sure you kissed me first." I slide three more cookies into the container.

"No way I would've had the guts back then."

"You did! You know I'm right. You told me you 'like-liked' me, and even asked permission before you did it. You were a perfect little gentleman." I pinch his cheek.

He watches me as I transfer more hot cookies to the

now empty cooling rack.

"Show me."

The air is sucked out of the room.

"What?"

"Show me how you remember it." His eyes turn stormy, it's a look of pure sex, and I want to drown myself in it. That was the best sex of my life. I try to remember why this is a bad idea, but I can't remember anything. All I see is a rugged jawline and those dark intense eyes staring me down. He steps into my space, crowding me against the kitchen island.

Fuck it.

"You walked up to me."

"Like this?" he asks.

I nod.

"You held my hand."

He follows along. "Like this?"

When he weaves our fingers together, I wonder if he feels the same spark I do.

"Like this?"

"Yeah," I respond in a whisper. "A-And then you kissed me."

"Like this?"

My pulse races as he leans down. It starts with a brush. His lips are soft yet commanding. His mouth moves over mine and causes my pulse to race. The pent-up feelings are finally being released and it takes over until our kiss builds into something heavy and potent.

It's different from the one at the hotel. When my breath hitches, he releases my hand and drives his fingers into my hair, deepening the kiss.

One hand lowers to the base of my neck, and the rough pad of his thumb strokes my collarbone. A spatula clatters to the floor when he grabs my waist and sets me on the counter, closer to eye level. His hands settle on my knees, pushing them open to stand between my thighs. The muscles in my core contract.

I fist the sides of his shirt but resist pulling him close enough to bring friction to my peaked nipples. Kissing him is like the first rain after a drought. It's something you've wanted for so long, and when it comes, you hope it floods. I bite back a moan when he parts my lips and traces them with his tongue as he did before. His palms drop to my hips, and he pulls me to the edge, kneading the flesh. Just before I wrap my legs around his waist, the oven timer buzzes and I jump. Our lips pull apart, leaving us panting, but our foreheads connect while we catch our breath.

"No," I answer his earlier question, "this kiss was nothing like that."

"Fuck . . ." He snickers. "No. It wasn't."

The timer on the oven goes off again, and it takes every ounce of self-control I have to place my arm on his chest and gently push him back. I'm lightheaded when I hop off the counter, but I turn off the oven, take out the cookies, and slide in a new batch.

I feel him watching me. Then he laughs, and it causes me to join in. We're punch-drunk off the kiss we shared.

"Wow, I need to get started on dinner." I giggle, attempting to fill the dead air. I'm very self-conscious of my movements around him after that. It's obvious, at the point, that he gets a rise out of seeing me embarrassed.

"So . . . what are we eating tonight?"

Are you looking for volunteers?

"Grilled chicken and vegetables, pasta, and some crusty bread I picked up from this cute little bakery nearby."

"I know that place. They have great cinnamon bread too." There's a lull.

"Can I help you chop veggies?"

"Sure." We stand in silence; the only sound is our knives hitting the cutting boards. I'm a lot faster at this than he is, and I cut all my carrots and cauliflower before he finishes the two sweet potatoes I've tasked him with.

Dinner is delicious, he makes a few appreciative grunts that cause me to bite my lip. I love how verbal he is. I can tell his thoughts are impure when he leans back in his chair, ripping off pieces of bread and flashing that straight white smile of his. It's mischievous. He's daring me to guess what he's thinking about, but I'm not taking the bait.

I'm a little surprised when he gets up to wash our

dishes after we finish. Not that he wouldn't offer, but he didn't hesitate to do it and made me sit back down when I tried to help. Aren't dishes part of my job description? I don't pay any rent, the least I can do is dishes.

After sliding the last plate into the dishwasher, he uncorks a bottle of wine. Shit, all this will do is give me the liquid courage to jump him again. *Vagina, it's a trap. Stay vigilant.*

He pours me a glass, and he lifts the stem of his to cheers. I clink my glass and pull my hand back.

"So, what's for dessert?" He swirls his wine in his glass. He's not even trying to hide it anymore.

"Snickerdoodles."

"These damn cookies."

Going against my better judgment, I pluck one of the cookies from the cooling rack and hold it in front of his mouth. I swallow, and a rush of warmth spreads through me when his eyes darken. There's a straight-up beast inside him. *I want to sharpen its teeth and let it out of its cage.*

He doesn't break eye contact when he slides his fingers through the belt loops of my jeans and walks me backward until my ass hits the cabinets behind me. He opens his mouth for me to give him a bite, and I pull my hand back just slightly. It's akin to playing with fire, I just want to see what happens. A growl rattles in his throat, and he slowly shakes his head, releasing a dark chuckle. "Don't tease me, Little Bird."

I'm done for. He takes a bite and watches me under hooded lids as he chews. He always gets what he wants. I'd give about anything to trade places with the cookie he's devouring. He encircles my wrist, his fingers resting on my pulse, which only causes it to quicken. Then he pulls away from me and turns toward the living room with his glass of wine. *What. The hell.*

"Come sit with me."

Really? We both know what's about to go down. My disappointment is compounded when he sits at the opposite end of the sofa. He angles his body to face me and picks up my feet to set them in his lap, rubbing the soles. I don't think anybody has ever given me a foot rub before. This is incredible. My back slumps into the cushions, and I snuggle in. It's not sex, but it's not bad.

Then we talk.

We talk for hours. About anything and everything. Exchanging stories of our shitty upbringings. Me with Julianne, and him with his mom before he moved in with my parents. I share what I'm comfortable with, but keep a few things to myself. But not him. He's letting his guard down for me, and I get the impression this is a side of Lonan he reserves for only those closest to him.

"Just because I make millions a year, doesn't mean I can spend it all. I only have a few years to work, I never know if I'm going to be dropped or traded, and I've been playing hockey at one level or another my whole life. It's a big check for my body to cash. I need to make this salary last the rest of my life." He takes his last sip of wine and stands to get a refill. He continues from the kitchen, "So far, I've been smart about my spending and investing. I have a few sponsorship deals, but I need to keep up appearances so that I can keep working after I retire from the Lakes."

I think about his reputation while reading articles and seeing pictures of him with random women. It's hard to believe that the guy from the tabloids is the same man sitting across from me. He returns with the almost empty bottle in his hand and sits next to me this time. We finish the wine, and he pulls me into his lap.

"Better."

I straddle his thighs and hope it plays out the same way it did last time I was in this position. He shamelessly checks me out, but instead of feeling shy this time, I welcome it. Allowing his stare to blaze across my body. His gaze follows his hands as he brings them down to rest where my thighs meet my hips, and I can already feel the heat pooling below. There's a heady buzz I get from being the object of his attention. My finger traces around the shell of his ear and behind his neck as I lean in to kiss him.

We pick up right where we left off this afternoon, this time a little slower and more seductive. He's teasing me with his lips. Every time I try to speed up, he slows down. He's savoring my frustration, slowly gliding his palms up and down the tops of my thighs. My muscles are tightening, and I'm so close to grinding against him —I want more. He knows I do. The growl he releases when I nip at his lower lip causes me to grip his shoulders a little tighter. Then his fingers are back in my hair —in the opposite direction of where I want them. I nip a little harder this time, and his hold on my hair turns into a grip. *Closer* . . .

My patience runs out. "Pull my hair," I whisper against his lips.

This earns me another growl, and a grin pulls at my lips as his control weakens. I'm winning. He slowly wraps my hair around his fist, building up the anticipation. When he pulls, all the nerve endings in my scalp light up with pleasure. My mouth drops open, and I gasp. He brings his lips to my exposed neck, dragging them down to meet my shoulder, and bites. I flinch and let out a small yelp when it sends a shock wave straight to my core. I've never been bitten before. It was more playful than painful. He exhales a small laugh at my response, then uses his tongue like a balm to lick it all better.

"You like it rough, don't you, Little Bird?" he asks against my skin.

Fuck. A small moan is all I can muster.

"Of course you do."

His length is straining against the clothing that separates us, its firm between my thighs, and I grind against him, stealing the friction I've been craving all evening.

200

"That's it," he coaxes.

I'm in heaven.

And then plunged straight to hell when a doorbell rings from his phone. You've got to be kidding me—how do we keep getting interrupted?

"It's just my dry cleaning from downstairs," he pants out. "They said it would be delayed. Don't stop, baby."

He taps a button on the phone screen. I start to get up, but he pulls me back down on him.

"Don't worry, they'll leave it in the hall and go. I promise."

I nod and ignore the interruption. Too busy getting back to kissing and grinding against him again.

I want to ride him. My legs tremble, and he slides his strong hands beneath my shirt, running his thumbs across my pebbled nipples. Oh my God. I might come from this. My walls tighten when the door to the elevator opens.

"Thank you!" he calls out. Then he drops his voice for me again. "Just like that, you're almost there."

I'm so close. I do everything I can to focus but then more background noise distracts me; it finally registers that I'm hearing the click of high heels on the tile floor. I clamber off him just as a blonde bombshell struts around the corner in a trenchcoat—carrying no dry cleaning.

"Oh, Daddy, I haven't done anything yet . . ."

NINETEEN

LONAN

hat. The actual. Fuck.

In every sense of the word, my *last* one-night stand, Nikki, is in red stilettos and a trenchcoat that she's obviously naked underneath. I can't believe this is happening.

"How the hell did you get in here?" I glower at her.

"You buzzed me in. I thought we could have some fun."

She sticks out her lower lip in a pout. It's not cute.

"I thought you were my dry cleaning." I get off the couch, clearly still hard, and take her by the arm, guiding her back to the elevator. When I look back at Birdie, she's sitting on the couch, hunched over with her arms wrapped around herself, looking at the floor. The flush of her almost-orgasm still on her temples. My heart sinks. She won't look at me. I want to explain, but first, I need this other woman gone.

I lead her to the elevator. "I'm seeing someone. It's serious." Not officially, but I have every intention to change that.

"She's pretty. I don't mind adding one more if you don't?" she offers.

"I mind."

"Why haven't you been answering my calls?"

"I blocked you. This wasn't something I planned to continue. I'm sorry if you got the wrong impression."

"Oh." She's disappointed, but I don't give a shit because my concern lies with Bridget. I look at Nikki, willing her to get into the elevator, but she won't budge.

"Look, I need to ask you to leave, or I'm going to have to contact security. You can delete my number."

"Oh, can I?" she says, backing into the elevator. "Asshole."

"Yup" is all I say as I usher her into the elevator. I don't have time; I want her out of here. And right now, I have earned the asshole title. I've just ruined whatever Bridg and I had going.

The doors to the elevator close, and I rush back to the couch, but she's nowhere in sight. *Fuck!* My jaw clenches, and my hands open and close into fists. Taking a deep breath, I head toward the bedrooms. Her door is closed, so I knock gently.

"Hey, I'm really sorry about that. Can we talk?"

"It's fine. Actually, I'm kinda tired, so I think I'm going to call it a night." It comes out casual, but I saw her face—she looked crushed. I need her to know she's the only woman I want, in my bed or otherwise.

"Bridg, please. Open the door, baby."

She pads over to the door, and it swings open.

"Yes, Daddy?" she mimics. It makes my stomach turn. I'm not a huge fan of being called Daddy, especially when she's only doing it to imitate a former lay. I'm not proud of my history with puck bunnies, and I want none of my old life to overlap with this fresh start with Birdie. Nikki has been texting for a hookup over the last couple of months, but I thought if I didn't answer, she would leave me alone. Eventually, I blocked her. I never expected her to show up here like that.

The second I saw her in that trenchcoat, I knew my old habits had died. Her sexy schtick did nothing for me. It seemed so vapid and detached. Now that I've had a taste of what it's like to have deep feelings woven in with lust, nothing can compare. I want Bridget in every way I can have her.

After calling me Daddy, she must see my lip curl in disgust because her phony smile falls.

"I'm sorry you saw that. You're the only woman I'm interested in."

"It's okay. I get it. It's part of your life. You don't have to apologize." I wait for the other shoe to drop. "But I think we should remain friends for now."

Goddamn it.

"No, it's not like that. That's not my life anymore."

"I believe you, really, I do. But it's a weird time for me, and I don't want to complicate things between us, especially since we're living together. I'm sorry if I led you on. I shouldn't have let it go that far."

She's lying. She can't even bring herself to look me in the eye when she says it. Why is she giving up on us so easily? I hold up my arm and lean against the top of the doorframe to restrain some of my anger.

"Nuh-uh. You don't get to lie to me," I sneer. "I know you felt the same connection I did, we both were into that!" I point toward the living room.

"I'm, uh, I'm going to go to bed. I've got that appointment with the team nutritionist tomorrow, so I need to get some rest."

I grip the trim over the door, and I want to rip it off. Instead, I look down at her and search her eyes for confirmation that I'm right.

"Good night, Lonan."

"This isn't over yet," I assure her as she gently snicks the door closed.

I want to shove my fist through a wall. There's no one to blame but myself. This is payback for sleeping around—bad karma. I need to regain her trust before she decides to leave again, because when our lips first touched at the hotel—and then again tonight—it was like everything snapped into place. She's it for me.

TWENTY

Birdie

W ell, last night was fun. That woman was so drop-dead gorgeous she didn't even look real. Is that what he goes for? I suppose those are the women that athletes and men like Lonan are used to. There is no way I can keep up with that. And she probably feels the same way I do about Lonan—who wouldn't? He's incredible. He's charming, funny, kind, brings his niece gifts, and is so fucking sexy I almost came from our little dry-hump session last night. Kissing him is an experience in itself. I need to shake off this crush and stay in my lane. It's not that I don't think I'm attractive, I do, but he lives in a different world, a world I know nothing about.

In some ways, it was for the best. Talk about post-nut clarity—or rather, pre-nut clarity. I should have gotten myself off before falling asleep last night, but I was too bummed to do anything about it. Seeing her walk in like sex on heels while I sat in jeans, a tee, and a slouchy cardigan was humiliating. No idea who she was, but I could tell Lonan was caught off guard as much as I was. I believe him when he says he's not interested in her anymore, but the whole thing has me rattled. It feels like a sign that I need to just focus on where I'm at right now. Shit, he's technically my boss, after all. And my roommate. And the only person I know from my old life. It's like a bad romance novel.

I pull up to the Lakes arena and meet the team nutritionist, Nate, at the security gate. I'm thankful he's the only person standing there, because my thoughts about Lonan have been so distracting, I accidentally left my phone in the Land Rover. He leads me back to the team offices, and we sit in one of the conference rooms. He introduces himself again and then we delve into it. We go over so many numbers it makes my head spin. Lonan's workout, his schedules, dryland training, on-ice training, macros, calorie intake, calorie burn. He hands off the dietary plans he's designed for him, and from what I can tell, Lonan's never actually followed any of them. Nate is thorough. We go on about how the team is doing this season, his history with the team, my background in cooking—casual small talk. It's pleasant. After wrapping up, he walks me to the exit.

"Hey, so, this is probably really unprofessional, but would you want to grab a drink some time?"

He's attractive, but in a different way than Lonan. Nate looks like he grew up in a yacht club. He's WASP-y, probably pledged to a fraternity in college and golfs on the weekends. But that might be exacerbated by his collared polo. We've had a good conversation; he's a bit arrogant, but it's delightful to know somebody that doesn't know me first. It puts us on an even keel. He's more my speed, and I probably don't have to worry about puck bunnies as much.

Some no-strings-attached fun might be good for me right now. At the very least, it would be a distraction and might help dissipate the sexual energy between Lonan and me. It's just one drink.

"Possibly."

"Let me give you my number."

I reach to pull out my phone and remember I left it in the car. Shit, I don't know the phone number yet. I got a burner phone at the airport to avoid all the roaming charges while I'm here.

"I'll write it down for you," he says, scribbling on the corner of my legal pad. "Old-school style."

He waves me off, and I head back to the Rover. When I look at the notebook, it reads:

LOVE YOUR LAUGH: 612-555-6734
—NATE

It's sweet. I really needed that ego boost after last night. Well done, Nate.

> Me: Hey, it's Birdie.

Nate: Hey Birdie, it's Nate.

> Me: Charming.

Nate: I know you are, but what am I?

Ugh. Less charming.

Nate: I promise I'll be funnier in person. Text you later?

> Me: Yup. Thanks for all your help today!

I return to the condo and lay out the paperwork, notes, and meal plans. I need to come up with a menu and schedule. I go through his home and away dates and create a calendar. Before I know it, I've got a menu set up for each day for the next eight weeks, along with my grocery days and a program for meal planning prep. Go me. I take out some chicken from the fridge to grill it for an asparagus pesto pasta dish I think he'll enjoy.

When the elevator dings this time, I do a much better job of extinguishing my excitement. He comes behind me and wraps his arms around my waist, leaning down to rest his chin on my shoulder. We haven't spoken since last night.

"Hey."

Sensing he's about to apologize again, I steer the conversation in a different direction.

"I finished coming up with a menu for the next eight weeks. Ready to take a look?"

"Let's see it. How much are you going to punish me?"

"It won't be a punishment. Just because you're following a dietary plan, doesn't mean you can't enjoy what you're eating. That's why you hired an incredible chef, remember?" I gesture to myself like a showcase model. I'm not sad at all.

"Oh, is that why?"

"Yeah. Now, pay attention."

I go over his away week schedule and his one for home. The lunches we'll be starting off with, baby steps to ease him into a better diet without crashing his GI system. He leaves tomorrow for four days while they play in Colorado, so I also discuss which foods he should look for on menus when he goes out to eat with the team.

Something catches his gaze, and he grabs my legal pad and slowly pulls it out from under some of the other papers. Pointing to Nate's note and phone number, his jaw tics. I forgot about that.

"What's this?"

I sigh, not wanting to discuss it. "He asked me out for a drink. It's nothing."

"Poor guy, what did you tell him?"

I shrug. "I'm considering it."

His face contorts like I've handed him a bag of cat food and said, *Enjoy your meal*.

"What is there to consider?" He angles his body at me as I walk to the fridge and grab a drink. "Tell him you're not interested."

That pisses me off. I don't like being told what to do in my personal life.

"Are you serious right now?" I scoff. "You have women dropping themselves at your feet every night— sometimes they even deliver themselves to your living room. And who said I'm not interested? Maybe I want to escape for a good time with someone who doesn't look at me with pity so I can forget I missed out on so many years with all the people I love. Just because my life is a mess, doesn't mean I don't still have needs—I have to live with some autonomy."

He stalks toward me and steps into my personal space, but I refuse to back down to his intimidation.

"Then you tell *me* what you need. Come on, let's hear it. Tell me what you want. You had no problem doing it the other night!"

"Don't patronize me. You don't get to tell me how to live my life because you think you know me."

"You don't give anyone a chance to know you! And I *never* said you were weak. You are far from it. Giving control doesn't mean losing autonomy. No one can control you unless you hand over the reins and let go. But for the record, I get the impression you like when I boss you around a little, and I know personally you're strong enough to take it too."

This motherfucker.

"You have no clue what I want."

It's a lie. I want all of that. My blood pressure is rising. Despite my attempts to push him away, he keeps pushing back. Why won't he give up already? Even in the face of my anger, I want to feel his hands and lips all over my body, grabbing, squeezing, and yeah, I get off on him telling me what to do. That pisses me off even more.

I'm aware this fight has become an outlet for all the frustration mounting over the last few weeks, but I can't stop yelling. It feels too good to get it all out.

"Sweetheart, you are smart and sexy and deserve whatever it is you want, but there's no fucking way Nate is getting a shot before me."

Ugh. I know it's wrong, but his possessiveness only adds to the sexual tension between us. *World's worst feminist.* But fuck him for saying it anyway.

"Oh, I get it. So maybe once you're finished with me, then he can have a go? That's what this is about, right? Whoever gets to be first? Jack has already talked to me about how you handle your relationships." I laugh without humor. "I won't be your next one-night stand. I told you I can't be that girl for you."

"But you can with Nate?"

"No, that's—it's different."

"Why? Because you don't care about him the way you care about me?"

"Go to hell."

My eyes sting, and a slight tremor has taken over my chin. I turn my back on him, but it doesn't make a difference. He can see right through me. He flips me back and cups my face with both hands, forcing me to look at him.

"You can yell at me all night long, but you're going to look me in the eye when you do it. Allow me to be perfectly clear. You will never be a one-night stand for me. There's more to us than that. We have history."

"Oh my God. Lonan, we were kids—those times don't matter. I hardly remember anything more than that day in the fort."

Hot tears brim my eyes. This is so humiliating. He keeps peeling back my layers and peeking underneath.

"I remember!" He stabs his finger into his chest. "I remember enough for both of us. Do you want me to prove it? You triple-knotted your shoelaces for good luck. You wore overalls all the time and your right strap was always twisted. You were scared of ladybugs, but not spiders—which is really fucking strange, by the way. You dreamed of becoming a marine biologist when you grew up. When we played house, you made your-self the armadillo—yeah, armadillo—every goddamn time. You had the coolest rock collection. Oh, and your favorite ice cream flavor was cotton candy."

The muscles in his neck are taut, and his glare bounces between my eyes. He releases a breath. "And I know you feel something when I kiss you. I feel it too. Don't you dare try to claim otherwise. We are good together, Bridget."

There's a pattern to him using my name. He calls me Bridget when he's talking to the woman locked deep inside my heart for safekeeping. It's not a name I've used in a very long time, but it makes me feel treasured when he says it. He's showing me his insides. This is him balancing out the scales of vulnerability.

I can't hold back tears any longer, they are streaming down my face, but the only thing I can blubber out is "I prefer mint chocolate chip now."

He drags me into his chest.

"Christ, you're even pretty when you cry," he says, irritated.

His arms hold me close for a moment and then push me away so he can level his gaze with mine.

"If you don't want to explore this, that's fine. But don't waste your time on some asshole that will probably buy you frozen fucking yogurt instead of what you really want. Don't waste your time on vanilla. You deserve the mint chocolate chip."

My eyebrows raise, and I stare at him, reflecting on

his words. *Did he just . . .?* Then I drop my forehead to his chest, and my shoulders shake with laughter. He mistakes it for more sobs and pulls me tighter into his arms.

When my laughter wins out, he shoves me to arm's length, confusion clouding his features. I can't help myself.

"That was the cheesiest—"

"Really? You're laughing at me. Right now? After all that?"

This isn't the reaction he imagined his thoughtful words would receive. They were adorable, but the ice-cream-themed suaveness sent me over the edge. A surprising contradiction to his usual masculine toughness. I loved it.

He tilts his head back and looks at the ceiling, his tongue in his cheek, trying to suppress the smile that could drop a whole room full of panties. "Such a brat."

"I'm sorry, I'm sorry. It was just so—"

"Stop talking," he commands. Gripping my chin again, he steals my lips, halting any train of thought or remaining laughter. The warmth in his kiss floods my senses and sends my heart into a quick rhythm. It's clear I've lost this fight—and I'm okay with that. Then, he corrects me with a restrained swat on my ass to put me in my place. My back straightens, and I bite my lip to keep from smiling.

His voice turns to that aggressive rumble, and he whispers in my ear, "If you give me a hard time like that again, I'm going to give you one right back." The promise of getting to experience his rough side again sends tingles down my spine.

Looks like I'm going to fuck the ice cream man.

TWENTY-ONE

LONAN

She's feisty. I never doubted her strength, but seeing the fire in her up close, close enough to burn me, is so damn hot. I stand in the shower, one hand bracing me against the tile wall and the other gripping the steel between my legs. Lately, every shower I take has resulted in me beating my dick like it stole from me. Tonight is no exception.

I can't stop thinking about her. Taking her in the hotel and making out with her on the sofa. How quickly the pulse in her neck was ticking, and how her body felt against mine when she straddled me and worked so hard to get herself off. The way she asked me to pull her hair and the noises she made when I did. I want to bury my cock deep inside her hot little cunt and wring every gasp, moan, and scream from her pouty lips.

"Damn it, Bridg."

My balls jerk, and I let out a groan as ropes of cum spurt onto the marble.

It's been forever since I've taken my time with a woman. Even at the hotel, it felt rushed. But no one else has wrapped themselves around my heart the way she has. If we're going to do this, it has to be at her pace. I've already had a strike against me from Nikki showing up. After our spat, she knows where I stand, but the next move is hers. I will give her space to figure out her feelings, but eventually, she'll realize she needs me as much as I need her.

Part of my attraction is biased because she was my childhood love, but she's not that same girl anymore—this woman is fierce, and a darkness has grown in her over the years. She makes me feel seen and alive again. Being in the NHL, the women I meet are so often like self-absorbed moths, fluttering around, only attracted to the spotlight I'm under. But none stand a chance against her—because pretty birds eat moths.

There's more to it than sexual attraction. She listens —we confide in each other our fears and dreams. I know she's holding back, but progress is still progress. She doesn't care about my career for any self-serving purpose. After games, she congratulates me and says she's proud of me, and I see in her eyes she means every word. She's genuine. She has her own hobbies and interests outside of me, and I love that. She's independent and isn't afraid to call me on my shit and make herself heard.

Tonight, she opened up and rained all hell down on me, and I could not have been more impressed. Some of that was her blowing off steam, but I didn't overlook that she trusted me to be a safe space for her to unleash that anger. Having someone listen and care enough to fight back, confused her. She'll soon learn I'm not going anywhere. Before coming home, I don't think she remembers a time when someone fought for her.

She's the woman I've been waiting for, someone I can have a future with, not just one night. But if that's all she wants right now, I'll be the one to give it to her. She's hard up for sex and attention. I can see it in her eyes every time I praise her. I want to show her how good we can be together, but first, I need her to show me she wants it. It's not only my heart on the line. If this goes south, it'll risk the whole family dynamic, and I'll disappoint the people I love most.

———

Our goalie, Kapucik, is rolling tonight, but his eyes are tired. Crosby—our other D—and I have been busting our asses trying to make his job easy, but we just can't seem to turnover the puck enough. They get another goal, and I brush it off. We can't let it get into our heads. I've still got hands, though my lungs burn. We're getting our hats handed to us. Kapucik squirts his water bottle into the air, and he tracks the falling droplets with his eyes, regaining some of his focus.

The puck is dropped, and thank God Conway snags it. He runs it up and passes to Banks. Their defense takes the puck and sends it up the boards to their forwards. I meet them and overturn it. There's a break-away. Banks and Conway rush, and we get our first goal of the night. There are only a few minutes left in the third period, and we're down by two. It gives the fans a shred of hope. It's a shitty feeling when you know people are spending money on seats, and we can't even give 'em one celly.

Thankfully, Winnipeg's forward shows his ass and starts a fight. He gets sent to the penalty box for a minor, giving us a literal last-minute power play. With less than sixty seconds on the clock, Sully subs in, and we storm the ice. Sulls snaps one in before the horn sounds. We lost by one, but at least we gave the fans something exciting to cheer about at the end. But now that the game is over, I'm ready to see my girl. I need to get my ass on the bikes. My legs feel like lead. No doubt, my on-ice drills will be more demanding this week.

Back in the locker room, we go over the mistakes we made and opportunities we missed. While we hit the stationary bikes to flush the lactic acid, the guys make their plans for the bar.

"Burke, you coming out with us tonight?" Crosby asks.

"Nah, I'm good," I say, adjusting the buttons on the bike. It's been days since I've been home.

A few of them side-eye me, others make whipping sounds—even they have noticed how bad I have it for Birdie.

"Laugh it up."

"Wait, are you serious about this girl?" Banks asks.

"Dead serious." I give him a glare to make it known he will not move in on what's mine.

"Have you locked her down?" Conway has turned into such a softy with relationships over the years.

"Trying to, but shit keeps getting in the way. I had her on the couch the other night and fucking Nikki walked in with her trenchcoat routine."

Jonesy spins around to look at me and yells, "Oh shit" the same time Conway shouts, "Shut the fuck up."

"Swear to God."

"How did she even get up there?"

"Thought she was my dry cleaning. I had blocked her number a while back and didn't know she was still making house calls. The notification came through that somebody was requesting access and my dumb ass approved it without even thinking."

Most of the guys are cracking up at my expense. Glad somebody finds it funny.

"That sucks, man."

"I know, it was bad. Think I've got myself out of the red though, she's coming around."

"Good luck, dude. She seems cool," Banks says. I hesitantly nod in response. I still don't trust him after he hit on Birdie at the bar, but I appreciate the support.

"Yeah, don't fuck it up, bud," Conway says. "Aren't you glad I told you to get her number that night?"

"You have no idea." When I get off the bike, I crack my back and throw my towel in the bin. "I'm heading out. Have fun tonight, boys."

"Go get 'em, Tiger!" Sully jokes.

I chuckle and give my best tiger growl as I shove the door open and make my way back to the lockers. I can't wait to get home to her.

This time when I step off the elevator, she's got a mean fuckin' burger waiting for me. I change out of my suit and into a comfy pair of basketball shorts and a sweatshirt. As I'm hanging the suit up, I take in how well this girl knows what I need. Whether it be a burger or a smile.

Back in the dining room, she cracks a beer and hands it to me without saying a word. It's so damn thoughtful and domesticated that my heart swells. I could get used to this. I love the way she can read me and anticipate my needs. I want to do the same for her.

She opens herself a beer, and we sit across from one another, watching each other in silence. She's observing me eat, and I'm attentive to those incredible gray eyes. After having them absent from my life, I'll never tire of gazing into them. It feels like home.

I realize, for the first time, that she's also had a big effect on my condo. Since she's moved in, her presence makes it cozier. The fireplace is turned on, but now it adds ambiance rather than only providing a heat source. She's turned this penthouse into a penthome.

We maintain eye contact. The burger is satisfying as hell, but when she tips back her beer bottle and swallows, it arouses a new hunger. *Is she fucking with me or is this an opening?*

"What are your plans for tonight?" I ask.

"Not sure. Probably watch a movie and go to bed."

"Want to play a game instead?"

She finishes chewing and swallows. "You're not tired from the game you just played?"

"I'm usually wired for a few hours after."

"What did you have in mind? Monopoly?"

"Truth or dare?" I suggest. It's the *only* game I want to play.

She laughs and narrows her eyes at me, she's on to me. When she rolls her eyes, it does something to me. It's slightly disobedient, and it makes me want to correct her behavior. Leave her on her knees, begging for more.

"You don't think we're a little old for that? I haven't

played Truth or dare? since I was a teenager."

"Well, we have a lot of time to make up for—including the teenage years."

And it gives her the illusion of control while I grill her on some things—without it feeling like an interrogation. She narrows her eyes while she considers it.

"Okay. But if you decline your dare or truth, you have to remove an article of clothing."

My eyebrows shoot up.

"Well, look who came to play," I exclaim.

She is even more hard up for sex than I thought. But I still want her to come out and tell me she's ready for us to become *us*.

"Be right back." She runs to her bedroom. When she returns, she's wearing a sweater; she's adding layers.

"Cheater."

She places her hand on her chest.

"I would *never* . . ." She's mimicking me from the night in her hotel room.

I walk into the living room and take off my sweatshirt and socks in retaliation.

"Ready?"

"Yup. Truth or dare?" she asks. *Guess I'm going first.*

"Truth."

"Why do you call me Bridget?"

"Because that's your name."

"Yeah, but everyone else calls me Birdie. You

usually call me Bridget."

"I'm only calling you Bird when I want to make you sing for me." I wink at her. "Truth or dare?"

There's that blush that gets my dick hard. Never gets old.

"Dare." She's got some truths she wants to hide. Good to know.

"I dare you to take off your sweater."

"Okay, *that's* cheating! And I decline," she says, peeling off a single sock instead. "Truth or dare?"

I poke my tongue into my cheek and inhale a long breath. She's playing with fire. The taunting smile she's beaming at me isn't doing her any favors.

"Truth," I answer.

She's got a question on the tip of her tongue; her mouth opens and closes again.

"Do you"—she looks down at her hands—"Are you seeing anybody else?"

"Not yet."

"What does that mean?"

I lean forward and wrap my fingers over her covered toes.

"That's two questions. I let you get away with it last time, but if you do it again, I'm taking this other sock."

My gravelly voice sounds aggressive, but she started this chase. Her little acts of rebellion are like bits of chum tossed overboard to draw out the shark.

"Truth or dare?"

She pauses, taken aback by my command. "Truth."

"Are you going to see Nate outside of work?"

"I don't know."

As soon as the words pass her lips, I reach across and snatch the sock from her foot.

"Hey!"

"'I don't know isn't an answer, Little Bird."

She glares at me and finishes her beer. "Truth or dare?"

"Dare."

She searches the room, trying to come up with ideas.

"Go to the kitchen and make me the best snack you can think of. You have three minutes. Starting . . . now!"

I hop up and walk toward the kitchen. My joints are popping and clicking like a senior citizen. I open the fridge. Damn, no whip cream. I choose a lime instead, grab a bottle of tequila from the cabinet, and a paring knife. Then walk back to my spot on the floor and lean against the couch.

"You were supposed to make something. Making something needs more than one ingredient."

I hold up the lime.

"Like when you made me an egg for my *snack* yesterday? Besides, have you already forgotten how I earned the nickname PB and J?" Her giggle only turns me on more.

After slicing out a wedge from the lime, I set it in my lap while I uncork the tequila, pouring a healthy shot into my mouth. The warm, smoky vapors expand in my throat. I crook my finger at her. She rolls her eyes and then she crawls. She fucking crawls toward me, and I almost swallow the shot myself. It sends all the blood to my groin. She gets to my thighs and goes up on her knees. Framing my face with her delicate fingers, she turns her head and locks her lips to mine, sweeping her tongue in my mouth and swallowing the shot. My fingers encircle her wrist when she reaches for the lime in my lap.

"No hands."

With a smirk, she innocently whispers, "Hold my hair?"

Yeah, she's got my number. This dare is backfiring on me. I grab a fistful of her hair and wrap it tight around my palm. Holding it away from her head just enough to put tension on her scalp—the same amount I gave her when she moaned into my mouth during our make-out session. Goose bumps break out over her neck, and she attempts to hide the shudder that moves through her.

"That's right, Little Bird. I'm the one that makes you shiver."

She drops her mouth to my groin and sinks her teeth into the juicy lime. This has become a game of trying to make the other more turned on, and I pat myself on the back for my genius. Though, if she doesn't hurry up, my cock will poke her eye out. When she sits up, there's a dribble of tequila on her chin, and I wipe it away with my thumb.

"Good girl." Her eyes turn from silver clouds to dark thunderstorms—my suspicions confirmed. "Truth or dare?"

She retreats, scooting back until she hits the ottoman she's been leaning against.

"Truth."

"I heard you masturbate the other day."

Her eyebrows shoot up at my brash comment. She crosses her arms but doesn't deny it.

"I want you to tell me what you were thinking about."

Say me. Say you were thinking about me.

"I don't want to make things complicated."

"No judgment zone."

Our situation is already plenty complicated. Her little fantasy will not change that.

She sighs and looks at the ceiling for a minute.

I hold my breath, praying she doesn't take off her cardigan instead. I want a peek into the hidden corners of her mind more than I want her naked.

She peers at me and tilts her head to the side before saying with defeat, "I was thinking about you watching me."

I exhale the huge breath I had been holding. *Yes.* I try to downplay my joy over her confession. "You have a bit of an exhibitionist streak, eh?"

"That's two questions. You have to take something off."

I grab my shirt from behind my neck and yank it over my head, her face transforms, and her gaze feeds on me. Fuck me, *those eyes*.

"Truth or dare?" she squeaks.

"Truth."

"What did you do when you heard me?"

"I put my ear to the wall, took my dick out, and got off to the image of you wet and spread open for me. I thought about eating your pussy and working you over. First, with you riding me and then flipping you over and taking you from behind. After I heard you come, I didn't last much longer. It was hot."

I pause for a second or two as I replay the sound of her muffled, raspy moans and rub the back of my neck. "Truth or dare?"

She doesn't speak; I can almost see the wheels in her head turning as she pictures the scene I painted for her.

"Truth or dare, Little Bird . . ."

"Truth."

She squeezes her thighs together, and I pretend not to notice.

"Are you wet right now?" As soon as the question leaves my lips, I regret it. My lizard brain is hijacking all rational thoughts. We're not playing a game anymore; this has turned into foreplay. I need to stop taking so many liberties and pushing her buttons. This has to be her choice to want something with me— beyond sex. All I'm doing is reinforcing the physical attraction, but I want her to imagine us becoming something deeper.

She stands up, and I think she's about to head to her bedroom. I've offended her. *Shit.* Just when I'm about to open my mouth and apologize, she hooks her thumbs into her leggings and wiggles them down her thighs. She could have taken off her sweater and still would have had a t-shirt on. She wants to strip for me.

"Dammit, Bridg," I mutter, crossing my arms behind my head to keep from fisting my dick.

I'm so hard it hurts. She sits back down on the floor. I'm speechless. I want to pull her on top of me and take her right here. But I don't want this to be something we give in to because we both feel it in the moment. Then she takes it one step further and bends her knee to the side, not-so-subtly exposing the damp strip of cotton between her legs.

She didn't strip to avoid the question. She stripped to answer it. The tent in these basketball shorts closer resembles the Leaning Tower of Pisa than it does anything you could find at REI. I smirk at her brazen move. As much as we need to downshift this game, I'm so proud of her bravery.

"Show and tell was always my favorite," I mutter, and she lets out a soft laugh.

"Truth or dare?" she asks, but all I hear is *Checkmate*.

I've got a million dares for her but I resist because she's not just some girl, she's Bridget.

"Truth."

"When you answered 'not yet' earlier. What did you mean by that?"

This is exactly why I won't sleep with her tonight. She wants to know if there's more to us than just sexual tension, and this is my chance to prove it. She's asking if I plan on pursuing something with her or just looking to warm my bed for a night. Now it's my turn to crawl to her. When we're close enough to touch, I sit up on my knees, towering over her.

"I meant that you are the only woman I intend on seeing."

I stroke her neck with my thumb and her pulse ticks faster and faster.

"Look at you, spreading your pretty legs for me, showing off your wet, barely covered cunt."

I meet her gaze and anchor my hand to her knee. Then slowly push it over to drop it to the side, butter-flying her leg for me, showing off that birthmark again. Her breath catches. Acknowledging the trust she's handing over, I continue staring at her face before I let my gaze fall and take her in. I want to see her needy like this for me every goddamn day.

I glide my hand from her knee to her inner thigh and

pause before leaning down to kiss her birthmark. I sit up again and continue the path of my touch until I reach the highest point and rub my thumb back and forth along the edge of the lace on her underwear. Her muscles clench and twitch as she releases the sexiest gasp. She's beautiful like this. Everything shifts into place when I look into her dark, stormy eyes. With every bit of willpower I can muster, I focus my brain and pull my hand back.

"When you're ready to let me in here"—I place my hand over her pounding heart—"Then we can keep going. As much as I want to do this, I don't want you to think that I'm willing to only settle for this." I draw my thumb over her clit and massage her just long enough to make her eyes flutter closed. I'm hypnotized by the pleasure on her face. I pull my hand back, aware that it was over the line. I'm an asshole, but her pleading eyes are my ultimate weakness. I want to give it to her as bad as she's asking me for it.

"What? Lonan, no. You can't do that!"

She looks . . . *not happy*. That's fair. She's pissed at me now, but I'll make it up to her.

"Well, have fun listening through the fucking walls tonight, knowing it should have been you."

Oof. She's not wrong. We go back to our respective bedrooms, and I exhale a breath. She caught me off guard. What was *that*? Where did her boldness come from? I'm reliving the yearning, submissive look in her eyes when I hear it—it's quiet—but there's no mistaking that subtle buzzing noise. I pull out my hard cock and pump in time to her sweet moans and cries. *Such a good girl.*

May 31, 2004

I've decided to treat myself to a shopping spree today. I deserve it.

Elizabeth made a rack of lamb for dinner. It was fine.

TWENTY-TWO

Birdie

That man gives me a fucking fever. I can't stop thinking about him. After I stormed off to my bedroom last night, I busted out my *toolbox* and had a DIY session. I've never been so turned on and pissed off at the same time. So much so, that I didn't censor anything that came out of my mouth. If he wanted to leave me high and dry, then I wanted him to know exactly what he missed out on.

I still can't believe how uninhibited I was during our game—which we both know was just a guise to act out on our desires—but when he speaks to me with that deep, commanding voice and flashes his wicked grin, I can't be held responsible for my actions. It's like nothing I've ever experienced with another man, and I don't want to. I want to surrender myself to him and completely let go. But he's not settling for just one part of me—he wants the whole package—and I'm not ready to give that away to anyone.

Flaunting myself in front of him was thrilling; anticipation was crawling all over my skin. His eyes were dark and wild as he watched me. And his erection—watching how hard he got for me, knowing *I* did that—will be enough masturbation fodder for the rest of my life. I've never been so bold before. All I could think about last night was teasing him until he could hardly stand it. I want to see him snap right before my eyes. Instead, he was the first one to pull back.

Today it's impossible to focus on anything but him. We haven't seen each other since last night, he left this morning for dryland training, and I stayed in my room until I heard him leave. I'm not prepared to face the aftermath of my actions—without the heat of the moment to mask my insecurity, I'm too easily influenced by our attraction. He'll be gone all day anyway, he has a ridiculous agenda. Training, game tape reviews, visiting the Children's Hospital, doing a press interview that's set to air tomorrow, and massage therapy.

I'm hanging around the condo today, finishing up some things on my own to-do list. My laundry pile definitely needed to be addressed. When I moved, only my favorite outfits came with me, so when I'm out of clothes, it means I'm *out of clothes*. Hence the light-pink sundress I'm rocking. Don't get me wrong, I love this dress, but it's also January and so not appropriate for this latitude.

I'm surprised to find Lonan does his own laundry too. When I went to put my wet, just-washed clothes into the dryer, it was full of his laundry he hadn't finished folding yet. Good for him. I decided to be nice and run his clothes through the dryer again to get the wrinkles out and fold them. If I'm honest, it's not actually because I'm doing him a favor; it's because I'm so damn horny today that if I run out of things to do, I'll drive myself crazy and spend all afternoon getting off in my room. There's a cloudy haze of horniness I can't lift. It feels like every nerve is vibrating under the surface of my hypersensitive skin. I need to keep my mind occupied with normal things. Like laundry, not Lonan.

Not him telling me I'm a good girl. Not him looking down at me with those dark dominating eyes. Not him hovering so close I can smell his cologne. Not him caressing my thigh just below where I *really* need it. My mind wanders. Even his hands are sexy. They're strong and masculine—and when he curls them inside me . . . *Damn.*

I've been waiting my whole adult life to find someone who can fuck me like he can, and as it turns out, the mythical beast is Lonan. My brother's best friend, my childhood crush, and my anonymous one-night stand. He's not willing to give me anything until I give him every other part of me too. It's tempting, and I can't deny the connection we share. My heart trusts him, but my brain can't. It's not safe. If he changes his mind one day and wants to move on, it would be crushing. How would I recover from that? Rejection is hard for me, which is why casual sex is so great. No strings attached means nobody gets hurt.

But, what if it worked out? What if he could accept me and all my broken pieces as they are—with no conditions? Could walk with me through all the dark times and all the good times? And what if it's the same guy who can reach into my fantasies and give me what I need? Give me his filthy praises until my ears ring. And supply all the frenzied, heated, uncontrolled sex—ugly sex—my aching body can handle? If anyone could be all those things, it's Lonan.

How long have I been standing in the living room holding his laundry basket? Time to stop daydreaming about getting railed and put these clothes away. *Focus, Birdie! Put the clothes away and go clean the oven or something. Jesus.*

I walk into his bedroom with the laundry basket resting on my hip; his bed is unmade. I quickly tidy it up —without thinking about him bending me over the side of it and having his way with me—and then make my way through his luxurious marble washroom and into the oversized walk-in closet. It's dark and quiet, and his scent surrounds me; everything in this closet radiates with cedarwood and spice.

I feel around until my fingers brush one of the light switches on the wall. In Vancouver, my closet had a small accordion door and zero lighting. His is an entire room with four light switches. I flip the first one and it illuminates the custom shelving with its built-in lighting. I take in the room; it's warm and inviting—two words I wouldn't normally use to describe a closet. This second switch is bright track lighting, and I turn it off. The third light switch makes the large mirror glow with a halo around the edge. The fourth light switch does nothing.

The custom woodwork is made of rich chestnut. I set down the laundry basket and take in all the masculinity. The smell, the tailored suits, the high-back leather chair. I carefully remove the stacks of folded clothes and set them neatly on the shelves. I hope he doesn't see this as an invasion of privacy.

The floor below my feet warms—ah, the fourth switch is in-floor heating! That must feel amazing after coming out of the shower. I'm in love with this closet. I set aside the laundry basket and sit on the floor, letting the backs of my bare thighs warm from the radiant heat. This is awesome. I close my eyes and breathe in Lonan's scent, and my mind wanders back to him.

Look at you, spreading your pretty legs for me, showing off your wet, barely covered cunt.

Screw it. I peek at my phone, and there's still an hour before he's supposed to get home. I pull up my dress and shove my drenched thong aside, closing my eyes. I imagine him with me and give in to my most salacious fantasies as I rub my clit. If I can get myself off one more time, that should help me keep it in my pants when he gets home.

LONAN

"How are things going with your girl?" Conway asks, spotting me while I bench press in the Lakes training room.

"Good. Really good." I huff when a bead of sweat trickles down the back of my neck.

"This the first one you've been serious about?"

I don't even have to think about the answer.

"Yeah."

"It's crazy, right? When you find that person that can make you imagine your life differently."

I do one more chest press, blow out a breath, and sit up.

"Exactly." He gets it. "So, where's your girl, then?" I pant. I use the neck of my shirt to wipe the sweat from my forehead.

He takes a swig from his water bottle. "No fuckin' clue."

I hesitate before asking, "Don't take this the wrong way, bud, but wasn't she a bunny?"

"Yeah, but so what?" He furrows his brow. "She was

different, ya know? Like how you are with Gray." I smile, recalling the nickname I gave her that night.

"I get that you didn't get her number, but you haven't seen her around? I'd think she would still show up at the bars and clubs or something, right?" If she's a bunny, there's probably another guy on the team that's fucked her. They might have her number. I have to say this cautiously. "Have you, uh, *asked around*?"

"Yeahhh." He sighs. "She's gotten around, but nobody's seen her. It's as if she's totally vanished. My guess is she moved away. This was years ago now. I gotta let it go."

"Aww, Big Bad Conway has a one-that-got-away." As soon as I say it, I wish I could take it back. I know better than anyone how it feels to lose somebody you care about. It's the worst.

"Oh, fuck off."

"You're gonna be good, though, right?"

"I'm fine, just one of those things. You always wonder, ya know?"

"Well, for all our sake, I hope you cross paths again. Don't know what went down between you two, but you haven't been the same since that night."

She must have been one hell of a lay to rattle someone like Barrett Conway.

———

My massage therapist canceled, and I'm glad. For two reasons: 1) I get to go home early, and 2) I know my mind would have drifted to Bridget, guaranteeing me a boner on the table. Today was difficult enough without a massage. I leave the press box where I got grilled for our last few games. We had two guys injured and it's not going well. When I get to my car, my thoughts are already on her. A cold shower would do me good.

Normally, I get a nap after training, but today was booked solid, so I'm wiped. As I step off the elevator, I'm reminded of how welcoming it feels to come home to her. I'm relieved to be home. It's quiet. I was hoping to see her face, but she's not in the kitchen or the living room. She's probably taking a nap. We were up pretty late last night, so I'm not surprised.

First priority is getting out of this monkey suit. Passing through my bathroom, I notice there's a dim light coming from the entrance of my closet. And a noise. *It can't be . . .*

The second my feet hit the door's threshold, they plant themselves firmly, and I can't move. She's sitting on the floor of my closet, touching herself. I can't take my eyes off her. God, she's my own personal centerfold. Her sexy little pink dress is gathered around her waist like cotton candy, and her arousal permeates the air mixed with my cologne. The combination has my mouth watering. My cock constricts against my fly.

Her hair is piled on top of her head in a messy updo,

and one of her thin straps has fallen off her shoulder as her fingers move quickly over her clit. Her charcoal eyelashes contrast her creamy skin as they rest against her flushed cheeks. She's biting the corner of her lip, and without context, one might think her furrowed brows were apologetic but she's chasing ecstasy. And she's definitely not sorry. One hand has pulled her thong to the side while the other is strumming her clit in small circles. Fucking hell.

Leave. You need to leave. Don't be a creep. Turn around and walk away.

On the other hand . . . last night she admitted she'd gotten off on the idea of me catching her like this. Is that what she's doing now? Why else would she be in here?

Yeah, I'm going with that. I smirk at her and lean against the cased opening, loosening my tie and pulling it from behind my neck. She startles, and her eyes fly open, showing me the stormy gray of her irises.

"Oh my God! What are you doing here?" she squawks.

Her fingers stall, and her legs press together.

"*I'm* getting changed. What are *you* doing here?"

"Sorry, um, I was—"

"Did I say you could stop?"

I saw how close she was to finishing. There's no way I'm letting a second orgasm get interrupted. She's going to come, and I'm going to watch.

She takes in a gasp of air and studies my face,

deciding whether to give in to this seductive scenario she's conjured up. I adore that little shred of shyness she can never seem to shed completely. As I walk deeper into the closet, I maintain a calm demeanor, though my pulse is pounding and I'm getting harder by the second. While hanging up my suit jacket, I can see her fingers have cautiously resumed in my peripheral. *That's my girl.*

I turn the leather smoking chair so it faces her directly in front of where she's sitting. As I roll the cuffs up my forearms, her gaze drops to my tattooed sleeve, like it always does. She stands. Ha—she thinks this seat is for her.

"Sit back down. This is for me."

I want a front-row seat to watching her come.

She plops down but is hesitant to begin again, so I remind her.

"You ready to be an exhibitionist for me? Lift that dress again, and show me how you make yourself come."

She blows out a long breath and grins at the ceiling. It's a mix of embarrassment and pure excitement.

"Oh my God, I can't believe I'm doing this."

She pulls up her skirt and spreads her legs.

"Take off your thong," I demand, holding out my hand. She presses her thighs together and lifts her ass to peel it off. My fingers close around it when she sets it in my hand, and I feel its dampness when I tuck it into my pocket. She won't be getting this back.

I lean back in my chair, my forearms resting on the armrests, and bore my gaze into her. When she spreads her legs, it takes everything not to react. She's plump, glistening, and bare, save for a small triangle of trimmed hair above. She's fucking perfect. My cock has been wanting to sink into her ever since our night together at the hotel. Instead, I torture myself and watch.

This is a lesson for me as much as it is for her. I want to know what she likes and how rough she wants it so I'll have her eating from the palm of my hand when she's ready to take this further. If I'm lucky, I'll be holding my dick.

She bites her lip and looks up at me with dilated pupils. Exquisite. The top rounds of her breasts are on display in the deep V of her dress, and her hard nipples pebble under the thin fabric I desperately want to rip off her body. I clench my jaw. I don't think I'll be able to keep my cool while I watch her.

She continues swirling her index and middle finger, sliding inside herself to gather more wetness and spread it upward to her swollen nub. She tries to massage her clit with one hand while fingering herself with the other, but she can't coordinate each hand to move the way she needs. It's the equivalent of her trying to pat her head and rub her belly at the same time. Her expression is pinched as she tries to focus on something on the ceiling. She releases a huff, and I can't help but chuckle.

"Something funny?" she hisses.

I unzip my fly and take out the thick erection straining against my zipper.

"It's cute when you struggle. You want to come so bad."

I fist my cock and glide my hand up and down. She rubs herself faster with one hand while the other pinches her nipple. Hard. *Noted.*

"Can I at least have a vibrator?"

"Next time. Right now, you're going to do it the old-fashioned way."

Her gaze flicks upward as she concentrates on reaching orgasm.

"Bridget"—her eyes drop to mine—"eyes on me, baby."

There's a spark reflected in those smoky eyes of hers. *That was something.* I clench my fist a little harder around my length when she shows how obedient she can be. She pants harder and brings her other hand down to pinch her clit. The bead of pre-cum on my cock slides down my shaft. She sees it, and her lips part as she says my name, and it's like a chorus of angels.

"Fuck." I chuckle. "Yeah, that's what I've been looking for. You love the attention, don't you?"

She answers with a whimpering nod. She's becoming less inhibited.

"Ahh," she whines. She's close. "Please," she begs.

It's tempting, but I shake my head, already regretting saying no. She needs to do this on her own. I grip my shaft hard, pumping to match her rhythm. I want to come with her again. Her muscles tighten so much she's lifting her ass off the floor, as if her pelvis is trying to grab the climax that hovers above her.

"Focus, baby. Just relax."

She grits her teeth. I do too. I'm ready to blow, but she's losing it. As much as I wish I could step in and draw one orgasm after another from her, this is her fantasy, and I want to give it to her. But the pleasure she's been chasing on the edge is getting away. She's so close,

She lets out a frustrated cry, and her ass drops back down. "I can't—"

I lean over and gently collar my hand around her throat.

"Yes, you can. Show me how you make that sweet pussy come all over your fingers. I want to see how pretty you look when your tight cunt is stuffed with every inch of me. You're going to milk every fucking drop out of this cock. Look how hard I am for you. Come on, Gray. Show me what a good girl you can be."

Her eyes turn into saucers, and it finishes me. She gasps my name, then she's silent. Her mouth drops open on a silent scream, and she pulls her fingers out, pinching her clit, letting out another wail, a tremor shaking in her legs. My cum shoots onto the top of her breasts. As she watches me come, she comes harder. Fuck, I'm falling for her.

"That's it, baby," I growl. "Such a good girl."

I realize I'm panting almost as hard as she is.

"Oh god, oh god," she mewls as her orgasm flows through her. Her pelvis undulates as she rides out the waves of pleasure. Her clit pulses as arousal trickles out of her.

My pulse is still pounding in my ears. Her breathing regulates, and the smile that spreads over her face grows until she laughs. She's breathtaking like this, relaxed and blissed out. I want to see her fall apart like this every day for the rest of my life.

"I've never done that in front of anyone before!"

Moving from my chair, I drop to my knees in front of her and cup her face, staring into the eyes with the power to both heal and break my heart. "You're so damn beautiful when you come. You did so well."

She bites her lower lip, and her eyes subtly glaze. I take her wrist and bring it to my mouth, sucking her fingers, then drop to the floor and lick her pussy clean. "Next time, you're coming directly on my tongue."

I stand, and hold out my hand. She takes it and follows me to the shower, where I turn on the steam and wait for the glass room to fill. I unzip the back of her dress, sliding it off her shoulders, where it drops to a small pool around her ankles. *This body*. I slide my palms from her shoulders to her ribs, sweeping my thumbs through my cum dripping down her chest and rubbing it across her nipples. She shivers. I continue my hands down to her waist and over her ass, watching the goose bumps break out across her skin. Her curves are so soft and grabbable. I can't help but give a restrained slap on her ass.

"Get in."

She steps inside, and the glass door closes behind her. After tossing her dress into my laundry basket with my shirt and pants, I stop and stare at it. I've never had a pink dress in my hamper, mixed in with my clothes before. It's a quick glimpse into what a future with her might be like. *If she would only let me in.*

Before I step into the shower, I remind myself this is only aftercare. This is me rewarding her vulnerability and bravery. I want whatever this is to be different—so I need to treat her differently from the women before her —which is also why I purchased a new bed and mattress last week. Eventually, I'll have her in my bed, and she deserves no one's sloppy seconds.

I step into the steam behind her and adjust the water to fall from above. I slide the hair tie out of her updo and lean her back to wet her hair. I massage her scalp with shampoo and conditioner, spending extra time rinsing out all the suds. Then I wash her head to toe, stroking every inch of her body.

Afterward, I stand behind her and wrap my arms

around her body, raising my hands to her breasts and kneading them before sliding them back down again. She is so goddamn irresistible—I never want to let go. My lips brush against the shell of her ear, and the smell of my shampoo on her is so sexy.

"This changes things, Little Bird. It might not be tonight, but this thing between us isn't going anywhere."

"Promises, promises," she goads.

I slide my hand back up her body and wrap around her throat as I press a kiss to her neck right over her quickening pulse. Her jaw goes slack, and I chuckle against her skin, scraping my teeth over her jugular. She shudders.

After turning off the shower, I grab a towel and robe from the warmer. While she holds the robe, I dry her off with the towel, dropping to my knees to finish her legs.

"Why don't you go pick out a bottle of wine and something for us to watch tonight? I'll be out shortly."

She wraps the thick fuzzy bathrobe around her and draws the thick ties into a bow around the waist. Her hands blot and squeeze her damp hair with a towel. Before she leaves, she does a one-eighty and returns for another kiss. Her tongue darts out to mine and she pulls me closer. Between kisses, she smiles against my lips, and it's hard not to reciprocate. She whispers a quick "Thank you" and trots out to the kitchen.

Bridget is like a cyclone. I don't know what she's

thinking or what direction she plans to take. I could be in her path of destruction and not even know it until it's too late. All it would take is one rogue move for her to rip me apart. After today, my feelings for her have more depth. I thought watching her get off would be hot—and it was—but it was also emotional, seeing her work so hard to please me, trusting me, and baring her insecurities with me. It was a big step for her.

I still have my own demons to work through, but she's made me feel more than I thought I could for one person. She's this strange enigma, a Venn diagram of trust and lust—two things I've never had at the same time before. Two things I know for sure, is I share a past with Bridget, and I want to share a future too.

TWENTY-THREE

LONAN

I'm finally home from my batch of away games. I'm exhausted. When I reach the penthouse, I toss my travel bags in the closet and strip down. I need a shower and a chance to sleep in my own bed. The hot spray from the shower is such a welcoming one. I look down and Bridget's hair tie is sitting on the shower floor from the last time we were together in here.

My mind wanders back to the image of her here. Water sluicing her body in rivulets, over her breasts, down her thighs. Her creamy skin and soft area just below her belly button that stretches to her curvy hips. She's so feminine, the soft to my hard. Our counterparts in perfect balance.

She's been spending some extra time at the Hayeses'

now that the media is backing off a bit. Bridg and I spoke on the phone every day I was gone. Every day I ask her how her day is. Nothing more, nothing less. It helps her to focus on the present and not become overwhelmed. This way, she can just tackle what she's feeling at the moment. Despite everything she's been through in the last couple months, she seems more *her*. It's something I can't describe, only sense. She's been sharing more with me this last week than she ever has before. It gives me hope for us.

I open my phone to our text message thread and reread the last text she sent me.

Bridget: I miss you.

The flood of warmth those three words give me is torrential. I won't get to see her much this week with my schedule, and it's killing me, but I'm glad she's taking some time to spend with her family. I know if I try to "keep" her, the results will be devastating. She's been held hostage for the majority of her life without realizing it.

To add more madness, her birthday is on Tuesday. Her real birthday—and Valentine's Day. I've got a game that day. I hate to miss it for a game, but I've already had her surprise in the works for a few weeks now.

After a little sleuthing, I found the famous Freya "Micky" McCoy on Facebook, and she and I have conspired to fly her in for Bridget's birthday. Jack will pick her up from the airport. The whole family is in on it, and I'm excited; I just wish I could be there to see her face.

I miss her too.

April 2, 2016

I need another vacation. Life can be so dull around here. Birdie has asked to go, but vacations are for me. Anytime we go do anything, all anyone talks about are her looks. Why would I want to hear that on MY vacation?

She says she wants to go to college. Truthfully, I don't even know if any college would accept her, but I'm too kind to say anything. Besides, then who would be here to take care of me? Birdie wouldn't want to leave me. She should just get another job instead. We could use an income boost around here.

TWENTY-FOUR

Birdie

A s I step out of the shower, my parents' doorbell rings. I peek out the bathroom window, no news vans. *Phew.* I pick out my favorite outfit to wear because I get to celebrate my real birthday today. My hair and makeup have cooperated today, so I know it will be a good day. I walk down the stairs and my mom tells me there's a delivery for me in the kitchen, so I turn the corner to see what it is and *whoa*.

There's an enormous bouquet of red roses. I've never received flowers like this before. A girl's first roses feels like a big deal. And there are thirty of them because, today, I'm thirty. Two years older than Julianne led me to believe. I feel like I missed two years of my life, but at least I'm truly where I'm meant to be.

I pull the small card from the envelope:

HAPPY 30TH BIRTHDAY, LITTLE BIRD.
THERE ARE SO MANY MEMORIES
I WANT TO MAKE WITH YOU.
SEE YOU SOON.
—LONAN

I read it three times and then slip the card into my pocket as my mom walks around the corner. She whistles at the bouquet.

"Now that's how you do it. Who are they from?" As if she doesn't know.

"Lonan."

"Smart boy," she says. "Those aren't friend flowers. Anything you want to tell me?"

"I like him." I bite my bottom lip. "The timing isn't great, but—"

"He has a kind heart, so be good to him." She's my mother, but it's wonderful to see her protective over him. Even if he was a playboy, she trusted him to take care of me, which speaks volumes. I've gone almost two weeks without seeing him. When I get back, I plan on being very good to him.

———

This is one of the best birthdays I've ever had. Not only did Lonan send me thirty long-stemmed roses, he flew

255

my best friend out to see me. That man is incredible. When she walked in the front door, I screamed.

We've been lounging around and getting caught up on everything. School is going great for her, and she's set to graduate in a couple months.

"You should move here, Mick. I mean it. We could get an apartment together and work in the city. It would be so much fun!" I squeak, still bathing in the high of being with my best friend again.

"It's cute that you think Lonan would let you live with me." She takes a sip of her bourbon. "That dude is gonna wife you."

"Shut up. It's not like that."

"*There are so many memories I want to make with you?*"

"I should have never shown you that. Redact."

"I'm serious. From what I've seen, he treats you well. Don't you think this is him laying the groundwork for something? And may I remind you that he and I have spoken a few times already? He likes you, Bird. He flew me out here to surprise you. That's not fuckboy energy. That's big-dick-husband-daddy energy. How do you feel about him?"

"I like him."

"You *like* him?"

"I like him."

"And?"

"I can't '*and*' anything yet. I don't even have a

living identity. I'm still on my Visa Waiver Program (VWP) from Canada. If things don't get fixed soon, I will probably have to go back to Vancouver until it is. I don't know when that will be—I was looking this stuff up online, some guy from Ohio went through this same process, and it took him fourteen months to be taken off the death list. Fourteen! This could take years, so I can't commit anything to him. Besides, I can't just mooch off him forever, enough people have already screwed him over, and I won't be one of them."

"That's the spirit . . ." she grumbles into her drink. "So, then, what's your plan?"

"I don't know, have fun? We have chemistry. Like *chemistry-chemistry.* He's so fucking hot, Mick."

I throw my head back on the bed, fanning myself. She laughs at me.

"That's no lie. If there's more of where he came from, I'll certainly consider becoming a transplant. Actually, this uptown area would be a great spot for the bar," she says, referring to her cocktail lounge venture.

———

I loved having my worlds collide between family and Micky and Lonan. Seeing everyone get along so well fills my heart to the brim. All I need is for this social security shit to work itself out and then life will be peachy.

We spent the afternoon watching old home videos. I got to see videos of Jack growing up, which was hard but also a beautiful way to see how my family still cared for each other in my absence. I even saw clips from past *Birdie Days*, which was one of the most depressing things I've ever witnessed. It was like watching my own funeral. No, thanks. I, hereby, forbid any more October Birdie Days. *Woof.*

We played pond hockey, something I hadn't done in forever. Jack took new home videos on his phone for us to rewrite some of the old depressing *Birdie birthdays*. Hockey is fun, though I suspect the ice Lonan skates on is in a little better condition than this. My skate caught a divot, and I was thrown on my ass. Good thing I have a big ass. Micky is also quite the skater, something I didn't know about her. I'm sad she has only two more days here, so I plan to spend as much time as possible with her.

After her full day of travel and the busy day, she trods up to the guest bedroom, and I stay awake a bit longer to finish watching the hockey game. He scores two goals. I'm in awe of him. Watching Lonan pant and sweat, being completely in his element, does something to me. I want to get him that worked up for me. I text him my congratulations with each goal, even though I know he won't respond until much later.

After I crawl into bed, he's still on my mind. I head back to his place on Monday. We've grown so much closer since being apart. Sometimes he calls me after a game, still wired from the adrenaline. We stay up talking into the early morning hours. Being at my parents' house and chatting all night feels like I'm thirty going on thirteen. However, the things I want to do to Lonan are definitely eighteen plus.

I slide my hands between my thighs and let my imagination run wild.

———

He should be home any minute, and I'm on pins and needles, trying not to pace. Yesterday morning, I had my wax, and I spent the afternoon getting all dolled up. I look hot. Under his jersey, I'm wearing some sexy lingerie that make my ass and tits look fantastic.

Operation Feed the Kitty is well underway. All systems are go.

I've decided I will make him an extra special dinner tonight—lobster ravioli. I found a quality protein powder to add to the pasta flour. And lobster is full of healthy omegas and vitamins that his usual lean protein, like chicken, is missing. It's the perfect special dinner. There's still a mixture of flour and protein powder coating the counter when the elevator dings, but the ravioli are made, and they just need to be added to my salt water. Hearing the familiar noise brings a smile to my face.

"I'm home!" he calls out, emerging from the hallway. He takes one look at me and drops his duffle bag. "Ohh, you're in trouble."

He removes his suit coat, tosses it over his bag, and unbuttons his cuffs, rolling up his sleeves. *Fuck.* The walls of my vagina constrict as soon as I see him. He's in his navy suit, freshly showered. That devilish smile beaming as he comes over to wrap his arms around my body. His scent envelops me, and I close my eyes, trying to imprint this moment forever. The feel of our bodies pressed together, his deep voice, the anticipation that hangs in the air . . .

I've missed him, not only physically but emotionally as well. He's been my closest friend since moving here. I miss our banter and jokes, playing cards, and the mundane things of living together, dishes, laundry, and seeing him in his sweats and tube socks. The thoughtful things he does, like rub my feet when I'm reading.

"I missed you," he says, tilting my chin up.

Then he kisses me. It's charged, his lips electric against mine. It's lustful and full of longing. Returning his kiss with the same enthusiasm, I cannot hold back a small gasp. When he growls in response, it goes straight to my center. Nobody turns me on like he does.

He spins me around, my back pressed to his front, and leans down, tucking his chin at the junction of my neck and shoulder. "What are you making? It smells terrific."

"Lobster ravioli." I grin.

I tilt my head, exposing my neck, and he gives me a gentle nip below my ear.

"Delicious."

He gropes my hips over the jersey, feeling the lingerie underneath.

"What's this? Did you get dressed up for me, Little Bird?"

Little Bird. That moniker continues to manipulate my hormones.

"Do you like it?"

"Is it for me?"

"Yes," I answer demurely, my shyness and confidence are warring. But after meeting his gaze, all my inhibitions melt away. I've been waiting for this for too long.

"Let me see you."

I lift the jersey over my head. Lonan drags his gaze over my exposed skin. I welcome his ogling. I enjoy every single burning second of it. How he fixates on me, and the way I can feel his appreciation of my body. He's not said anything yet, so I bravely reach up, running my fingers over the cups of the sheer bra, hardening my nipples.

"Yeah, I like it. I really fucking like it." He grabs me under my thighs, picks me up, and perches me on the cold countertop.

I immediately jump when the frigid marble hits my

skin. "Shit! The counter is freezing!" I can't stop laughing at the shock.

He chuckles in reply and widens my legs so he can stand between them. That sobers me. His thumb brushes back and forth across my bottom lip.

"Are you hungry?" he asks.

I salivate at the thought of taking him in my mouth. I bite the tip of his taunting finger, and he slides it past my lips. I want all of him. I swirl my tongue around his thumb and suck. He pulls his finger out and skates it along my neck and between my breasts. Goose bumps fan out from the line he's drawing down my torso. He stops at my fleshy hips, and he squeezes. My insecurities move in like heavy storm clouds, and I place my hands in my lap, attempting to cover my stomach. He wastes no time pushing them aside and digs into my curves again.

"This area, just below your navel, makes me crazy. It's so hot."

He worships me like a goddess. I'm delighted that the part he loves about me is the part I'm most critical of.

He continues, "It's feminine and soft. You drive me fucking wild. And I've dreamed of these hips for weeks, so don't try to withhold them from me."

His thumbs hook under each side of my black panties.

"Lift," he orders, and wetness floods my center.

I look up at him through my eyelashes, savoring his greedy hands on me.

I raise my ass, which unintentionally causes me to thrust my pelvis toward him. Dragging the underwear down, they fall at his feet. His big palms settle on my knees and he parts my legs, farther this time. The cold counter makes me gasp again. Next to me, leftover flour is shoved to the side by my spread thighs. I can feel how soaked I am when the air chills every wet part of my exposed pussy. He takes me in, and his rich-brown eyes turn obsidian.

"This for me too?" he asks, swiping a finger through my folds, catching the arousal on his fingers and bringing it to his mouth.

"Mmhmm," I pant as my chest rises and falls. "I've been wanting you since you watched me get off."

"Did you touch yourself while I was gone?"

"Yes."

"When was the last time you got yourself off, Princess?"

I hesitate.

"This morning."

He smiles, and my heart somersaults.

"Oh, yeah?" He looks down and strokes the pad of his thumb up and down my clit with a feather touch. "Like this?" he asks, his eyes meeting mine.

The second he touches me, in the exact spot I've

wanted it for weeks, the coils inside me tighten, and I squirm, trying to grind into his touch.

"More," I plead.

"Look at how starved you are for me." He tips his head back, cocksure, and smirks at my fidgeting like he's enjoying my torture.

When he slides a finger inside, it only increases my desperation. "More, Lonan."

"So wet," he approves, adding another finger.

I squeeze my eyes shut at the relief that rushes to my sex, and my mouth drops open.

Finally.

He grasps the nape of my neck and tugs me toward him, exploring my mouth with his tongue while he does the same between my legs with his other hand. It's almost too much. My heart skips and my vision clouds. Tears prick at the corners of my eyes. It's the culmination of all the desire and emotion that's been accumulating between us, now colliding all at once.

I refuse to come early. I'm going to extend this pleasure for as long as possible. His fingers pump into me, and the sound fills the space. His lips curl into a smile against mine, and I know he hears it too. My palms press against the cool countertop, and he removes his hold from my neck and brings it to my entrance, drawing it back up to circle the tight nub. I lean back on my elbows and rock, trying to ride his hand even harder.

I catch his eyes on my breasts as I send him deeper with each movement.

"That's it, baby."

Observing his fingers disappear into me sends a charge up my spine, and I mumble a curse at how erotic it looks.

"You going to watch me like this when I'm fucking you too?"

A quick "Yes" is all I can muster.

He chuckles. Then drops to his knees, pulls my ass to the edge of the counter, and latches his mouth onto my clit. *Holy shit.*

"Fuck, I've missed this."

"Like that. Just like that, Lonan. Don't stop," I beg.

I push my hand through his hair and graze my nails over his scalp. He lifts his gaze to mine and there's only adoration in his eyes. Watching him work between my legs is breathtaking. I'm close—his fingers plunging inside me, his lips locked down on every nerve in my body as he sucks. I moan his name, causing his lips pull into a smirk, and he winks at me. He actually winks, and my dropped jaw transforms into a euphoric smile at his arrogance.

When he curls his fingers to hit that spot inside, it's game over. The tower of blocks that have been stacking inside, sway and slip. He pulls his mouth away and firmly brings a clap down on my clit. The sting vibrates through my body—I'm insatiable for him, and I clench my teeth.

"Lonan!"

When I look into his eyes, it feels like falling. My panting turns to moans as my walls grip his curved fingers as he strokes the orgasm out of me. My hips rise and he stands, pulling me against him and pressing his forehead against mine as my legs quake. He takes my mouth again. The flavor of him and my arousal mingles on my tongue. His lips lazily tease mine as he pulls his hand away, his thumb gently brushing over my still twitching clit.

"Yeah," he says, watching me. "So fucking pretty."

Tasting myself on his lips makes me hungry for more, like a fire being stoked from embers. It's my turn to watch him come apart at the seams. My desire for him grows into a fever pitch, and there's nothing I want more than to watch this incredible man shatter for me.

TWENTY-FIVE

LONAN

I've never been one to come from getting a woman off, but I had to fight to keep it together. She's luscious and sweet—visions of her riding my face flood my mind. I want to devour every inch of her.

My cock jerks when she unfastens my slacks and her fingers brush over it. The anticipation of what's to come sends my heart racing. The number of times I've imagined those full, pouty lips wrapped around me is too many to count. She hops off the counter, then hurries into the living room. *The hell is she doing?* She steals a cushion off the couch and brings it back with her —adorable.

She tosses it down in front of me, lowering to her knees on the firm cushion and a grin pulls at the corner of her mouth. Moving my boxer briefs out of the way, she releases my length and bites her lip.

All for you, Little Bird.

Fisting my girth, she licks her lips and works me up and down. The drop of pre-cum glistens on my tip. Mouth open, her tongue draws a warm trail from my base to my crown.

"Christ, you look so fucking sexy right now," I groan, her tits pushed up and rounded in that lace bra with no panties. A meek smile etches her face, hinting a sense of pride. She clenches her thighs together, gliding her smooth palm over me one more time.

I'm eager to find out how well her curvy little body takes me this way. Fingers knead my ass while the other encircles the base of my cock. She opens her mouth and paints her flattened, glazed tongue with my tip, back and forth like an ice cream cone. The lingering bead of pre-cum is picked up by her tongue, and she swallows with a wicked smile. *Tease.*

I tilt her chin toward me and push her bottom lip down with my thumb. "Open up, baby."

Her eyes darken, and I love seeing my girl like this. So eager to please.

"Yes, Daddy," she whispers right before her lips wrap around me. The possessiveness in her eyes brings with it a frisson of excitement. She's erasing the memory of any other woman using that word on me.

"Bridget," I growl.

Her warm velvet tongue massages my cock as she acclimates to the sensation of me filling her mouth. It's pure bliss. She pushes deeper, and a rumble works its way up my throat. Bending, I release the clasp on her bra; she lets go of my thigh, pulling her arm from the strap. I straighten to my full height and look down at her. *Electrifying.* I could marvel at this for days. Watching her take my cock with her mouth, her nipples pebbling. She looks up at me with those gray doe eyes, and I melt.

"So beautiful."

Her tongue flicks and swirls around the tip.

I cup her face and stroke her cheek with my thumb. "Are you going to give me some of those pretty tears when I slide down your throat?"

Her thighs squeeze tight, and she releases a moan that reverberates around my dick. I peer beyond her lips, down to her full breasts, and watch as they heave every time she takes a pull from me. She twists her grip as she sucks, adding more lubrication.

"I want you to tap my leg three times if it's too much. Show me."

She looks up.

Tap. Tap. Tap.

"Good girl."

She hums, and I glimpse the hunger in her eyes before they flutter closed when she guides me toward the back of her throat. *Fucking hell.* I brace one of my arms behind me on the counter and gaze at her through my lashes.

"Ready?"

At her subtle nod, I continue.

"Show me how well you can take me."

She draws me in, and I skim the back of her throat. Pulling away, she leaves only the tip in her mouth and inhales through her nose. Closing her eyes, she nuzzles to push me deeper and angles herself to accept all of me. *Goddamn.*

"Look at me, baby. There you go, just like that."

I wrap her hair around my fist and pull her back. When she sucks in a breath, I thrust into her mouth as deep as I can go. Her upper lip kisses the base of my stomach, and I hold her there. I want to see how she handles it. Seeing her work so hard to please me stirs something deep inside me.

"That's my pretty girl. Take it all."

Her temples and cheeks turn rosy as the oxygen burns up in her lungs. When I feel her grunt against me and a single slap to my leg, I release and pull away from her lips, a thread of saliva connecting her lips to the head of my cock.

"Again," she says, licking her lips. I can't help but beam down at her. She's every wet dream come to life.

"You're unreal . . . Deep breath, Princess."

She does as she's told, and I sink into her throat

again, the muscles flexing around me as she tries to swallow my entire length.

"Fuck."

I tug back on her hair, bobbing her mouth over me a couple of times to let her get another breath of air through her nose. I'm in awe of the view in front of me.

Her tits bouncing as I glide in and out, the shine in her eyes, the welling tears on the rim of her waterline, waiting for me to claim them. The sticky wetness glistening on her inner thighs only fans the flames of desire. I love how turned on she is when she's choking on my cock. Those thirsty, pouty lips wrapped around me, suctioning until her cheeks hollow. Her need to surrender and submit to me tugs at my heart. How is this woman mine?

She moans, shooting waves of pleasure from my core, urging me to quicken my pace. I pick up speed until I'm fucking her mouth.

"You're such a good girl," I praise as she takes me like a damn champ.

A muffled whimper sends a shiver through me. Watching her saliva pool at the edge and drip off her lips is intoxicating.

Spreading her knees, one of her hands falls and disappears between her thighs.

"That's right, show me how much you love this. I wanna see you make that perfect pussy come again while I'm buried in your throat."

I pull out.

"Inhale. Then relax," I command.

When she does, I drive my hands into her hair on each side of her face and push myself back in, holding her firmly there. She gags at first but quickly recovers control over the reflex. I slowly slide in and out, watching the red at her temples blossom to her cheeks. She can't breathe when I'm this deep. She frantically rubs her clit and lifts her hips higher, chasing her own need.

"That feel good, baby? *Allllmost there*, you're doing so well. As soon as I let go, I want you to take big inhale and come for me." I hold her for three more seconds, and when the tears spill from her eyes, it does me in.

I swiftly pull from her lips. She coughs, and the rush of oxygen into her lungs barrels back out of her on an orgasm. She gasps and takes a deep breath before bringing me back to her mouth. Grinding and squirming as she moans around my cock. I plunge into her over and over again. I admire how determined she is. She's stunning.

"You're going to swallow every drop, aren't you?"

I let go of the pressure building inside me. Her fingers dig into my ass, and she burrows into my pelvis as I pump into her. Her muted cries add even more sensation, and the tension inside me explodes. My thrusts lose their rhythm, and I break—cum spurts down her throat and a growl rips out of me. I unclench her hair, and she slides off my cock, licking me clean. Her face flushed, chin wet with saliva, hair tangled. She most beautiful chaos.

"God, you're gorgeous." I drop to my knees before her and sink my hands into her hair. My kiss is full of adoration, tasting myself on her tongue and wiping my thumb below her lip to clear the drool from her chin. She's magnificent when she's a mess. I kiss her temple and curl her body into mine, still breathing heavily.

"You did good, baby. You did so fucking good. I'm so proud of you."

TWENTY-SIX

LONAN

With her legs wrapped around me, I can feel she's ready to go again. I'll need a few minutes. Carrying her into the bedroom, I drop her onto the thick fluffy comforter and unbutton the wrinkled dress shirt that's been bunched up on my stomach for the last twenty minutes.

Her fingernails scrape down my abs, and my lips curve into a grin as I furrow my brow.

"Sorry, I've wanted to do that for a while now."

"Oh, yeah? Did it live up to your expectations?"

"I don't know. I always imagined doing it while you were inside me."

"You're killing me."

Her laughter's relaxed, she's happy and sated. This woman doesn't have a care in the world right now. I love it.

I kneel on the bed, straddling her thighs. My hands move from her thick chestnut tresses to her delicate neck, over her breasts and peaked nipples that rise with each breath. I drag them lower, over her stomach. Fanning out my fingers, I dig into her hips and lean down to press a kiss to her stomach. That part of her body triggers some primal feeling of lust deep within me. The softness makes me crazy. Her fingers thread into my hair, running her nails over my scalp. A new ache climbs up my throat. It's full of emotion—fear that something this good won't last and desperate hope that it will. I want this to never end.

I brace myself on my elbows so I don't crush her. Her hands find my neck, and she brings my mouth to hers. I lick the seam of her lips, coaxing her open with my tongue.

"Fuck me, Lonan," she begs in that breathless, raspy voice against my lips.

"Let me grab a condom." I sit up to reach into my nightstand.

"I'm on birth control." A weighty pause passes as I consider what she's offering. "I'm clean."

"I'm clean." I fight to keep a smile off my face, and my dick comes alive again. "I've never gone bare with anyone."

I bend her knees, lifting her calves and separating them so I'm kneeling between her thighs. Her exposed pussy is so ready. I want to taste her again. I crouch and lick from her core to the top of her clit. She tastes like tart honey, and I'm addicted to it.

"We don't have to if—"

I grip my cock, leisurely stroking it in my fist. She watches with eager eyes as it slides through her inner lips and over her swollen nub, bringing forth a soft exhale. I sit on my heels and look down at her through hooded lids. Lying there for me like a seductive angel on her cloud of pillows.

"No. I'm taking you like this."

I trace her opening with my thumb, working in one finger, then two, stretching her wider. I drop my chin to my chest, letting a drop of spit fall to the head of my erection. She's wet but tight as hell and already trying to clinch down on my fingers.

Our gazes meet, and a moment of trust and compassion passes between us.

I grasp her hip in one hand and nudge my cock at her entrance. I slowly sink into her until she's filled with every inch of me. It feels like a promise. This is where I'm meant to be, I feel it firmly in my chest. As if this moment had been planned for lifetimes and our being together was always inevitable. It's different from the hotel. It's emotional and raw.

Her lips part, and her eyes widen.

"Lonan. This is . . ."

"I know, baby."

We fit like our bodies were made for one another. I

swallow the feelings clawing at the edge of my thoughts and focus on the task at hand. Her body stretches to accommodate the sudden fullness. My self-control wanes as I drag out and thrust back in again. Nothing has ever felt like Bridget. *My Bridget.* Her arousal coats my cock, and my movement becomes more fluid. I'm trying to take it slow, but it's too hard to maintain with her. She looks down at our bodies connected and curses. She bites into the corner of her lower lip while watching me slide in and out of her, again and again. Seeing her get off to *us* is thrilling.

"Oh my God. Please, don't ever stop fucking me." She lets out a moan, and her eyes squeeze shut. No more taking it slow. I place my palm at the base of her neck, and her eyes pop open and her breath catches.

"Eyes open, sweetheart. I'm done going easy on you. It's time to show you who you belong to."

"Uh-huh." She nods, lifting her ass to give me access.

My hand wedges a pillow under her. I encircle her wrists and hold them above her head, lacing our fingers together. I drive into her with long strokes, pulling out to the tip and thrusting back in. A smoky moan escapes her lips, and it might be the sexiest sound I've ever heard. I pull one of her nipples in my mouth and gently increase the pressure between my teeth until she cries out, then I use my tongue to heal the pain. I nip under her breasts, marking her with my teeth.

"You're so deep." She exhales.

"And you take every inch so well, baby."

She clenches around me, and I groan. I need to change positions, or I'll finish before we even get started.

I drop her hands and sit back up on my heels. When I place her calves on my shoulders, they tremble, and I flash her a smile. Those little involuntary movements are so precious. My dick bottoms out, and she flinches —*too deep*. I pull one of her legs off my shoulder and cross it over the leg on my other, twisting her to the side and exposing the side of her ass to me. Her eyes flutter at the new position.

"Lonan," she whines when I drive into her again. "I'm going to come."

The crack of my hand on her ass fills the room, and she grits her teeth and shoots me a look, daring to do it again.

"Ohhh, darling . . . not until I say so." I tsk.

I look down and watch her pussy take my slow, unhurried strokes, testing her patience. When she pleads for more, I pull out, flip her on her stomach, and drop another clap to the other cheek to match the first, before massaging my palm over the rosy handprint.

Her head tilts to look back at me, frustrated, waiting for me to push into her again. I wrap my arm around her stomach and hoist her onto her knees. She spreads them quickly, eager for relief. My cock slaps her clit from behind, and her arousal spatters. *Damn.*

"So wet," I mutter.

She tries backing into me, grinding against my dick, hoping I'll give her reprieve from my stalling. When it doesn't work, a frustrated snarl comes out of her, and I chuckle.

"God, you're needy. What's wrong? Are you hungry for this?"

"Starving," she grits out. The sexy, surly side of her is hot as hell, and I want to fuck it out of her.

"Let me hear you beg for your dinner."

"Damn it, Lonan!" I bite my lip to keep from laughing. She doesn't see how big I'm smiling. "I need to come. Please. Please, I'm so close!"

Bending down, I move my mouth to her shoulder and whisper, "I'll fill you up, but your cunt is going to feed until I say it's had enough, understand?"

She nods.

I slap her ass one more time before I descend into her dripping pussy. She joins in my momentum, rocking on her forearms and propelling herself against me over and over. Soft music is drowned out by the sounds of flesh hitting flesh, gasps, and moans. I increase speed and she matches it, holding the quick pace for as long as she can. When she clenches and her movements become erratic, I grab her hips and hammer into her, keeping us on the same rhythm. From the side, I see her mouth drop open and her eyes squeeze closed.

"There you go. Show me how you come on this cock."

And she does. Her walls are like a vise.

"Bridget. Fuck."

Listening to her moan and feeling her pulse around my erection has me redirecting my attention to anything but how good this feels. I fist the base of my cock tight to keep from blowing my load early, it's right on the edge. I can't move, or I know I'll finish. I wasn't prepared for how intense this was going to be.

She relaxes around me and gets up on her knees, wrapping her hand behind my neck for balance. I rove my hands over every curve, one hand toward her breasts, the other finding her clit.

"You're going to give me one more," I order.

She turns her head to kiss me, and a smile spreads across her face. She is perfection.

"Let me ride you."

Fuck yes. The next time she comes, I want to see it on her face.

A dark chuckle breaks from my throat, and I pull out of her one slow inch at a time. She whimpers from the emptiness.

Leaning against the headboard, she climbs on top and ever so gently lowers onto my dick with a cheeky smile. Giving me a taste of my own medicine.

I catch her off guard with a sharp spank on her ass.

"I don't like to be teased."

A devilish grin rises on her face, and she lifts her chin. "I'll keep that in mind."

Fingernails scrape down my abs again, leaving soft tracks.

"Much better," she says matter-of-factly.

She plants her hands flat on my chest and takes over, grinding her clit as she gyrates, occasionally sliding up and down my shaft. My large hands stretch over her ribcage, and I thumb her hard pink nipples. She leans back, jutting her tits out and resting her hands on my knees as she rocks on top of me. So beautiful.

"That's it, baby girl. Take all of me."

I pinch the sides of her exposed clit, and she calls out like a siren. Reaching behind, she tugs on my balls. *Shit.*

I groan her name and give her another spank. Her movements become more passionate as she closes in on another.

"Hold on to the headboard."

When she does, I grip those luscious hips and thrust up into her, making her breasts bounce. I love how soft she feels in my hands, how grabbable she is. She's white-knuckling the wood as she holds herself steady.

"Lonan, I'm going to come." She tucks her face into the crook of my neck, but I don't let up. Every pant, mewl, and raspy whimper fills the room, and once her cunt swells around me, it's utter hell holding off.

"Let go. I've got you."

I reach behind her knees and spread them wider, sliding her up and down, fucking her in long strokes.

"Don't stop, don't stop," she sobs. Her trembling legs quake, and each cry of pleasure sends me over. I concentrate and keep at it until I feel that hard pull from her. She's right on the brink.

"You have the sweetest goddamn cunt."

When Bridget stiffens and purrs my name, it's over for me. We capsize. I bring her mouth to mine and kiss her like she's my only source of oxygen. I send my hands into her hair, breathing heavily and heart racing, I kiss her with everything I have. Each swipe of my tongue is drawn out as we gradually rise to the surface again. Her body collapses on mine. I'm speechless. Skimming my fingers up and down her thighs while pressing my lips to her neck. We lie together and catch our breaths.

I carefully slide out of her, already missing her warmth, and she releases a soft exhale. Forcing myself out of bed, I bring back a warm, wet washcloth from the bathroom. Before cleaning her up, I take in the X-rated image of my cum leaking out of her. So good. Her hair is wild, face flushed, and eyes still full of ecstasy.

She's all mine.

I crawl under the sheets, wrap my arms around her

warm body, and pull her against me, her back to my front. I drop kisses onto her shoulder, and she smiles.

"Are you hungry?" *Because I'm fucking emaciated after that.*

"The food!" she panics.

"Relax, just tell me what I need to do."

She gives me instructions and sends me to the kitchen on a mission.

I come back to bed with two bowls of damn good lobster ravioli. *How is this woman real?* She's snuggled up in my covers with a few movie options picked out. I pass her a bowl, and we devour them.

The rest of the night is spent with her curled into my body, feeling her breath against my skin, her feet brushing my calves, tracing lines and circles over her back. I'm not paying attention to whatever show is on. I just want to eternalize this moment with her and how perfectly she fits into my arms, into my life.

TWENTY-SEVEN

LONAN

"**D** change! D change," Coach shouts to our bench.

My legs take over, and I jump the boards before I have time even to think. My skates hit the ice, and I fly through the neutral zone to catch up with the action.

Our forecheck kept the puck behind their net while Hanson and I made our change. Hanson is already positioned on the left and just in time for Conway to poke the puck away from one of their guys. The puck rolls along the board where Hanson takes control just inside the blue line. I'm flying into the zone, and Hanson sends the puck right to the tape of my stick like we've done it a million times before.

The other team swapped defenders the same time we did, but Hanson and I had a step on both of them, so when the puck hit my stick, there was only one skater between the goalie and me. Conway and Banks were still tied up in the corner with a couple of their guys, but Sully was open, closing in on the net, waiting for an opportunity, and that's exactly what I would give him.

The opposing skater in front of me knows I want to go right for a slap shot or a wrist shot. I deke right hard, and he bites. Off balance but still in control, I dangle, and I'm in the clear.

Shit! I went too hard, and I'm moving too fast. I've got no chance of pulling back for a forehand shot. Hell, I've got no chance of keeping this edge for another second, let alone a respectable shot. I give up trying to regain my balance, and as I start to fall, I send the best pass, well, the only pass I can muster, over toward Sully.

I hit the ice and slide headfirst toward the scrum of skaters, including Conway and Banks coming out of the left corner. I can't see shit other than the wall I'm about to hit, but I can still hear.

Wood smacks against hard rubber and then a split second later, ringing metal fills the rink. It's the sound that makes every player and fan hold their breath.

I crash into the boards, keenly aware of how out of position I now am, but then I'm enveloped in the deep and glorious resonance of the foghorn. It's a goal.

Holy shit, I can't believe that worked. Ten minutes to play, and we're finally up 1–0.

I get to my feet and am slammed against the boards once more as my teammates surround me in celebration.

"Atta boy, Burke!" Conway shouts.

"Hell of a pass, buddy!" says Sully.

"Thanks for putting it in. I would have never made it back in time if you hadn't."

———

"Madaroni and Cheese! What do you want for dinner?"

"Chicken nuggets!"

I open the cupboards and pantry, searching for some panko breading or cornflake crumbs for her requested dinner. Maddie comes over and weasels her way under my legs to peek inside the fridge next to me.

"Aunt Birdie, do you know how to make chicken nuggets? You got any chicken in here?" Mads shouts.

"I do," she says, squeezing between us and the fridge. She opens the freezer and pulls out a bag of frozen dinosaur-shaped nuggets. For a chef, that feels like cheating.

"Two hundred degrees Celsius for twenty minutes. Not everything needs to be homemade. Besides, they taste better when they are shaped like dinos. Right, Mads?"

"Yup!" Maddie yells as she runs back over to the TV to watch her movie.

When Bridget turns her back, I pinch her waist and

wrap my arms around her from behind. I bite her neck and whisper, "We need to work on your Fahrenheit conversions, Little Bird."

"You need to behave yourself, Maddie's—"

"Never." She turns and glares at me, trying to suppress a smile.

God, I love this girl. It's just a figure of speech. It's not *love-love*. Right? I give her a peck on her lips so she doesn't question the way I'm staring at her.

Maddie is having a sleepover at our condo tonight, and Bridg and I have everything planned out from finger paints to fruit snacks. Well, she did most of the work. Hell, she even had dino nuggets locked and loaded. But Maddie wants to surprise her Aunt Birdie with something special, so I told her we could send her out on an errand while we bake her cupcakes. Okay, it's not so much baking them as it is scraping frosting off a twelve-pack of store-bought ones and re-decorating them with new frosting and sprinkles. I can't bake for shit.

I sent Bridget out to buy more ketchup. She swears up and down we had some in the fridge, and she's right. It was in the fridge, right before I stuffed it under the sink.

I nod to Maddie as soon as Bridget steps into the elevator.

"Ready for cupcakes? We gotta move fast."

"Let's go!" She tears through the kitchen on her little feet, grabbing all her things.

I bust out the new frosting—at least it's the good stuff you get from the bakery and not the shit from a can. Maddie does her best to frost the cupcakes, but between the two of us, we probably get more on our hands than we do on the cupcakes. It's the thought that counts. I'll blame mine on the four-year-old.

I look over at how she's doing and find her adding sprinkles to a cupcake heaped with an absolutely disgusting amount of frosting. My pancreas is stressed out just looking at it. I tried to make a bird on mine with pink icing. At least, I hope she thinks it's a bird. It could also pass as a trailer hitch. It's either a shitty bird or a really good trailer hitch. Whatever.

When Birdie arrives with the ketchup, I'm wiping up the last of the frosting from Mads's fingers.

"Maddie! What is this? Did you make cupcakes? They are beautiful!" She's so good with her.

"Lo-Lo helped me," she announces, chin held high.

She shows off her cupcake piled with enough frosting to choke a horse.

"Wow!"

"This one is for you!" She thrusts the monstrosity at Bridget, and I stand there trying not to cringe as she takes a big bite out of it. *Fucking yuck.*

"Do you like it?!" Maddie squeaks.

She can't speak with her mouth full, so she deflects her wince and puts two thumbs up.

Best. Aunt. Ever.

I bite the inside of my cheek to keep from laughing at her well-disguised suffering.

"Lonan, this tastes *amazinnngg*, you have to try it!" she says before shoving it in my mouth. Jesus Christ. My teeth are ringing.

"Yap. So good," I say between chews.

"I'm really super at cupcakes, huh?" Maddie hops up on the chair and swings her legs back and forth while happily peeling off a polka-dot liner from her sugary creation.

This time, Bridget is trying not to laugh, and she finally swallows her last bite of frosting. I use my thumb to wipe away the frosting smeared on the corner of her mouth, then bring it to my mouth to suck the sugar from my finger.

"You taste so damn good." She spins around to see if Maddie heard me. The Kool-Aid man could smash through the wall right now and that little girl wouldn't blink. She's far too infatuated with her cupcake to care about what's going on around her. Bouncing and chattering as she tries to count all the sprinkles.

"How come you don't wear rings?" Maddie asks.

Huh?

"What do you mean, kiddo?" she asks her.

"You and Lonan don't wear wedding rings. On your fingers."

Bridget side-eyes me for a moment, then tilts her

head and responds matter-of-factly, "We aren't married, so we don't wear wedding rings."

"But you live together. And all my friends' aunts and uncles that live together are married," she says, trying to understand.

"Uncle Lonan and I are just friends."

My eyebrows shoot up.

Excuse me?

"Do you want to get married?" Maddie asks.

"Someday," I respond, keeping my gaze fixed on my future bride.

Bridget clears her throat. "Are the chicken nuggets ready to go in now?"

"Nice segue. You and I *will* talk about this later."

———

After dinner—and some animated movie about cats—Mads is out cold. I peek over at them, and she's snuggled up with her head in Bridget's lap. Thoughts of what our kids might look like slink into my mind. I knew I wanted children someday, but seeing her with Maddie makes it seem like my dream of having a family is actually attainable.

"She looks so peaceful." She smiles down at our niece and brushes the hair back from her face.

"Ready to put her to bed?" I whisper.

She nods.

I bend down to scoop her relaxed little body into my arms and carry her into the spare bedroom. We work together to tuck her into bed and ensure the night-light and sound machine are on. Bridget tiptoes out behind me.

As soon as the door clicks shut, I push her up against the wall.

I kiss her, parting her lips, and ever so slowly press my tongue to hers.

My lips curve into a smile against hers as a sugary flavor floods my mouth.

"You still taste like cupcake frosting."

"I snuck one during the movie."

Grabbing her ass, I hoist her up to my middle so she can feel how hard I am.

I sweep my tongue through her mouth again. "Naughty girl."

She wraps her legs tight around me, and I carry her into my bedroom.

I grip her sides, and a small yelp slips out when I toss her to the bed's center. She sits up on her elbows as if waiting for a show. Gripping my shirt at the nape of my neck, I pull it over my head. She draws in a sharp breath when I unbuckle my belt, and a wide grin spreads over my face as she presses her thighs together. Wrapping my palms around her calves, I yank her to the edge of the bed.

"Strip for me, angel."

After quickly removing her sweater, she lies back down, arches her back, and lifts her ass to shove the leggings down.

She pulls them off her ankles and flings them across the room.

"What if she wakes up?"

Her shoulders relax when I nod to the baby monitor I set up earlier.

I think back to what she said before dinner. *"Uncle Lonan and I are just friends."*

I don't know if she did it to irritate me or if she really feels that way, but it's only going to confuse the poor kid later on when she sees me kissing her aunt.

I drop my jeans and boxers, stepping out of them while lazily stroking my erection. Her ragged inhale makes me harder. She crawls into my lap when I sit on the side of the bed and straddles my thighs, positioning her cleavage at eye level. I tug her bra lower and take each of her hardened peaks into my mouth, gently biting and swirling my tongue around each one. Her hands move to the nape of my neck with feather touches.

Now seems about right.

Without warning, my hand connects with her ass— loud enough that the resounding smack rings off the walls, this one, a punishment.

"Ow! What was that for?" Her voice catches. She drops down on my thighs and rubs the sting. I knead the pink blotch of my handprint to soothe it.

"That was for telling our niece we're *just friends*. Thought I told you to strip." I slip my finger into the top of her G-string and snap it. "What're these still doing on?"

She's already soaked. I felt it as soon as my dick brushed against the small scrap of lace separating us. She rises to her knees again and smiles, shaking her head, making no move to take them off, and I'm growing impatient.

"Make me."

A rumble crawls up my throat, and I shove her panties to the side, spearing my full erection inside her. Her mouth drops open as she takes every inch like the extraordinary woman she is.

"Lonan!" she gasps, her arousal dribbling around me.

"Look how wet you are for me. Still think we're just friends, baby?"

I nip at her lower lip.

"I promise you. We will never be just fucking friends. You can try to lie but your sweet pussy"—I apply pressure to her clit—"is begging to be more than friends."

Her legs quiver, but I don't let go yet. I kiss her, placing every bit of affection on her lips.

"Am I still your friend when I spank your ass? Kiss you like this? When I'm buried inside your dripping cunt so far that you tremble and shake when you come?"

She slides up and down my length.

"Lonan," she warns.

"Are you just my friend when you're riding my cock like it's made for you?"

Her muscles contract, and she plants one of her feet for more leverage. I reach between us and rub the sensitive bundle of nerves between her legs. Her eyes go wide, and she stares straight into my goddamn soul. Her muscles are taut, and she clenches around me on her last down stroke. She pulsates and softly groans, grinding her pussy into me. Now I'm ready to get mine.

I collar her neck with my hand. "That's it, Princess. Milk every drop of cum from me. Show me how you think we're just friends."

She's slippery and tight and feels so damn good. Her mouth drops open in a silent scream. *So gorgeous.*

"Don't stop, right there. Don't stop, don't stop," she whispers.

It feels like she's pulling me inside her deeper as she squeezes. I continue to massage her under my thumb. When I rub my fingers back and forth, I slap my hand over her mouth in time to smother her raspy wail.

As she comes, her stare bores into mine. In this moment, I would do anything for her. The connection between us sends me into my climax.

I love her.

———

Her head rests on my shoulder while her leg lays over mine. She's tranquil as I stroke the soft skin behind her knee. There's a comfortable silence, but my curiosity forces me to break it.

"Do you want kids someday?"

She looks up at me.

"Maybe. Do you?"

"Yeah."

"Your mom . . . she wasn't around much, was she? You lived with my parents?"

I clear my throat. Talking about my mother is never easy.

"My mom was an alcoholic. She wasn't a happy drunk. When she got pregnant with me, my dad left. She always blamed me for it. Whenever she went off on a bender, she would spend the weekend berating me. She was a bully."

"I'm so sorry," she says, closing her arms around me tighter and nuzzling closer.

"The first time I showed up at Jack's—your parents'—with a black eye, they called Mom up and made some kind of arrangement. I'm not sure if they paid her or what. To this day, I don't know what was said, but I lived as a Hayes until college."

"I had no idea it was that bad, Lonan. I'm glad they

were there, but I wish they didn't have to be. That's awful. You were just a kid."

"They are the closest thing to real parents I have. And I always imagined having a family someday that looked like theirs."

"Hopefully better than what they went through."

"You know what I mean. It's rare for a marriage to withstand the loss of a child for obvious reasons. But somehow, they got lucky. Theirs did." They have something unique. Their love is unshakable. That's the love I want with Bridget.

"You know I can't promise you any future plans right now, right? I have no clue what's happening with my social security status. I'm running out of time. Getting involved with anyone is a bad idea."

It feels like I just got checked into the boards.

What the fuck?

"How so?"

"It would be selfish. I'm deadweight. I don't have access to loans, cars, or any jobs, a house—Lonan, I'm scrounging off literally everyone I know."

"That's not—"

"You talk about marriage and kids because those things are possible for you right now. I couldn't even get a marriage license if I wanted to. I can't get health insurance. How the hell am I supposed to have a family when I can't even take care of myself?"

"You have a job with me. I will get you a car. You don't need a loan. You live here."

"Lonan."

"Bridget."

"It's not the same. I need my independence. I've spent most of my life thinking I was unwanted; I've learned to be dependent on myself. It's what I know. It's safe."

God, this woman has trust issues on top of trust issues. She's shutting us down before we even begin. The walls she has put up are tall and wide, but I know she feels something for me. I can see it in her eyes every time our gazes meet. Every time I touch her, she's looking at me for more.

July 25, 2018

I'm not speaking to Birdie. Ever. She went behind my back and not only applied for college, but somehow got accepted and registered for classes. Apparently, she has been squirreling away her wages all this time. That money was supposed to be for us to live off of. Selfish little bitch. Well, good riddance. She'll be crawling back here asking for forgiveness in no time once she realizes she can't stand to be away from me and can't hack it in school.

TWENTY-EIGHT

Birdie

I open my laptop and check my emails. My heart sinks. Looks like the US Government is on their shit again. Are the SSA and Homeland Security working together to bend me over? This is one hell of a welcome home present. The last couple of weeks have been some of the happiest in my life, why does it have to be like this?

ATTENTION!

Your travel authorization via the Electronic System for Travel Authorization (ESTA) will expire within the next 30 days. It is not possible to extend or renew a current ESTA.

If you enter the United States under the VWP you are not permitted to extend your stay in the United States

beyond the initial admission period. You must depart the United States on or before the date on your admission stamp when you entered the United States.

Staying beyond the period of time authorized by the Department of Homeland Security, and being out-of-status in the United States, is a violation of U.S. immigration laws and may cause you to be ineligible for a visa in the future for return travel to the United States.

Fuck.

Fuck, fuck, fuck. Where's my phone? The contents of my purse scatter all over the table as I shake it upside down. My phone clatters out, and I snatch it up. I need to talk to my parents.

"Mom? I just got an email that my VWP is expiring. What should I do?"

"Shit." This is my first time hearing her swear. *Well done, Ma.*

"I know. What do I do?" I repeat.

"Let me talk with your dad. We need to figure this out. I would have thought that your social security documentation would be overturned by now. Why is it taking so long? Can you come over tonight? I'll make dinner, and we'll go over everything."

"Yeah, yeah. I'll bring all my info."

"Have you told Lonan?"

"Not yet."

"Mmm." I know I should tell him, but I'd rather go to him with solutions, not problems.

"I will. I just need to have a plan first. There has to be a way we can speed up the social security office. We have police reports and documentation. And . . . and . . . I'm breathing and alive! God, it's like trying to convince someone the sky is blue."

"We'll figure something out."

———

After two hours of trying to find a loophole, we are stuck. There are papers strewn across their dining room table. Three open laptops, a pile of newspaper clippings, there's even an open encyclopedia. Who even has an encyclopedia anymore? Oh yeah, *rich people.* The four of us, Dad, Mom, Jack, and I are at a stalemate. I spin in the office chair. Isn't there something about movement that makes your brain figure out problems?

I pick my phone up and I see six missed calls and a handful of texts from Lonan. My phone was on silent. *Shit.*

Before I can text him back, he strides through the front door with purpose.

"Birdie, what the hell?" He holds up his phone, then freezes.

"Whoa. What is going on in here?"

"I'm sorry I missed your calls. We've just been working through some stuff."

"Like? Care to elaborate on your vagueness?"

I go back to spinning in circles. "I need to find out how to get me off of the Master Death File quickly."

Lonan simply stares. "The Master what? Is that a band name?"

"The Master Death File, it's like this big list the social security people manage of everybody who's cashed their chips," I explain.

"Pegged out," Jack adds.

"Gave up the ghost."

"Bought the farm." We're getting punchy.

I stop spinning and smile at Jack, getting sucked into the playful reprieve.

"Bit the big one."

"At room temp."

"Didn't pass go; didn't collect two hundred dollars."

"Jesus, are you guys finished?" our mom cuts us off, exasperated with our bullshit.

"Oooh, met their maker!" I couldn't help myself.

"Paid the ferryman!" Jack shouts.

"Enough!" Dad booms.

Damn, he used the dad voice, I mouth to Jack, and we stifle our laughter.

My dad hands Lonan a printed copy of the email I received. His gaze darts back and forth over the words. When his eyes reach mine, he looks hurt.

"Bridget, when were you going to tell me about this?"

I shrug. "I didn't want to tell you until I had a plan and knew what I was going to do about it."

LONAN

What? I sit and listen for the next hour, trying to get caught up on the mess. I didn't realize how short on time we were. Something drastic needs to happen.

Bridget stands up. "I need a break. My head hurts. I'm going for a walk."

Jack rubs his face and leans back in his chair to look at the ceiling. The rest of the family is still digging through information like they will suddenly find answers that weren't there five minutes ago.

———

I'm so thankful I don't have a game tomorrow. I stay up late, pulling all the information I can think of about Homeland Security and visas from the internet. Our immigration system is an absolute holy mess. I don't know how anyone gets a visa when everything is so confusing.

A Green Card won't work because she needs to have applied a long time ago and would have needed a sponsorship anyway. Plus, those take up to twelve months to process, and she would have to go back to Vancouver and start over. Nope.

B-1 visa is out. She would have had to apply for that early on too. And she wouldn't even be eligible since you can't get one without proof that you're not planning on abandoning your old residence—Bridget had sold half her shit. She didn't *have* a residence when she moved here.

For everything else, she needs a sponsorship through employment, and the whole thing is a big Catch-22 that goes round and round again. This is so exhausting. I will not sit and take this day by day until she's gone. That'll be agony. *There has to be something.*

I hate using my fame to get things, but maybe somebody who works at the SSA is a fan? Could they speed the process along? I know I could get the rest of the team to help if need be. But who would we even talk to? It's not like you can call the Social Security Administration and say, *Hey, I'd like to bribe one of your workers to process some paperwork quickly. Are there any fans of Lonan Burke that work in your office?* This whole thing is such a clusterfuck. I mean, how do people survive this?

Finally, at 1:00 a.m., I strike gold: the Fiancé Visa.

We have to be married within ninety days of applying for the visa, but during that ninety days, she doesn't have to leave the country. She can stay in the States on her old identity so she's able to keep her Canadian insurance while her paperwork processes. It gives us extra time for her social security shit to turn up. Should she be taken off that Master-Death-List whatever, the only thing changing is the name on our marriage license. I would never take back my proposal. Bridget is mine. She always has been and always will be. I'll call my lawyer in the morning and see what he can do to get started. And then I need to talk to Ken and Lori—and Jack.

———

"I could marry her."

"What?" they say in unison.

"I know we're all trying to find a way to get her identity back so she can stay here as Bridget, but what we need to be focusing on is keeping her home—here— even if that means she stays Elizabeth Fournier."

"Dude, no. This is getting out of hand. You have her living with you already. There's clearly something going on between you. That's taking it too far. What about afterward?"

"Look, this is an opportunity for me to do something for this family. You gave me shelter and a place to live when I was ten. Let me give your daughter a place to live—a home. She's safe here. Besides . . ."

Silence. *Come on, man up.*

"Besides . . ." Ken prompts.

"Besides, I love her."

"Lonan, this is really generous, and I should decline this offer, but if we look into it and it's possible, I'm not going to tell you no. I need my baby home," Lori says, her voice catching.

"I had my lawyer look into it this morning. It's legit."

"Okay. So, when does she find out she's getting married? That'll go over well," Jack adds, rolling his eyes.

"Can we keep this between us for now? I don't want to make it sound like some kind of financial arrangement or scheme." She'd bolt immediately. "I'd like to have a proper proposal." I almost whisper the second half.

Lori tilts her head with swoony eyes.

"Don't look at me like that, Mom H."

"I'm sorry, you're right." She shakes off whatever gooey feelings she has brewing. "I'm not. I'm not. It's just very romantic, Lonan."

I can't think of a proposal under less romantic pretenses.

"I'm going to head home. I've got homework to do. Mind keeping her here tonight?"

They nod, and I head out to the foyer to leave.

"I'll walk you out," Jack says as I grab the door handle.

Jack has been fairly silent throughout this whole proposition. *Big-brother talk in 3 . . . 2 . . .*

"Is this for real?"

See?

"Yeah, man. It's real. I haven't told her I love her yet because your sister has major fucking trust issues, but I do. I would marry her "dead" or alive. Obviously, I didn't plan on it happening this way, but if all it's doing is moving up the inevitable, so be it."

"Just . . . think this through first, yeah?"

I decided to marry Bridget when I was eight. I don't need to think anymore.

August 30, 2022

A body was found in Ontario this morning. I don't know why anyone would have torn up that gorgeous landscaping I had put in. It was perfect. Something tells me this is going to cause problems for me even though none of it is my fault. I've proven myself to be a wonderful mother. So wonderful, in fact, that Birdie has come back to live with me since money has gotten tight and she doesn't want me to lose the apartment. Having her here should help me prove my innocence even though I shouldn't have to do this in the first place.

TWENTY-NINE

Birdie

I t's just after 8:00 a.m. when my phone rings. I barely lift my head to see the screen.

Social Security Administration—oh my God! I thrash, trying to escape the sheets twisted around me, the phone rings and rings, and it feels like I'm moving in slow motion. It's hard to get my fingers to swipe fast enough on the screen and answer.

"Hello?"

"Hello, my name is Cheryl. I am calling to speak with Bridget Hayes regarding case number 379814D."

That's one hell of a case number, Cheryl. How many people have you guys wrongly added to that Master Death File each year?

"Yeah, yeah, I'm Bridget," I rush.

"Could you please confirm your birthdate for me?"

Shit, she means Bridget's birthdate. Think, think.

"Two fourteen, nineteen ninety-four." My heart is racing.

"Social security number?"

"Uh . . . uh . . . Yeah, I have it. One second." I open the Notes app on my phone and carefully read the ten-digit number Mom gave me.

"Thank you. Bridget, I'm calling about your open case regarding an erroneous death. I have some good news."

———

Lonan is gone all day. Again. He's practically been gone from sunup to sundown lately. We barely see each other between practice, games, and his other responsibilities. He's usually gone before I even wake up. Thankfully, my family has been great about coming here to help go through all the paperwork with me regarding my social security status. But I've missed his hugs.

Jack picks me up to take me over to my parents', and I keep my mouth zipped for most of the drive. I'm too afraid I'll leak the information to them. As far as they know, we are going through day four of the loophole search. We're all exhausted. I can't wait to tell them it's over. It's time to move forward. Delaying this is not an easy task, there's been a smile on my face since the call came through this morning. When we arrive, my mom is alone in the kitchen finishing the soup and sandwiches she's making.

"I'm sorry—I should have come earlier to help you prepare lunch."

She shoos me away. "No need, I'm letting the flavors *get to know each other*, as you say." I'm proud of her.

"Way to go, Mom. Where's Dad?"

"He had to run to the store. He'll be back soon." She points her elbow to the backyard while she stirs the soup. "Why don't you go take a walk before we sit down to eat?"

Come on, people! This is eating me alive. I have news I want to share. Where the fuck is everybody? If I stay, I'll ruin the surprise, and I'd really rather present my news to them altogether.

I nod. "'Kay. Be back in a bit."

I head out the French doors that lead to the backyard. It's calm. The birds are chirping and it's the most welcoming sound after a long winter. I love being in the woods. The fresh spring air is light and soothing. Full of new beginnings. I inhale as much as I can. On the ground, the soft damp leaves beneath my footsteps seem to have been pressed down by tire tracks or something big. *That's odd.* I go back to focusing on all the nature around me, twigs snapping, birds singing, squirrels scurrying around the otherwise quiet forest. Pushing through the yellow fern branches from last summer, I notice there's something new. There's a raised garden box in the clearing off to the side.

And, oh my God. *The fort!*

It's transformed from a kid's tree house into a very legit, adult-sized version. Still similar to before but on a much bigger scale. I'm not crazy. It's noticeably larger. It wasn't that long ago I was out here. *Who did this?* I climb up the tree, step over step, and flip the hatch open.

"Hey." The gravelly voice startles me, and I scream. My footing wobbles, and I grasp onto the side as Lonan reaches down to grab my arm.

"Jesus, Lonan, you scared the shit out of me! What the hell are you doing up here? I thought you were supposed to be at that charity thing today."

He just chuckles and helps to pull me to my feet.

Whoa.

There's a whole other section that's been added. For the first time, I can see how massive this tree truly is. Not only has it been given a new addition but the inside looks like something you could actually live in. There's a fancy propane stove set up and a narrow countertop. A small table and two chairs. There's a love seat. *How on earth did that even get up here?* And there's a bed—a whole bed—with a big fluffy duvet and euro shams. I laugh. This place is outrageous. It looks like one of those luxury glamping tree houses that are always booked out.

My fingers fan out across my breastbone as I walk

around the space, fairly certain my jaw needs to be picked up off the floor.

"Yeah, I've been working on it for a few days."

"*You* did this?!"

"Well. I may have gotten a little help from some general contractors who are Lakes fans."

A tentative smile on my lips builds as my gaze leaps from one enhancement to the next. This is unbelievable.

"This is what you've been doing all week?" I shove him.

He grabs my wrist and spins me so my back is pressed to his chest. His arms cover mine, and he wraps them around my stomach, curling me in a hug as we stand and admire the craftsmanship.

"Early on, everybody wanted to tear the fort down. It was a point of contention in your family, but I wouldn't let them. I fought hard to keep it and told them I would take care of it if they left it up. Every spring, I come by after the snow thaws to inspect and make any repairs. This has been a sanctuary for Jack and me to come out here and feel close to you. It's where all three of us played as kids, where you and I shared our first kiss."

I don't know what to say.

"Your to-do list wasn't the easiest, and I didn't get everything . . . but"—he drops one of my hands and points to the largest addition where the bed sits—"I added on to make it bigger, and there are garden boxes outside where we can plant—and I quote, '*all the good vegetables and none of the gross ones.*'

"Your skylight to watch the stars." He points above, and sure enough, there's a skylight I had yet to notice.

He rubs my shoulders and steps away. His tall stature leaves little headroom, but he still walks through the space without ducking down.

He points out the window. "The bathroom you requested was not so simple. Apparently, there's a lot of zoning and soil-grade stuff that needs to happen. However, I did get a rain barrel to install an outdoor shower."

Our childhood "deal" creeps into my brain. No, that's not what this is. But I know he's got something up his sleeve.

"Lonan, why did you do all this?"

A smirk forms on his lips as he strides over to me. His gorgeous smile grows, and those white teeth bite into his lower lip. He reaches out, grabs one of my belt loops, and jerks my hips into his. His touch relaxes me as he slides his hand into my hair. *The way he's looking at me. . .* My body missed his touch this week. I lean into him and sigh.

He places a soft kiss along the sensitive skin below my ear.

"Do you *like-like* me, Bridget?"

The smile on my face grows.

"*I like-like you.* Is this the part where we kiss?*"* I finish his cute bit.

He chuckles and drops a small bite onto my neck. *God, I've missed this.* He brings his mouth to mine, and his tongue laps at my lower lip, seeking entrance to my mouth. My hands find the edge of his shirt and slide underneath up to his chest, where I draw my claws down his stomach. My need twists tighter and tighter. His kiss is patient and slow, and torturous.

"The last time I was kissed here, it was you giving me my first kiss."

He tilts my chin up, and I stretch on my toes to meet his lips, but he pulls his head back. I try to shuffle back, but his arm keeps me locked in place. Instead, he searches my eyes, clearly lost in his thoughts—I would give anything to hear what he's thinking out loud.

He clears his throat. "Can I give you your last too?"

I cock my head at him. My body stalls as his words sink in. Does he even know what he's saying? Stepping back, he produces a ring box from his pocket, and my hand slaps over my mouth. *Oh. My. God.* Tears well in my eyes as he gets down on one knee. This can't be happening. No, this isn't happening.

"I know you think you'll be returning to Vancouver, but there's no way I'm letting you go that easy. I won't let your family lose you twice. I'll never let that happen. I'll never take for granted this second chance. A second chance to fall in love with you for the first time. Making you live with me was the smartest decision I've ever made; it's made me realize how much I love you."

The admission causes my eyes to widen. My heart explodes into pieces.

When he cracks the box open and the lid lifts, the most beautiful ring I've ever seen sparkles before my eyes. A clustered starburst of smaller diamonds halo around a classic oval-shaped diamond in the center.

He takes my hand, and the tears build to a swell.

"Bridget Hayes." My hands are shaking in his. "Will you marry me?"

I steal this moment for myself. Memorizing every word from his mouth. Every fleck of gold in his eyes. That incredible smile—the one that makes me ache. I imagine a life with him, getting married, going on a honeymoon, and making love from sunrise to sunset. Starting a family. Watching him become a father. Teaching his kids to skate. I think of the fights and the make-up sex. The good and the bad. Seeing him spend the rest of his life loving the woman of his dreams. I want all of that for him with every part of me, but I can't offer him that.

Selfishly, I don't regret spending so much time together and falling in love with him—these have been some of the happiest weeks of my life—but he's doing a service to my family by asking to marry me. *I won't let your family lose you.*

I look into the eyes of the man that holds my heart.

Within my motionless body, I'm imploding. This is the hardest thing I've ever had to say no to, because I do want it. But not for the same reasons he does. I retract my hands, wrapping my arms around my stomach.

"No."

His eyebrows raise and he blinks.

"No?"

"I'm so sorry." The tears swell until a warm drop spills down my cheek. I wipe it away before it reaches my chin. "I can't let you do that."

His forearms drop to rest on his knee as his head falls between his shoulders.

The silence is suffocating.

It feels like an eternity until he stands. When he does, his unwavering stare is dull, lacking emotion. I would rather he glare than regard me with apathy. Everything tells me to look away, but he doesn't deserve that from me. And I don't deserve him.

"I've stopped you once, I'll do whatever it takes to stop you again."

There it is. I feel sick. This proposal is his "whatever it takes."

"What do you mean 'you stopped me once'?"

Silence.

"I leaked the story to the press."

"You *what?*"

"I heard you talk to Micky on the phone about going back to Vancouver. You said you were moving back. I figured if the press got involved you would have to lay low for a while."

"And how convenient that you had a place for me to live, right? So, all of this has been set up by you. Were my parents in on it too?"

"No. They didn't know. It was something I did," he rumbles.

I'm so stupid.

Is this what everyone came up with for their grand plan to "keep me"? They thought we could have some kind of Green-Card wedding? Whatever it takes to make the paperwork appear legit, right? Like when Julianne kept me. I was a placeholder for someone else. Existing only to look good on paper.

What if I had said yes? I can't even imagine how painful his rejection would be after he realized he made a mistake—I'd never recover. This was never his long-term plan, it's another temporary solution. How temporary is his love? How long did he think he could do this? Eventually he would meet someone he truly wanted to spend his life with and I would have to step aside. I'd rather go back to Canada than go through that pain. Luckily, I don't have to.

"I got a call this morning," I begin, swallowing my tears. "My social security paperwork came through."

"What?" he sneers.

The anger he has toward me says it all, *why the hell did you make me go through all this work for nothing?*

Pressure builds all around us.

"I was hoping to tell you tonight after you got home. But now . . ."

I don't want to ask my next question, but I need to know.

"If I had told you this morning about the phone call, would you have proposed to me today?"

His eyes narrow. "Is that what you think? That I wouldn't propose to you on my own?"

"Would you have proposed today?" I repeat.

He hesitates. "Probably not. But it doesn't matter."

"It does. You asked because you *needed* to, not because you wanted to," I snap back. This proposal was nothing more than a Hail Mary.

He stalks toward me, and I shuffle backward until my ass hits the thick tree trunk that spears through the center of the tree house. He advances until the bark digs into my back and scrapes my skin. The blaze in his eyes consumes me. *He's pissed.*

"You don't think the last few months have been real?" He presses against me. "This isn't real?" He grabs my chin, parting my lips, and sweeps his tongue through my mouth. Everything in me wants to return his passionate kiss, but I don't. Instead, more tears.

"I would have fucking married you whether you were going to leave or not. Hell, we would probably already *be* married if you had never gone missing."

"Why? Because of some childhood promise? Why

won't you give up on that?" My response is bitter in my mouth.

"Because, you and me, we are goddamn inevitable. You just haven't realized it yet!"

"You never said *I love you* before today."

He snatches up my wrists and lifts them above my head, pinning them against the cool bark of the tree.

"Darling, you were made for me. Look at you, even now you give your body to me so freely. But why is it that the second I ask for your heart, you shut down? Do I need to make you fall in love with me again? Is that it?"

"You already have!" I shout.

I'm exhausted and going to double over any minute. This hurts too much.

"Then what the fuck is the problem!?"

"Goddamn it, Lonan, stop making this harder than it has to be!" I sob.

He drops my hands and backs away from me. Composing myself, I clear my throat and try to relax my shoulders, speaking as calmly as I can.

"Lonan, I love you," I choke out. "You are incredible. You're funny and charming and thoughtful . . . so damn thoughtful." I wince, looking around the room to observe his hard work.

Every day this past week, he's come home with aching muscles, and it wasn't the extra practices he said he had, he was getting here early to start working and coming home late.

"It's selfish and irresponsible for me to say yes when you have options for something better. If you're being honest about how you feel, then you need to consider this decision *without* the pressure of me leaving."

"So, what? You're giving me a chance to back out? That's real fucked, Bridg, you know that? I call bullshit. This is *you* backing out because you're scared of opening up."

"You're only asking me to marry you because the threat of my deportation was looming over your head! The responsibility fell solely on you. I won't let that be the foundation we build our life on."

No little girl grows up imagining her marriage proposal will be motivated by logistics rather than love.

His nostrils flare, and he shoots his arm out like he's about to make another argument, but no words form when he opens his mouth. He knows I'm right. When our gazes meet, his hands drop to his sides. The crushing sadness I feel is reflected in his eyes. He slowly shakes his head.

Swallowing hurts. My throat bobs, trying to push down all the feelings on the cusp of spilling over at any moment. *Don't show him how much this hurts you.* If Lonan and I are meant to be, I have to trust it will happen someday. If I said yes now, I'd always wonder if he did it for my family or me.

Because, yeah, there's some truth to what he said—deep down, it is hard for me to trust. But he loves my parents and Jack more than anyone. He would do anything for them.

He scrubs his hands down his face. "So, what now?" Bitter sarcasm on his tongue.

I feel like my insides have been scooped out.

"I don't know." I subtly shake my head, my voice solemn. "I guess I'll stay with my parents until I can find another job."

This time I don't look at him. My eyes stay fixed on a knot in a floorboard, it's all I can do to keep from sobbing.

Heavy footsteps cross the space to the open hatch on the floor.

"You can pick up your shit from the concierge."

He's gone. And I'm gutted.

———

My parents are thrilled that I'm officially "alive" and will use the name Bridget Hayes on new documentation. They knew about the proposal, which only gives more weight to the argument that he did it for them. This was the loophole they found. They know something went down between the two of us, based on the way they said he peeled out of here, but nobody has said anything. I don't have the strength to talk about it, so I'm glad for their understanding. Today should have been a great day, but instead, I'm here. Alone in a guest bedroom, obliterated. Will I ever feel happiness again? The empty pang in my gut multiplies, and I worry it will swallow me whole. *I wish it would.* My throat is raw from crying, and I have a headache from all the tears, but I stand behind my decision to put him first, even if he doesn't see it that way.

He was so wrapped up in this that he was willing to throw his future away. Stepping back was the right move. If we are inevitable like he says, I won't fight it. But I don't know that. He admitted he wouldn't have proposed today if my visa waiver wasn't in jeopardy. And sure, we'd have a few good years, but eventually, after he tired of the sex, he would see there's nothing more to me than broken pieces. I would end up even more busted than before.

He deserves someone that will fit into his life better. I've seen the hockey wives. They are so put together, as if they stepped out of a magazine. They have pressed designer dresses, while the few outfits I own are well-worn. Where their bodies are tall, tight, and lean, mine is short, curvy, and soft. Their lives are organized; mine is a mess.

On top of that, I have been relying on everyone for everything—*which is never safe*—I have zero control over my life. Now that I can get a job, I'll be able to take care of myself. I can get my own place, and people can stop feeling like they have to take care of me. I'll be able to get my bearings and figure out where I stand.

My trust issues aren't something that can be cured; this ugly part of me is permanent. Eventually, he'll see that he dodged a bullet. The hard part is moving forward; it's not like we can just split and go our separate ways. Seeing him when I'm with my family will be like twisting a knife through my heart. There's no avoiding him. He's my parents other son. I hate that I hurt him, but I needed to pull back before I destroyed us both.

THIRTY

LONAN

he Macallan 18 isn't cutting it. I shouldn't even be drinking since we have a game tomorrow. But what else is there to do? Jack told me not to fuck this up, but I'd say it's well within the realm of fucked. I'm tempted to go out and take home the first bunny that looks my way, but none are Bridget. And I know it would only be out of spite, so there's no way I could follow through once I got her back here.

I don't know how to get through to her. Nobody has made me as crazy as she has. Maybe I messed this up by proposing so soon, but it wasn't because I didn't want her. She probably thinks it's a favor for her family. An eye for an eye. They saved me, so I save her. That's bullshit. We belong together.

She calms me and makes me feel cared for. At least

she did. Ironically, all I feel now is rejection. *Ain't that some shit.* I can't just move on with my life as if nothing happened. The worst part is I know I'll see her around. I sure as hell don't want to see her right now, though. I've already packed up her things and dropped them off at the front desk. It was a dick move to drop her stuff with the concierge, but I'm not ready to see her.

Deep down, I'm just hurt and want her to hurt too. She doesn't seem nearly as affected by this split. I suppose that's no surprise, considering it was her idea. When she said she would stay with her parents and get another job, it was like getting kicked in the gut. She didn't even want to *try* to work through it. When we're married, I'll teach her it doesn't work that way. She can't cut and run when things get tough. If she wants to fight, then we're going to fight. I'll stay up all night arguing if that's what it takes. And then I'll fuck her until the sun rises, just to show how much I love her.

I'm not giving up as easily. I'll wait. I'm a patient man. How can she not see I'm all in? Baggage and scars, I want it all. I'll take her issues, her trauma, her bad days. Because I know we'll also have good ones. We'll have a life full of everything she's ever dreamed of. There's a lot of happiness ahead of us, if only she could see it.

This isn't over yet. Not by a long shot. But right now, I need another drink.

———

I'm playing sloppy, which only makes me more angry. Stayed up too late drinking. Rage radiates from me. I'm not one to start fights, but I'm waiting for an excuse to drop gloves or throw one of these assholes from Texas into the boards.

My shitty skating doesn't keep me from chirping at the other team. I want everyone to be as pissed off as I am. Especially this forward who keeps trying to deke on me.

"Aye, Ehlers, my left nut dangles better than you do." I throw my shoulder into him.

"I bet it does. You ready to age out yet, bud?"

I get him out of my zone, but before long, he's back again.

"Age out? That's big talk for someone who's been riding the pine for the first two periods."

"Funny, that pretty brunette of yours was riding my pine last night too."

There it is.

I drop my gloves, and so does he. I release blow after blow, giving him every bit of my aggression. The second that stupid fishbowl gets knocked off his head, I lose control. The boys are banging their sticks against the boards as I throw my shots. He dodges the first few punches but on the fourth swing, my fist connects with his face, and it's glorious. He's gotten in a few jabs, but

I'm numb to them. There's too much adrenaline coursing through my veins to feel anything.

We each have a firm grip on each other's sweaters, slowly circling as we throw as many balanced punches as we can.

"Come on, hit harder, bud!" I fire at him.

"I'm going to beat your ass, old man."

He's definitely not, but I am getting tired. I'll give him that.

I prove my point with a couple of haymakers. As soon as I drop him to the ice, I'm getting hauled back by the refs.

I try to lurch for him one more time but Sully grabs me.

"The fuck's your deal tonight?" He shoves me toward the penalty box.

"Just trying to have some fun, baby." Damn, that felt good.

The ref escorts me off the ice. They give me ten whole-ass minutes. I didn't hit him that hard. Five would have been sufficient.

I look over at Ehlers, he's getting his eyebrow stitched up. He has a black eye forming, and my lips curl into a smile. After squirting water in my mouth, I spit it back out, but it sprays red all over the mat under my skates. *Perhaps I deserved the ten.* I kept my head down for most of the fight, so it's nice to see my hard work paid off. I still came out with a busted lip, and I know I'll be sore tomorrow. But this was the wrong night for him to bring up Bridget. I've been chirped at before about the women I've been with, but they were always bunnies; no feelings were involved.

Texas scores on us while I sit in the sin bin. Now that the fury has died down, I feel like an asshole. Had I been in the game, I might have prevented that shot. Why not pile on more guilt to the steaming pile of self-hatred brewing inside me? When my time's up, they bench me until the game ends.

"Look who's riding the pine now?" Ehlers shouts as he skates by. *What a dick.*

"You want me to give you a matching set, mother-fucker?" I say, referencing the deep purple lines under his left eye.

My hand hurts, so I'm thankful I can't.

We lost that game, and it's my fault.

When we get back into the locker room, Sully grabs my shoulder and spins me around.

"What the hell was that?"

"Dunno. He pissed me off." I shrug.

Banks cuts in. "Bullshit. Guys chirp at you all the time, you hardly ever let it get to you. And I've never seen you throw punches like that. So what's going on?"

"I proposed to Birdie."

The last thing I want to do is tell Banks, but what do I care anymore? What's he going to do? Make me feel worse? Impossible.

He shrugs. "Okay. Congratulations?"

"She said no."

There's a silence in the locker room. Nobody knows what to say. I don't blame them, it's rare to ever hear about a rejected marriage proposal, and it's unheard of for athletes. Banks doesn't give me shit, he just stares at me with pity. If I didn't know any better, I'd say that was sympathy in his eyes. Nothing like getting sad eyes from the biggest asshole on the team.

"That guy's a prick," Banks murmurs, not looking at me while he loosens his skates. "He had it coming."

———

Me: Hey.

Me: Have you talked to Birdie?

Micky: Yeah. Dude, wtf? You proposed???

Me: I was trying to keep her here.

Micky: You do realize that she's essentially been "kept" her entire life right?

Me: Kept?

Micky: Let me break it down for you. She's been held hostage for like 20 years by a deranged garbage person that never showed her an ounce of compassion or love . . .

Micky: Now in walks you, trying to tie her down with a ring, telling her she doesn't need a job, a place to live, a car. You're going to handle everything. Sound familiar?

Micky: Let's paint another picture. She and her family have been spending the last 4 days trying to come up with a loophole that allows Birdie to stay.

Micky: 4 days toiling day and night to find the perfect solution, legalities be damned.

Micky: Now in swoops you—the person she loves—and he's got a solution. If she marries him, it's the perfect loophole. How romantic. 😊

Micky: I mean, you basically sprung an arranged marriage on her. What the fuck were you guys thinking? Did no one see this backfiring?

Holy shit. I should have seen this coming. Bridget is still wrong on her assumptions, but I'm starting to understand why she said no.

Me: Shit.

Micky: Yeah.

Micky: She's a huge pain in the ass when it comes to affection. I'm her best friend so I understand your frustration all too well. She's infuriating.

Micky: But that anger should be directed toward Julianne. That woman gaslit her for 20 years, convincing her that she was unlovable. It fucked her up.

Micky: Thank Christ she's FINALLY starting therapy.

Micky: Anyway, she needs to know you would still marry her as Birdie Hayes and not Elizabeth Fournier.

"I've been trying!" I shout into the empty room. I don't know how I could have made it more clear.

Micky: It's obvious you love her. You've showed her a million times. Now that she doesn't have to deal with loopholes and she starts working on herself, she's going to come around.

Micky: Just don't give up on her. Give her some space and let her figure out her shit. I know you care about her, but she needs to be cared for a little differently. She's special.

I know how special she is. Taking a break from her will not come easily. Especially when we've been living together for weeks. But I'll play the long game if that's what she needs.

> Me: How is she?

I miss her so much. We've spent weeks apart before, but these have been the hardest days ever because there's no guarantee we'll ever be what we were.

Micky: Pollyanna? Oh, she's fucking fantastic.

Micky: She's just as messed up as you are

> Me: I can't believe I didn't see how stupid this was.

Micky: Don't beat yourself up. You meant well. I'm coming in May and I'll help point her in the right direction.

> Me: Oh yeah? Going to spend longer than a weekend this time?

Micky: Actually, I'm moving there. Well, if I can get an apartment that is . . . so far it's not looking great. But, I miss my girl and I can't go back to Seattle.

Micky: Besides, the market is perfect for the bar I want to open.

> Me: No shit? That's awesome.

> Me: Hey, I'll get you that apartment if you help me get Birdie?

Micky: Granite countertops sound lovely! Thank you!

Me: Done.

Micky: Don't worry man. She'll come around. Don't forget, she loves you too.

THIRTY-ONE

Birdie

I don't know if I can watch much more of his game. He's not playing like himself.

"Not sure what's gotten into Burke tonight, but the crowd is loving it, Randy. He and Ehlers are still going at it. Ehlers is getting in a few punches, but he seems unprepared for the haymakers coming from Burke. He's throwing bombs out there! I don't know why lines haven't stepped in yet, they're going the full twelve-rounds and—and Ehlers is down! Refs finally have stepped in and Burke is getting escorted off the ice for a penalty. Looks like we have a little blood on the ice tonight, folks."

The color commentary is ridiculous on this fight. What the hell is Lonan thinking? Usually, Banks is the one out there stirring shit up. I get that they are trying to hype up the viewers, but watching him get hurt is unbearable. I shouldn't be talking, considering I'm the one that may have hurt him the most. They show a close-up of him in the box; every time he squirts water into his mouth, he spits out blood.

I hate it. I want to say that his little stunt on the ice tonight was unrelated, but I can't help feeling some blame. My fingers itch to text him, but I resist. First, I need some time to get my feelings sorted out. Based on how we left things, I don't know if he'll ever want to speak with me again.

———

Fuck. Therapy was a bitch today. Lots of heavy topics and lots of tears. Or as my therapist Carol calls it, a "productive session."

Unfortunately, now that I'm acknowledging some of the trauma that's happened, I'm becoming familiar with my tendency to run away from my problems. I need to work on myself and make some progress before I enter a relationship—much less answer a marriage proposal. It would be too easy to slip into old patterns and end up right back where I started. There's only so many times someone like Lonan will allow himself to be hurt by me. I will not burn through my strikes until I'm ready to give him what he wants. What I want. I just hope he can hold out for me.

I flip open my phone and check out his Instagram.

He's not posted in a while, other than team promo stuff. He looks good. Healthy, a lot better than he looked during that fight a few weeks ago. He's smiling, but it's not the same as the one I'm used to seeing, it doesn't reach his eyes.

THIRTY-TWO

LONAN

I got Micky her apartment. The guy who owns our hockey bar, Top Shelf, has a couple of apartments above it that he normally only rents to rookies for dirt cheap. Most of us have lived in those units at one point or another, and because of that, we've gotten used to going to the bar for our usual hangout. In exchange for the cheap rent, we show up and bring in more customers. Everybody wins. Since we only have one new rookie next season, Rhys something-or-other, the other apartment was available, and I talked him into renting it to Micky. I've held up my end of the bargain, now it's her turn.

> Me: Let me know when you plan on getting in town. I've got keys for you.

I send her a pin drop with the address so she knows where it's at.

> Micky: Seriously? How? I haven't been able to find any vacancies!

>> Me: I pulled some strings.

> Micky: You're the best. I'm still working on her. How are you holding up?

>> Me: I miss her.

> Micky: Ugh, you're both so cute it's gross.

Has Bridget been saying she misses me too?

———

Our press box lasted longer than usual. We lost the first game of the playoffs. We're out. Everyone on the team is feeling the heavy slump of our loss. Funny how I started thinking this year would be one of the best. I was way off the mark. I can only go up, right? Hope so 'cause I'm fucking counting on it.

I enter the auditorium as the lights are dimming, thankful I got into the doors to Maddie's dance recital before they closed them. I pull my ticket out and squint to see what row I'm supposed to be in. Row 12. I quietly make my way down the aisle, when I reach the seats, there's only one left open on the end. And Bridget is in the other seat.

This is the first time I've seen her since I asked her to marry me. It's like I've been coldcocked. I take my spot. She doesn't look at me but she sucks in a breath when I sit. I can smell her shampoo or perfume or whatever it is that makes her smell like fresh citrus. I've been going back into the guest bedroom every now and then to get a hit of her scent. It's faded over the last month, but right now I'm surrounded by it. I close my eyes and commit it to memory. My jaw tics. After this recital, I don't know if I'll ever be this close to her again.

I check the program they handed me, and Maddie's group goes second to last. We'll be here awhile. I shrug off my jacket and get comfy. I've gone from seeing her almost every day to quitting her cold turkey. I'm jonesing, so there's no reason I should make it easy on her either. I roll up my sleeves and rest my arm next to hers on the armrest.

Like I prayed she would, she welcomes my touch. It's pure relief. I let out a long exhale. She keeps her arm right where it is. Not only that but goose bumps burst across her skin. *That's my girl.* It's the game we've always played. When my body brushes against hers, she never pulls away. She's still holding feelings, same as me.

I take it a step further and stroke the back of her hand with my tattooed knuckles. My touches are butterfly soft but she reacts. She crosses her thighs, and even though the speakers are blaring with some shitty pop remix, I heard the sigh slip from her lips. She tries to cover it by clearing her throat. There's not a sound she makes I haven't memorized. The connection between us is so charged, and we're so starved for each other's touch that this feels like foreplay.

If I keep it up, I'm going to have an issue. For now, I'll just keep my forearm pressed against hers. I'm not pulling away.

———

Me: It was good seeing you today.

Bridget: You too.

Me: You know this isn't over, right?

Bridget: I know.

September 14, 2022

I have already filed a complaint with the chief for all the harassment I've received from police. They can't treat me like this. Now, there's an order in place for me to give a DNA sample. They also want one from Birdie. Too bad she just moved out. Maybe if they were better at their jobs they could locate her, but everyone over there is completely incompetent. Don't they realize I pay their salary? To think I had something to do with that murder is laughable. Do they have any idea how much I've done for Birdie? What about what I've had to go through? I did nothing wrong. These people have no idea who they are messing with.

THIRTY-THREE

Birdie

Job hunting was a good distraction from the pain. There are enough restaurants in the metro area that need chefs, so I have a few options. My top choice is Alloy. It's a trendy restaurant that offers a pop-up style menu—something like that is perfect for me since there are so many more opportunities to play around in the kitchen and present new ideas to the executive chef. On top of that, I can work in a variety of cuisines at the same location. It's an awesome concept, but I wish I could be more excited about it.

I impress them with my cooking demo during the interview and am thrilled to accept their offer. Once I get my first pay stub—and some insurance—I'll be able to sign a lease. I've got my eye on an apartment within walking distance to the restaurant; it's not available yet, but there's a tenant moving out soon. I told the restaurant manager it would be a couple of weeks before I could join the team, and I'm very appreciative of their patience with my start date. There are a few other things I need to take care of first.

I wish I could tell Lonan about everything. We've had the occasional text here and there. And the moment at Maddie's recital. I can't stop myself from checking in on him online. I need to stop because every time I find a photo he's tagged in, he's not alone. There's a woman with him, though never the same one. It's a push and pull of wanting him back and wanting to give up. But that's why I meet with my therapist multiple times a week.

In the beginning, therapy was difficult. I'm not good at asking for help. But I noticed a pattern of behavior in myself, and it's not healthy. I don't think I even realized it existed until Lonan pointed it out so bluntly. I do cut and run. If there's one thing Julianne taught me is that to avoid getting hurt, you hit first. I know there's a lot of baggage to go through, but I always thought trying to go through it was useless. Better to just set the whole thing on fire and walk away. Therapy can't go back and change what has happened, but it's not about changing the past. It's how I react in the present. I'm putting in the work and am learning how to accept love.

Unfortunately, as soon as I used Bridget Hayes on my paperwork, it didn't take long for the media to catch up with me. The phone has been ringing nonstop for interviews. I had to get a new private number. I don't need the attention right now. I'm trying to get my life back on track, and it's not something I enjoy talking about.

The local news has gotten involved, but now national news and morning shows are sending reporters to my parents' house and blowing up their phones. Their networks' resources are endless. I've decided the only way to get through this is to give them what they want so I can become old news, and they'll move on to something else.

I'm thankful my dad is here to help me navigate contact with all the broadcast networks. We have a family lawyer that's been incredibly helpful too. I'm not yet used to the level of encouragement from my family, but it's another thing I'm working on in therapy.

After much back and forth, we will release the story with one of the national news shows, *Headline*. I'm told they have the most respectful, least exploitative interviews. Quite an accolade, "least exploitative." I meet with *Headline*'s host, Charlotte Stanard, in two days. They are flying the whole family to the film studio. Our lawyer has sent over some things we are willing to discuss and what we're not. I'm trying to get packed up for the trip, and this whole thing feels surreal. Thankfully, I still have a therapy appointment before we leave for New York City.

By next week, I will have gotten a job, moved into

an apartment, interviewed on national TV, and have left the man I love. My hair is falling out because of the stress. My life is in a tailspin, but at least I'm trying to pull up this time. I want a vacation, but that would just be an escape. I need to learn not to run away from things when they get hard.

I wish Lonan were with me. He had become such a close friend and confidant. I want to text or call him constantly. I miss hearing about his day and how he's feeling. It hurt when I saw photos of the team out partying. He didn't seem too upset to have a woman's hands all over him, whispering into his ear. The big smile on his face made his feelings apparent. Those are the consequences of my actions, and I will live with them forever. Although I'm hurt he moved on so quickly, I hate my jealousy over that photo. This is what I wanted, right? This is what I told him to do. I pushed him into this.

I shake the thoughts from my mind. No, those are simply negative thoughts. I repeat my positive messages to myself.

I release my past and am ready to accept people into my life.

I deserve fulfilling, authentic relationships.

I am letting love into my life.

———

Flying into New York City is bananas. We have been put up in the most luxurious hotels and have eaten at some of the most famous restaurants in the city. I've even had the chance to meet a few of the head chefs and see their kitchen operations. It's incredible. Unfortunately, now comes the part I'm not looking forward to— the big interview.

Walking into the studio, I take a moment to think how different my life was just six months ago. The story has been released, and my picture was plastered all over the internet last week, but this is the first time I've sat down to do a nationwide interview.

I didn't realize the real Elizabeth Fournier had been murdered until I opened the journals. When I read her words, it made the hair on the back of my neck stand up. It made me sick. Julianne lacked empathy and cared for no one but herself. I'm learning that her lack of love wasn't because I was unlovable; it's because she didn't have the capacity to love. There wasn't a person inside. She was a monster. The majority of my life was spent in the care of a child murderer. A few wrong steps and I could have had the same fate as Elizabeth. Instead, I survived by forgetting my family and keeping my head down. I was obedient and lonely, but it kept me alive.

Her death was her escape. She was too cowardly to face the consequences of her actions. How anyone could be so malevolent is beyond my comprehension. I was the one to convince officers she fell asleep at the wheel.

I was an idiot. It was right in front of me; she wasn't wearing her seatbelt, and there were no skid marks leading to the crash. This was all part of her plan. It makes me nauseous to think I painted her in such an innocent light; the funeral where I worked so hard to make sure she was remembered—I was glorifying a murderer.

I had no idea that a murder case was unfolding when I left Canada. Thankfully, the police here have been able to prove I was also a victim. My existence was a cover-up for her. She needed a body to play Elizabeth, and it was an unfortunate coincidence I had a striking resemblance to her daughter. Wrong place, wrong time to be found by Julianne.

When the studio staff hand over my credentials, I'm ushered into makeup and hair. It feels like so much makeup is being added to my face, but when I see the result, I'm thankful it looks natural and not gaudy like I was expecting. My parents and Jack are being spackled with bronzer so our fair skin doesn't look washed out under the camera lights. In other words, *you all look like corpses*. Minnesota winters are brutal, we look like mole people seeing the light for the first time.

Walking back into the studio, I notice my therapist and lawyer are seated along the side of the stage—a pretend living room set up on a raised floor surrounded by soft lighting. The producer tells us the seating order she wants us in when Charlotte Stanard walks in.

Someone from the wardrobe department is trying to get her attention, but she beelines for me and gives me a big, sincere hug.

"I am so honored that you have chosen to trust us with your story. If anything becomes too much, just let us know, and we'll take a break. Do you need anything? Water? Snack?"

"Water would be great. Thanks."

My throat feels dry as a cob now that my nerves have settled in. I'm glad my family and team of supportive people are here, but I wish Lonan was too.

————

I bring the water bottle to my mouth with shaky hands and take one last swig. After we all are mic'd up and sound checks have been performed, the interview begins.

"Bridget, can I call you Bridget?"

"Yeah, Bridget's fine." I laugh nervously.

"How are you doing these days? What have you been up to since your return?"

"Um, I'm busy. Lots of therapy." More nervous laughter. "I've been spending most of my time with family and getting to know old friends. It's been a lot to get used to."

"I can imagine. Your abduction is unique. What is it like to be one of the longest-held captives on record?"

"It's strange. Mostly because I didn't know I was abducted. I had always been told it was a type of adoption. That I'd been sent away."

"Do you remember the abduction now that you're home?"

"No, I've been diagnosed with dissociative memory loss. My brain just hid all the memories of the event. I couldn't handle the trauma, so they were tucked away to keep me safe."

"We have to ask, were you abused in any way? Were there times you didn't feel safe with Julianne?"

"No. I didn't encounter any physical abuse, as far as I know. If anything, I was ignored. Perhaps neglected. I don't think she wanted Elizabeth or me."

My mind wanders into the many ways she showed that she tolerated me but never wanted to engage with me. I was just . . . there. Like a piece of furniture she couldn't get rid of.

"Why do you think she abducted you if she didn't want you?"

"Because she needed me. She needed a body to fill the place of her daughter. I happened to look a lot like Elizabeth—"

"It's remarkable, we've seen the photos, and it's bizarre how similar you look."

"Exactly. I was an alibi for her, a way for her to keep anyone from questioning. She kept that secret from everyone, including me."

"What is your earliest memory of Julianne?"

"It's kind of weird, but I remember wanting her to like me. I just wanted her to see me." She never did, though. That woman should never have been allowed to mother children.

"Why did you want her to like you?"

"I thought she was my new mom. Who doesn't want their mom to like them? To love them? And . . . maybe a part of me knew she was dangerous, and pacifying her —making her happy—was a survival instinct. As if there was safety in flying under the radar. I don't know."

At hearing that, my mom reaches her arm behind me and pulls me into a side hug. She's looking down at the floor, trying to mask her emotions. I turn back and give her a hug. This woman loves me. Her emotions bleed into mine, and my vision blurs. Charlotte hands me a tissue and gives Mom and me a moment to gather ourselves.

"Were there any fun times with your abductor?"

"Not particularly. I remember being bored a lot." My chuckle makes me sniffle, and I dab my eyes with a tissue. I don't want to break down on national television. "I think that's fairly normal in childhood, though. But she homeschooled me enough to get me to secondary school, and she taught me how to cook. I fell in love with cooking."

"And you're a chef now?"

"Yeah, I graduated last year from Vancouver Culinary Academy."

"Congratulations, I hear it's quite a prestigious culinary school.

"Thank you."

"What about your name? You kept your nickname."

"I did. She called me Elizabeth, but eventually accepted that I wasn't losing Birdie. It made her angry in the beginning, but I knew I was Birdie. Even as a child I wasn't willing to give her power over my name. It was a nickname that was given to me by my real family. It was my connection to them. I let go of a lot of memories but not my name."

"And what about the real Elizabeth?"

I look over to my lawyer, and she nods. "I've been told she has been given a burial in Ontario with extended family. But I'm not allowed to say much more since the case is still in progress."

"Do you feel like you have given Elizabeth justice?"

"No, I think the police and the people who decided to landscape their backyard gave her justice. I can't take credit for that. I'm so happy she was found. She deserves to have her story told." What happened to that little girl is vile, and my stomach turns when I think of an innocent child being hurt by their mother, the person who is supposed to protect them above all else.

"Let's talk about the moment you discovered you

weren't Elizabeth. You find a website, see your picture all over it, then what?"

"It was wild." I shake my head, thinking back only a few months ago when I received the results from that genetic test. "I found the website and thought I was losing my mind. It was too far-fetched to imagine but the pieces all fit. So, I decided to go see them in person."

"And what did you say when you finally saw them?"

I laugh and look over at my parents. "Oh god . . . it was really emotional for everybody."

"Jack, what was it like hearing your sister was back again?"

"Honestly, at first, I thought it was a hoax. But then we saw for ourselves the genetic test match. When she used my childhood nickname, it got real." We all laugh a little. "I thought . . . this is it." His voice breaks at the end of his sentence.

"Dude, stop," I say, trying to make him laugh.

"Lori and Ken, what was it like for you?" Charlotte smiles.

This is the happy part of the story. I'm smiling too. I haven't heard about it from their perspective before.

"Oh, wow, I remember my hands shaking, and I just broke down on the floor. Then I called Ken and started yelling, 'She's home!'"

"What was that like that, finally having your daughter back after such a long time?"

"It was the best day of our life. We were whole again," Dad says.

I smile through the tears.

We discuss the social security snafu and what my goals for the future are, and they want to know where I've been hiding since I got back. I was with a "family friend." It's so hard not to bring up Lonan, he's been such a huge part of my story since coming home, but I don't want to create a media circus for him. It would only lead to more questioning, and he doesn't deserve to be made a spectacle of.

"It sounds like things are finally getting put back together. What has been the hardest thing for you to overcome?"

"Trusting people. I've made a lot of mistakes and have hurt people that I care about most. I have regrets. I had been programmed most of my life to believe I was unwanted, and it has taken a big toll on how I viewed myself. At first, I was scared to trust anyone because I thought that love was conditional. I'm in therapy now and working hard to break those cycles. It's a journey."

At the end, they ask me something I hadn't thought about before.

"Do you forgive Julianne Fournier?"

I pause for a long time.

"I don't believe Julianne possessed a conscience to forgive. It's not in her nature to ask anyone for forgiveness unless it served her in some way. I want to leave

354

her in my past. If that means I must forgive her for my mental health, then sure. But she has no power over me anymore. She's nothing."

It's like an epiphany.

"What about you, Lori and Ken? Jack? Do you forgive Julianne?"

"Never," Dad responds.

"Never," Mom responds.

"No, never," Jack responds.

When we leave the studio, the sun seems to shine brighter than before. This interview proved more cathartic than I realized. I'm glad I did it, it gives me closure.

———

When we board the plane back to Minnesota, it gives me time to think. I watch out the window as the plane's wings cut through the wispy vapors. Julianne doesn't have control over me or how I see myself. My negative thoughts were always in her voice, not mine. I am still here, still living. She's dead and gone. She was a horrible person, so why would I care about what she thought of me? But I had been letting her disapproval fester in me without realizing it.

Everything that told me I was damaged, broken, and unfit for love wasn't true. My self-doubt was poisoning me, and I never stopped feeding myself those messages.

Just because Julianne didn't love me, doesn't mean I'm not lovable. My parents love me. Jack loves me. Audrey and Maddie love me. Micky loves me. And at one time, Lonan loved me, and maybe he still does.

For most of my life, I've believed I'm not worthy of someone caring about me the way Lonan did. He laid it out for me, and in return, I said, "*No thanks, I'm good.*" Not only that, but he's probably struggled with the same unworthiness, and I've gone and reinforced it. Even after he said he loved me to my face, I rejected him when all I truly wanted was to allow myself to give him that same love back.

September 23, 2022

They refuse to see this as a misunderstanding. The police are making me go in this afternoon to do a DNA swab or they are going to send out an officer to "escort" me. I'll not be humiliated like that. The audacity of this city's detectives is staggering. They want to ruin my life. I've never been so insulted. They are undermining everything I have worked so hard to build. What is the point of even trying? This was all Elizabeth's fault. It was an accident. Doesn't matter. This will never be pinned on me. I'll make sure of it.

THIRTY-FOUR

Birdie

Three weeks later . . .

My story is finally dropping off the media circuit. I've had my fifteen minutes, and I'm ready to have a somewhat normal life again. Though nothing about my situation has been normal in the last six months. There's pressure to find a publicist and write a book. What the kidnapping was like, what living with Julianne—the child murderer—was like, how it's shaped me as a person, yadda yadda yadda. I don't want to. At least not right now. The focus should be on Elizabeth, not me. This is about her. I was an unfortunate victim in her tragic story. I was a filler, a prop. All I've ever wanted is control over my own life. Which is why I'm done with all the media interviews and talking about it. I want to move forward. I want to experience life.

I haven't made many friends yet outside of work, but I anticipate that will become easier once I've been out of the headlines for a while. Thankfully, I was able to distance my story from Lonan and not involve him. It gave me a tiny taste of the attention he receives daily, and I don't know how he does it. Privacy has always been important to me; now that I know what it's like to give it up, I can't imagine living like that permanently.

My new apartment is working out swell. A little small, but I don't need more than a studio right now anyway. I don't mind the size; it's nice and cozy. Micky says that's another way to say rathole, but whatever. It's not like I need a fancy kitchen now that I have a state-of-the-art one at Alloy to play around in. Most of my dinners happen at the restaurant anyway. Unlike my neighbors, who apparently eat orgasms for breakfast, lunch, and dinner. The walls here are a bit thin.

I mean, truly, more power to them. I'm just jealous because the few vibrators that can still get me off are only because of my memories of Lonan using them on me. This leaves me still getting off to the image of him, and that's not doing me any favors. It's a bad habit I can't seem to break. I keep telling myself to stop, but I can't. Anytime I try to finish without his image in my mind—nada. No stars, no fireworks, nothing.

Sure, I could try to find a hookup, but what's the point? None will be Lonan. It's like my vagina has betrayed me and only responds to him now. How am I supposed to get over him when he's in control of my orgasms too? I hate him for that. I'm sure he's not having the same issues. After all, I've seen even more social media posts of him out with the team. He's certainly not lonely. There's a hot woman on his arm in every. Single. Picture. I know I have to move on, but I'm not ready. Job security for my therapist, right?

There's a gala coming up that I'm expected to be at with my family. And guess who else is going? That's right. I refuse to be a fifth wheel in my own family, though. It's bad enough I'm going "with my parents." Technically, we all get a plus one, and although Mom and Dad have cautioned against asking someone to go with me, there's no way in hell I'm showing up alone. Not if I have to look at him with someone else all night.

Nate is the only other guy I know that isn't a coworker or relative. Nate, who I told Lonan I wouldn't go out with. But he also said he didn't plan on seeing other women, and according to the internet, he hasn't done a good job of holding up his end of the bargain either. Besides, the whole Lakes organization is going, Nate would have been there anyway, and even though I made it clear numerous times we would only be going as friends, his excitement level makes me worry he's reading into it.

It doesn't matter who my date is for the gala. It

won't change the deep ache that will be inflicted when I see him with someone else. Being in the same room to witness his hands on another woman will be so much worse than seeing the photos. My brain plays this horrid game where it pretends there's still a chance he secretly loves me, and all the pictures of him with other women are just something that's been fabricated by the tabloids. Once I see him in person, that daydream will be smashed. The truth will be revealed and will play out in real time in front of my eyes. His distance from me is due to my own request, but that doesn't mean I'm mature enough to sleep in the bed I made.

There is one thing I'm looking forward to, though—Micky will be moving to Minneapolis in four days. Four! I can't believe she kept it from me for so long. I wish she had told me before I signed my lease; we could have gotten an apartment together. Unfortunately for me, her new one-bedroom is above Top Shelf, the hockey bar where the guys hang out. I could have sworn those apartments were reserved for Lakes rookies, but somehow she snagged one. What are the odds? My mouth has stayed shut about it; there's no way I can burst her bubble. She's beyond thrilled to have an entire team of hot-as-hell hockey players practically hanging out on her doorstep night after night.

LONAN

The familiar beep of swiping my ID card sounds as I pass through the turnstile at the arena. My footsteps are the only sound as I stride through the empty walkways. Most days I enter through the back, but I like to walk through the arena when it's empty every now and then. One of those things I miss from before joining the NHL. I see one of the janitorial staff ahead pushing a broom.

"Hey, Earl." I nod at him. "How's Janice?"

"Oh, you know, same old. Good days and bad. Just celebrated fifty years, though."

"Shit. Congratulations, man."

"Thank you. You decide to settle down yet, hot shot?"

I laugh and spin around, walking backward.

"Working on it." He's always busting my balls about finding a '*good woman*.' "Any advice?"

"Yeah, quit dicking around. You're burning daylight, son."

"Noted. Send Janice my love."

"Will do, will do. You take care now."

"Stay out of trouble, Earl," I say, turning back around.

I've watched every interview she's done, and she hasn't mentioned me—or us—once. Her story is dying down, and I'm thankful. Not only does seeing her on TV every day torment me, but I know how much she hates being the center of attention. At least from the media. She loves it when she's the one holding my attention. I'm sick of missing her. But she needs time to figure out her feelings, and I have to respect that. For now.

My patience with her won't last forever. It also won't keep me from stalking her Instagram. I keep telling myself I'm just checking in on her, but it's more than that. Shit, it's not even conscious anymore. Half the time, my fingers open the app and type in her name before I realize what's happening.

I push open the door to the locker room as my phone dings. There's an email about the annual Children's Hospital gala and the expectations for our behavior during the event. As if we're a bunch of rowdy frat boys that can't get our shit together. Every year I buy a table and invite the Hayeses. They're my family and support the cause as much as I do. I suppose that means she'll be there too. As much as I want to see her again, it scares me. This gala will only end in one of two ways: really good or really bad. I'll finally see firsthand whether there's a chance for us. I can't make her choose me, and I wouldn't want to. I want to get back together because *she* wants to. Because *she* sees a future with me and realizes *she* can't live without me as much as I can't live without her. And she needs to come to that conclusion all on her own.

Just as I always do, I absentmindedly find myself on

Instagram. When I search her name, her profile is gone. I double-check my spelling and try again; this time, I notice a new account listed, B. Hayes. The profile picture is a woman facing away from the camera, only the back of her head shows. It's her. It's the same view I had every time I took her from behind. No question, that's Bridget. I had that hair wrapped around my fist enough to memorize the exact shade of chestnut brown.

I click on the account. Private. Her 432.8K followers are now down to 39. For the last few weeks, she's been a bigger celebrity than me. Her social media accounts exploded overnight. I suspect this is her attempt to regain some solitude from the media spotlight. But she can't hide from me. My thumb hovers over the *Follow* button. What the hell do I care? I click it. She already knows I'm keeping an eye on her. Locking my phone, I stuff it into my gym bag and finish lacing up my skates.

As I hit the ice of the empty rink, my mind drifts to what I want for us. Without thinking, I begin a bag skating. Why does our relationship have to be so hard? I don't realize how mad I am until I'm sprinting back and forth, barely able to catch my breath. My college coach used to make us bag skate until we puked. It was a punishment for playing shitty. Part of me questions whether I'm trying to punish myself for losing her.

No. We both made mistakes. She's it for me. I know the only reason she tries to push me away is because she's scared. It doesn't matter how many times she tells me to see other people. It's futile. That woman has ruined all other women for me. Sure, they hang on me like they do every other player, but outside of getting too drunk and letting them sit on my lap, the only thing I've fucked is my fist. And it's her face I picture when I come all over my hand. I skate for an hour. Not running defensive drills or shooting at the net, just bombing up and down the ice.

My legs feel like anvils, and it takes me tripping on the ice to see that it's time to go home. When I get back to the locker room and shower, I meditate and let the high of the endorphin rush wash over me. I think of how she used to look at me and how her eyes drank me in when I was buried inside her. That was love. It can't be washed away so easily. It's going to be okay.

After wrapping the towel around my waist, I head back to my locker and fish my phone out of the bag to check for any calls, specifically from Bridget. The only notification I have is from Instagram—she's accepted my request to follow. She still wants my attention.

Careful not to double-tap any photos or click any hearts, I scroll through to see what she's been up to. I zoom in on the last one she posted. It's a selfie of her standing on a cliff overlooking a lake. I know that spot well. It's on the north shore. It's where I used to go to think when I was in my twenties before fame and game schedules ruled my life. It's not an easy hike, but the view is rewarding. In the photo, she's surrounded by pine trees and huge boulders. Her hair is tangled, whipped from the wind. Her forehead is glistening with sweat from climbing over all the rocks. She's not done up by makeup teams or put into dramatic lighting for one of her interviews. Nope, this is the real Bridget. Her eyes are sparkling, and the sense of accomplishment on her face is evident. She's a knockout.

I'm about to comment on it when I see another person has beaten me to it.

Looking forward to the gala, cutie. I hope you wear something a little more formal for me than your hiking gear, just kidding.

Seriously? Nate, the piece-of-shit nutritionist, is her date? There's no way she's going out with him. That guy's a douchebag; I've heard the way he talks about women—he's not as nice a guy as he pretends to be. She's gotta be messing with me. That comment is probably the reason she accepted my request to follow her in the first place. She *wants* me to see it, payback for how much I've been in the spotlight lately at bars.

A sarcastic laugh rips from my throat.

"Oh, sweetheart, you don't even know what I'm going to do to you now."

I finish getting dressed and grin as I toss my bag over my shoulder. If she wants to play games and trifle with me, that's fine. But she should know it's a two-person sport. I shoot off a quick text to Micky because I know they're grabbing drinks tonight, it might be fun to show up and remind her who she's dealing with.

Next, I open my contacts and scroll until I find what I'm looking for and pause. Perhaps this is taking things too far, but I enjoy seeing her riled up. Besides, I plan to make it up to her by the night's end. I unblock the phone number and type out a message.

> Me: Hey. I need your help with something.

Nikki: Oh, now you need me?

> Me: Not like that. I need a date to the gala for an hour or so. This is NOT a hookup.

> Me: The rest of the team will be there . . .

Nikki: Is Rhys Kucera going?

> Me: Probably.

Nikki: K. I'm in.

Vancouver Police Department

Office of the Chief Constable

Accident Report - September 23, 2022

Agent: Andrea Lavoie (LA-4987)

Report on fatal car accident involving Julianne Fournier, driver of the 2021 Lexus sedan on September 23, 2022. Driver was only occupant of the vehicle. Julianne Fournier-64 years of age, found dead on arrival.

LA-4987 responded to a medium sedan car fire on the northbound side of Trans-Canada Highway near exit 25 at approximately 11:48 hrs. Officer blocked traffic on northbound side. Point of impact was made when the victim's car hit a tree, but it should be noted that skid marks were not present. VFD-81 arrived on scene at approximately 11:52 hrs and a dry chemical extinguisher was used to extin-guish the remaining fire inside the car interior.

Fournier struck a tree on the northbound side of Trans-Canada Highway near marker 25. The angled collision struck the left fender of her car at approximately 90 kph. It has been determined that the fire in the car was due to an airbag explosion on the driver's front airbag upon impact. Victim was not wearing a seatbelt and head and neck shown a partial ejection from the vehicle.

Fournier was removed from the vehicle and pronounced dead on arrival by the Vancouver Memorial Hospital staff. She suffered a frontal fracture of the skull and severe burns over her 75% of her body. After further investigation, it has been determined that the driver was conscious and attempted to escape the vehicle after it caught fire, but was unable to exit the vehicle due to her posi-tioning and partial ejection, where she succumbed to her injuries.

THIRTY-FIVE

Birdie

"Let's get a drink!" Micky grabs my arm and yanks me toward the front door of Top Shelf.

"Wait, what? I thought you were going to give me a tour of your new apartment?"

"I will, but first, we need to celebrate!"

Normally, I'd say no way, but since it's the offseason, the chances of seeing any players in here are slim to none. Still, I don't want to hang around too long.

"Okay, but only one drink. I get that this is basically your backyard, but we are not going to become regulars here."

"Aww," she pouts with her lip out. "But I thought this could be our home base. Our *Cheers*." She begins to sing the theme song.

"You don't want everybody to know your name. Trust me, it loses its charm."

"Um, I do if they are hot hockey players . . ." I glare at her.

I wrap my arms around her and lean into her side.

"I can't believe you're here! I'm so excited for us to have our Tuesday nights back."

There's a pause, and I look over at her.

"Well, we may need to change our Tuesday nights to Monday nights," she says, stretching her arms in front of her across the table.

"Oh?"

"I got a part-time job bartending."

"Already? Way to go, Mick! Where at?"

She pauses again. I turn my head slightly and give her the side-eye. *You better not, Micky.*

"Don't be mad."

I knew it.

"Here. This bar. Top Shelf. The bar where the team hangs out. That's where you're bartending?"

Why the hell does she have to work here? It's bad enough she lives above it. Now she works here too?

"Yeah." She cringes. "Here."

My face falls, but I quickly regain my smile and feign happiness for her. That's fine. It's fine. Everything is fine.

"Why would I be mad? That's awesome! I mean, you can't beat convenience, right? When do you start?"

"Next week . . . Are you seriously still avoiding him?"

I give myself time to answer. It's complicated, I'm still working on myself.

"I wouldn't say I'm avoiding him. But I'm not seeking him out either. I don't keep tabs on him."

She fake laughs like a hyena. "Whatever."

An eager server pops over to our table before we can set our purses down.

"Can I get you ladies something to drink?"

"Two French 75s. We're celebrating," Micky says, slapping the table.

"You got it." He winks at her and turns to make the drink.

"He's into you."

"He's about to be my coworker. Stop deflecting. Why don't you just ask Lonan to the gala and then bang his brains out and make up?"

"First of all, aggressive much? Second, I'm going with somebody else . . ."

I look around the bar so I don't have to look into the green eyes burning a hole in my face right now.

Micky tosses her hands up and barks, "Because you want to self-sabotage or . . .?"

My sigh doesn't seem to be an acceptable response for her, so I continue, "No, but I don't want to show up empty-handed and watch some other woman have her hands all over him all night. I don't know if I'm ready yet. When I make my move, I want to be stable, I don't want to begin a relationship and run out on him again because I'm scared. I thought that this way—"

"This way, you could make him jealous and show him what he's missing out on. Maybe it'll provoke him to hurry up, shoot his shot—again—and you can get back together?"

"I didn't say that!"

She's not wrong, though. I want to know he still wants me. I want to undo all the things I said to push him away. I want to be good enough for him.

"Playing hard to get is for bitches, Bird. You want something? Go get it, then!"

I fold my arms on the table and drop my forehead to them. "I know." My voice is muffled as I groan into the table.

"What has gotten into you? This is the kind of shit I would expect from you while you were living with Julianne. You hide and wait for the other person to be vulnerable first so you don't have to."

I lift my head.

"Jesus fuck, okay! Will you stop yelling at me now?" I whisper-shout.

There's a quiet break in her interrogation. She's giving me tough love to show she cares, I know it's coming from a place of kindness.

I'm well aware I fucked up. I made a lot of assumptions, and they were all based on messages I fed myself.

He constantly encouraged me to get out of the house, to explore, to do whatever I wanted. He wanted me to spend time with my family. He wasn't trying to "keep" me. Marrying Lonan is nothing like the hell I went through with Julianne.

"So, who is your date?"

"This guy named Nate."

She's staring at me again. Her raised eyebrows and smile convey equal parts disappointment and amusement.

"Nate, who-works-for-the-team Nate? The one who wouldn't stop checking out your ass? Who Lonan hates?"

"That's the one. We're going as *friends*. He was already going, I was already going. It's not a big deal. You make it sound like we can't all act like adults here."

She cackles. "That's cute."

"Why are you laughing? He's nice."

I know what I'm doing. And yeah, maybe I don't want to look weak if he's moved on. The server sets our drinks in front of us, and I already want to order a second. Micky is grilling me, and I need some reprieve, even if it is in the form of a cocktail.

"Does Lonan know?" Her eyes are big.

"I dunno. I told my family, so it's possible."

"You probably just signed that dude's death certificate," she says, taking her first sip. "Needs more lemon," she mutters.

"He's not a caveman, Freya."

She sets her drink down and raises her eyebrows at me for using the F-name.

"He is for you! Listen, I know you're trying to play hard ball right now because you don't want your inner feelings exposed, but that man wants yours exposed . . . he wants it *bad*," she adds, looking into her 1940s champagne glass as she takes another sip.

I want her to be right. Talking about him makes the butterflies in my stomach stir, and I hate that it's giving me hope. I don't want to be naïve about the situation.

"I'm almost ready, I just need to make sure I'm in the right headspace. But what about all the women he's been seen with?"

"What about them? And, plus, also, how would you even know if you're '*not keeping tabs on him*'?"

"There are pictures of it all over!" I turn around and point to the round VIP area. "Right there, last week, a woman was sitting in his lap, and he looked *very* happy. I messed up, I know. I pushed him away. So, ease off me. Maybe a rebound is what I need? Would that be so bad?" My eyes sting with the threat of tears. "Goddamn it."

"This is what he wants from you." She gestures to the tears welling in my eyes. "This. Just consider it, 'kay?" When I look at her, she sees the hurt and hops off her seat to hug me.

"Love you."

"Love you more," she responds.

We finish our drink, but when the server comes by, she orders another round instead of asking for the check. *Fannntastic.*

Thankfully, Micky senses I've reached my limit with the tough-love stuff, and we move on to discuss her plans for her cocktail lounge. She has the whole vibe narrowed down and tells me all about the patisserie items she plans to sell and what cocktails will complement them best. This is her dream. Listening to her talk about it is captivating, she has so much passion. I can't wait to see her conception come to life and thrive. There's no way it'll fail with the homework and research she's put into her business plan. As soon as she gets the capital, she'll be unstoppable.

As our next round of drinks arrive, the door to the bar opens, and six guys from the team walk in. Including *him.*

"Shit."

Her eyes follow mine, and she turns around to see what I'm staring at. We're tucked off to the side, but my body still tenses as I will myself to become invisible.

"Well, speak of the devil, and he doth appear." Her lips curl into a smile.

I glare at her, and she gives me those ridiculous innocent eyes.

"Did you do this? I know you still have his number."

"It's fate, babe."

"No, it's *late*, babe," I grind out, reaching for my clutch. "Let's get the check."

"Yeah, no."

I freeze. "Pardon?"

"I'm having a marvelous time, and I want to finish my drink." She leans back in her chair, settling in.

"Freya," I warn.

"Bridget," she parrots back. Her neck straightens. "Oh my God, that was the first time I called you *Bridget*. Was that weird?"

If I wasn't so stressed out seeing Lonan, I'd probably laugh at the look of shock on her face. Instead, I shake my head. It's my name. Having Micky say it feels like worlds colliding. She's been with me on this journey from the beginning but hearing her say it somehow makes it feel more legit. As if we've come full circle. I like it.

I take a big gulp of the second French 75 to take off the edge. After a while, my anxiety begins to lift. I can exist in this space just as much as he can. I look hot tonight. If he sees me, who cares? I have nothing to be afraid of. Eat your heart out, Lonan Burke. We have a clear view of the team as they sit down in a round corner booth. Micky and I chat more about her new apartment, and how she plans to furnish it and what new furniture she still needs. I'm distracted from our conversation when a woman sashays up to Lonan and sets her palm on his chest, bracing herself to sit on his lap. *Great. Here comes the ick.*

"So I'm going to need to pick that up from IKEA, but first, I have to find someone—girl, are you seeing this?" she asks as if I'm not already staring.

He shrugs her off, shakes his head, and turns away.

"*See*? Do you see how I'm right?"

My heart is racing. *Yeah, I saw it.*

My thoughts are put on hold when the server walks up with two ice cream sundaes.

"Oh, I'm so sorry, we didn't order these," I say. Micky glares at me for rejecting the desserts. I'm a Minnesotan that's been raised in Canada all my life. It's a wonder my DNA results didn't say *83 percent Sorry*.

"These are from the gentleman sitting over there."

I don't have to follow her gaze to know what table she's looking at. He saw me.

I swallow, not knowing how to respond.

"We accept!" Micky happily pipes up. "Please tell him thank you and that she'll eat anything he gives her."

"Micky!"

I shake my head toward the server and apologize again. "She has a condition."

"I'll tell him you said thanks," the server replies, blushing.

When I muster the courage to look up, he's staring at me. His eyes dance with amusement even though he doesn't smile. Those are fuck-me eyes. He leans back in his seat, one arm extended, the other holding a beer. He balls his hand into a fist and releases it again.

Choose wisely, he mouths.

The rush of emotion that swells in my throat is almost overwhelming, and I have to fight like hell to hide it. I know he wants vulnerability, but we're literally communicating across a bar. I look away but can see that big white smile out of the corner of my eye.

Micky digs in, she eats one bite, but then pushes it away. "Gross, this one's frozen yogurt. Let me try yours."

I look down at the ornate glass dish. Mint chocolate chip. *That fucker.*

THIRTY-SIX

LONAN

Adjusting my cufflinks one more time, I check myself in the mirror. The bespoke tux fits perfectly, but it can only take me so far. I'm fucking nervous. Tonight is the night.

I told Nikki to meet me at the gala. She knows she's there as arm candy and that there will be nothing happening between us. I'm 99 percent sure she only agreed so she can rub shoulders with the new rookie, Rhys Kucera. He seems to be on every woman's radar, but I haven't seen the guy take one piece of pussy home yet. Usually, the young ones want to party and throw themselves into the spotlight; I certainly did. Not Rhys. He's quiet and keeps to himself. I can't get a read on him. That is probably why the ladies want him so bad. It makes him "mysterious," and they all want to be the one to break him.

After one final look, I grab the keys for my Bentley Continental. A little classy, a little sporty. When I drop it off with the valet, I tell him to keep it close. I plan on taking Bridget home tonight, and I don't want to waste any time. We need a quick getaway before she starts overthinking.

I walk into the spacious Landmark Center Ballroom and scan the room, Lori and Ken are already chatting with some of their friends, and I stride toward them when my eyes catch on Bridget. *Goddamn.* She's stunning. She's wearing a one-shoulder gown; the top half is tight and form-fitting, showing off every curve. The bottom half of the dress is long and flowing, with a big slit up the side. Good. That'll make it easier to shove up when I fuck her in the coat closet later.

Seeing her with Nate pisses me off. Her gaze meets mine and she inhales deep.

That's right, baby. I'm the one that takes your breath away. Not him.

Just then, Nikki saddles up to me and hands me a champagne glass. I keep my eyes on Bridget. I might be standing next to this one, but Bridget is the only woman I plan to go home with. Her chin lifts and she purses her lips, tonight they are painted in a deep cabernet color to match her dress. They would look so pretty wrapped around my cock. She slides her arm through the crook of Nate's elbow. *I see how it is.*

Jack walks up and claps me on the back, pulling my attention from her.

"Hey, man." He glances to Nikki and then back to me. I'm sure he's wondering what kind of bullshit I'm up to. And he's right, this is some bullshit.

"Hey. Good to see you."

"Mind if we chat for a minute?"

Nikki smiles and walks away. Off to find the new rookie, I assume. Honestly, I don't care if she's gone for the rest of the night. I only wanted one appearance in front of Bridget to get her blood pumping a little. Hate and lust aren't that far apart.

"What's that about?" he asks, nodding toward my date as she wanders toward some of the other players.

"Nothing. What's the deal with her and Nate?"

"I dunno. But considering she's paying more attention to you than him, I'd say it's nothing of concern."

It's hard to take my eyes off her.

"How's she doing? Really?"

"Okay. She got a place in the city, loves her new job."

I suspected she had moved out but didn't know for sure.

"Where at?"

"Nuh-uh. I'm no snitch. You can ask her yourself."

"What happened to pals before gals?"

"Sisters before misters, bud."

"You got me there."

He looks back toward my date. "So . . . is this you giving up, then?" He seems pretty annoyed that I came here with someone else.

I laugh. "*Hell* no. I told you, she's it for me. I'm just giving her space to figure that out for herself."

He purses his lips and nods slowly. "I see. You're trying to expedite the process with jealousy. Bring around a bunny so you can woo my sister. Makes perfect sense."

I mean, when you put it that way . . .

"You're a fucking idiot," he says before walking off. He's not wrong.

———

Sitting through dinner is a master class in patience. I have to sit with the team and Nikki. Dinner is excellent. I haven't had a good home meal since Bridget lived with me. Even my stomach misses her. Though, I'd probably be enjoying this steak more if she was sitting next to me. Though my appetite isn't very present tonight.

As fate would have it, our tables are next to each other. She's in my line of sight and it's hard to keep my eyes off her. She looks incredible. In the middle of my gawking, Nate whispers something to her. Whatever it was, she wasn't into it. I cock my head and narrow my eyes. I know we're playing this little tit for tat, but seeing her next to him is bad for my blood pressure. He can play pretend all he wants, but his date is going home with me.

Dinner wraps up and the auction begins. We have a few Lakes player items like private lessons, player-led tours of the arena, dinner with the team, season tickets, game packages, etc. Obviously, those don't need my bids, but when they begin auctioning a trip to the Maldives, the five-night stay on a private island in a romantic water villa for two perks up my ears. I start at seven grand, and Nate jumps in with eight. I respond with sixteen. *Fuck all the way off.* I'm sure he imagines taking Bridget there, he's probably envisioning how sexy she'll look swimming through crystal-clear azure waters. And she absolutely will. I'll be sure to send him a postcard.

I lean back in my chair while my fingers trace lazy figure eights on the tablecloth. The price continues to climb, it's for a good cause. Somehow Nikki seems to think my bidding has something to do with her. She's finding more reasons to touch me; lean her head on my shoulder, whisper something in my ear, intertwine our fingers. Everything I specifically asked her *not* to do. I forgot how flirtatious she is with a glass of champagne in hand.

When I bid twenty-five thousand, Nikki slides her fingers into my hair and presses a kiss to my neck. Anger flashes on my face and she quickly pulls away, but it's too late. When I peer at Bridget, the hurt on her face tells me the damage is already done. *Damn it.* Between bids, I unlock my phone and order a rideshare for my date. I win the auction at the bargain price of forty-two thousand dollars, but after Nikki's little stunt, it may have cost me much more.

After the clapping dies down and the band strikes up, I escort her down the hallway.

"Are you taking me to the Maldives?"

"No, I'm taking you to your Uber."

"What, why?"

"I told you when I got here, not to put your hands on me. We are not a thing. You knew the deal."

She picks up her pace alongside me and whines that I'm not fun anymore.

"This was a mistake," I mutter to myself.

Pushing open the heavy doors, I'm relieved to see the waiting car. Like a gentleman, I help her in, confirm her home address with the driver, give him a cash tip, and send her on her way.

Good riddance. What was I thinking bringing her here? She was rude all night, constantly cutting down other guests and playing fashion police. *Did I really used to put my dick in her?* Doesn't matter, she's gone. I need to find the woman I came here for.

Climbing the shallow outdoor steps to return to the ballroom, I hear the band playing inside. I know this song. The memory of it is so fresh in my mind. This is what played in the background when I made love to Bridget. My fingers threaded in her hair, our bodies completely in sync. I'll never forget that desperate look in her eyes. The zap as our gazes met—it was as if the significance of that moment had sealed our fate. At that moment, I knew I would never love another like I love her.

I reach the entrance doors the same time Bridget is hurrying out. Head down, she runs right into me. God, she's even more gorgeous up close. She immediately apologizes, but when she looks up and sees it's me, her face freezes. Her eyes are glassy. It's like déjà vu. Same song. Same big eyes. Same love.

"Bridg." There's so much I want to say.

She plasters on a fake smile. "Good seeing you. Have a nice night."

"Where are you going?"

She tries to rush past me, but I grab her elbow.

The smile on her face turns sad. "Why her? Of all people?"

"I know. I sent her home. Shouldn't have brought her in the first place. I was pissed off when I found out about Nate, so I thought it might be fun to get your hackles up. There's nothing sexier than seeing you fit to be tied."

She won't look at me.

"You thought I was leaving with Nikki?"

Oh, come on. She knows better. How could she think I wasn't leaving with her tonight?

I reach for her hand and glance above her head to nod at the valet. He hustles off to get my car. *Smart kid.* Threading my fingers through hers, I lead her toward the valet pickup.

"We need to talk. Now. I'm done playing this game." This ends tonight.

My car pulls up, and I hand him my ticket and a fifty.

"Lonan, I think—"

"Get in."

The valet opens the passenger door, and she climbs in, pulling the remainder of her gown in before the door closes.

"I just want to talk," I say.

When she clicks her seatbelt, her perfume fills the space, and I inhale as casually as possible. My eyes meet hers one more time before I pull away from the curb. There's no sign of protest.

"Where are we going?" she asks quietly.

I don't know yet, so I don't answer. When I see a vacant-looking parking garage, I enter and drive up each level until I reach the rooftop. Relieved to find it empty, I take off my seatbelt.

When I turn off the car, I grip the steering wheel tight. *Now or never.*

Her sultry voice breaks the silence. "What are we doing here?"

"We're making up." I unbuckle her seatbelt and haul her into my lap.

The slit in her dress spreads open, and I reach up to stroke her thighs, reveling in the feel of her soft creamy skin. She straddles me and presses her forehead to mine. A tear falls, and I brush it away.

"Do you still love me?" she asks. How could she ever ask me that? It hurts to think she could ever doubt my love for her.

My throat feels thick, and my voice comes out gravelly. "I could never stop loving you."

A relieved laugh cuts off her sob, and gentle hands bracket my face.

"I love you, Lonan."

The exhale that leaves my lips takes with it the weight that's been heavy on my shoulders for months.

"Say you're mine."

My lips take hers, and the kiss we share is fierce. Demanding. It pulls at my soul. It rips me apart and mends me back together. She sighs so softly, and everything is right in the world again.

"I'm yours."

My hands dig into her thighs, and I slide them up to grope her ass. My lips pull into a smile against hers.

"You look incredible tonight. Did you wear this dress to drive me crazy?" I smack her ass.

"Maybe."

"Were you going to let Nate touch you wearing this?"

She grinds against me. "No. He tried to get me to go to the coat closet with him. Classy, huh?"

"He's a dead man." I easily find her clit through her already-damp panties. "Who are you soaked for, baby?"

She grinds against my knuckles, seeking gratification.

"For you. Always you," she gasps.

"That's right. Now take it off and show me how wet you are."

She pushes down her thong as I recline my seat so I can see all of her, then she spreads her pussy apart for me.

"Fuck yeah." She was made for me. I glide my thumb up and down her clit, her dewy flesh becoming glazed before my eyes.

"Please," she purrs.

"Tell me what you want," I say, shoving two fingers inside of her. Her burgundy lips drop open, and watching her ride my hand has me so hard it hurts.

"God, this. I want this. You. All of it."

I pull my fingers out of her and suck them clean, then grab the back of her neck and bring her mouth to mine so she can taste how fucking sweet she is.

"Do you get why I love eating your pussy so much? You taste like you belong to me. We belong together."

She sits up so I can unzip my pants and push them down. My cock springs free, twitching when it slides along her tight bundle of nerves.

"I was wrong, I was so wrong. I'm sorry."

My heart pounds, she takes my breath away. It's everything I've wanted to hear.

"You don't ever have to apologize. I know how hard you've been working to accept yourself and accept love. That's all I've ever wanted, baby. For you to let me love you the way you deserve to be loved."

She presses into me, locking her lips on mine. Her tongue brushes the corner of my mouth, and she works her way down to my neck. Every part of me is aching for her. But sorry or not, she'll still need to pay a little retribution to gain her redemption. I grasp her jaw and bring her back to my face.

"Who's going to fuck you tonight?"

"You are," she whispers.

"Say it."

She groans and I smile. Her frustration causes me to chuckle. She's dripping for me.

"Come on, tell me again. Use your words."

"Lonan, quit fucking around. Give it to me."

"What's the magic word?"

"*Please*. Please fucking give it to me," she rasps against my temple.

I fist a handful of her hair close to the scalp and tilt her head back to see the blissful smile on her face.

"Next time, I don't want to have to ask you," I growl.

I slide inside her, and she immediately constricts around me.

"Fuck." I push her thighs down on me, shoving myself deeper inside. Her little hoarse cries fill the car's interior, sending chills up my spine. I've been craving this. I lower her down on me again and unzip the side of her dress, exposing her full breasts. She's unreal. She slides up and down my cock like a goddamn dream. I'm tempted to fold my arms behind my head and enjoy the show. But I regain focus and grab her thighs, pinning her so she can't move.

I flick her clit, and she draws in a sharp breath.

"Whose pussy is this?"

"Yours."

I grip her waist as I lift her, then thrust her back down on me, plunging myself further. Her moans and whimpers are enough to get me off right now.

"And who decides if you're going to come?"

"You."

Thrust.

"Will you be a good girl for me?"

"Yes."

Thrust.

"Will you be a good wife for me too?"

She pauses.

"What? Lonan, I . . ."

I don't move. She clenches her jaw and grips my shoulders, trying to hold off her orgasm.

"Come on, sweetheart—I'm done playing. Whose wife are you?"

She clenches up on me like she's going to come. *Oh, hell no.* I pull out and pinch her clit. Hard.

"Don't you dare come until I say so."

I cup her face in my hands. "Listen closely to me. If you think what we're doing right now is just a hookup, you need to open those big gray eyes and look around. I'm all in with you. So I want all of you in return. You are the only woman who will ever own my heart, but that doesn't mean I'm going to let you tear it apart either. I won't accept anything less than forever from you. Do you understand?"

She chokes out a sob, and her eyes mist over. She nods frantically. *Here we go.*

"I'm going to ask you one more time, so you better answer me this time, or this hungry little cunt will starve tonight." I swipe a tear with my thumb. "Ready?"

"Yes."

Her hands gently tremble, and she bites her lip. We stare at each other, both preparing for what I'm about to ask.

"Bridget Hayes, will you marry me?"

"Yes," she cries, smiling. Hooking her arm around

the nape of my neck, she kisses me with more emotion than I've ever felt in a kiss.

I sink my cock as deep as I can, and a tremor starts in her core and wraps around my length. She's trying so hard not to come, but I'm done making her wait.

"Come for me, baby."

She's unable to confine the scream that bursts from her throat, and I fall right after her.

"You are mine." She pulses around me. "You will always be mine."

"Forever," she answers.

She collapses into me, and we shower each other with deep, slow kisses.

"Take us home," she hums.

Then she kisses me again, sweeping her tongue across my lips and turning me on all over again. Her fingers run through my hair, and I hold her body to mine, feeling her warmth and memorizing everything about this moment. The smell of her perfume mixed with sex, the feel of her naked skin pressed against mine, the sound of her breathing, the taste of her lips, the beating in my heart filled with adoration for her. My Bridget.

EPILOGUE I

LONAN

S tanding on a ladder, I plug in the final strand
of bulbs in the tree, then I climb the board on
the tree trunk leading into the tree house.
Bridget and I have spent the last several months in
these woods, clearing dead trees and raking away the
old leaves. These woods are where it all started; it
only makes sense we make our vows to each other
here too.

Long heavy swags of fabric are draped across the
massive tree's large sturdy lower limbs that will serve as
the backdrop of our ceremony. We had eight benches
made for our guests to sit on: four on each side of the
wood-chipped aisle. A set of tall old church doors are
freestanding at the end of the aisle for our guests to walk
through before they enter the sanctuary of these trees. A
few ferns have been transplanted outside each bench,

which serves as a nice pop of greenery next to the tall square lanterns.

We kept the wedding small and private, only inviting around thirty guests. A mix of friends and close family. I chose not to invite my mother. Jack is my best man, and Micky is her maid of honor. Maddie will be our little flower fairy. After we presented her with the dress-up wings she gets to wear down the aisle, she put them on right away, and Auds says they can barely get her to take them off at home. She is taking her role very seriously.

I think back to the day we walked away from each other in this very spot. The gut-wrenching memories of her rejection have been replaced with new ones filled with love and the promise of our future. I look out the tree house window and survey all of our hard work. I'm shocked at how well this has all come together. It's a simple layout, but she's done a terrific job bringing her vision to fruition. Bridget pads across the floorboards in the tree house and wraps her arms around me from behind.

"Do you think we have enough wood chips?" I ask her.

She grabs my sides and turns me to face her. I drop a kiss on her temple. There's a smudge of dirt on her cheek, and her messy ponytail is barely holding together. Some of the strands pulled loose by tree branches, as evidenced by the small stick trapped in her hair. We've been hanging strands of globe lights in the pine trees to light the long aisle we'll walk down as husband and wife. I carefully untangle it from her hair and drop it back to the ground.

She's wearing overalls, like she used to as a kid. The metamorphosis of young Birdie to grown makes my heart swell. I hate that we missed out on so many years together. I would have preferred to have been childhood sweethearts, though I can't imagine all the trouble we might have gotten into in this very tree house as teenagers. Instead, I plan to make it up by giving her every one of my days for the rest of my life.

"I think the two truckloads are more than enough. Aren't I the one that's supposed to be all wrapped up in the aesthetics?"

"Yeah, you are. But since you refuse to go all Bridezilla on me, I've had to step into the role. I want this to be the wedding of your dreams."

"In the wedding of my dreams, I get to marry the man of my dreams. I've already locked that down, the rest is just details." She waves her hand.

"You think you can lock this down, huh?" I joke, gesturing to myself.

"*Please.* Like a penitentiary."

It's true.

"That so, warden?" I muse, unclicking one of her overall straps.

"Haven't you heard? I've ruined all other women for

you. I'm Bridget-fucking-Hayes."

"Not for long," I remind her, unclasping the second overall strap, the buckles slide off her shoulders and the bib falls, exposing that soft spot on her stomach I find so goddamn sexy.

"I can't believe I love you so much that I'm willing to walk back into the social security office and ask for another name change."

My gaze falls to her lips as she darts her tongue out to wet them. I notice her chest rising and falling quicker, and it causes me to smirk. I reach up and pull out the loose hair tie, letting down her hair.

"I can."

When I drop to my knees in front of her, she threads her fingers into my hair and draws her nails from the nape of my neck to my forehead. It's something she absentmindedly performs every time I eat her pussy, and now she's got my dick trained to get hard every time she does it. I push up her t-shirt and grip her sides while I lay kisses across her stomach and hip bones.

"Lonan . . ." she breathes. "Everyone is home. They could come out and check on us any minute."

I untie the laces of her shoes and slip them off her feet. Then grasp the denim and pull the overalls down to her ankles so she can step out of them.

"With the way you scream, they'll definitely be coming out here to check on us." I chuckle, giving her a hard nudge onto the plush bed behind her. Her hair fans out around her like a sunbeam. Lifting herself on her elbows, she gives me a soft smile. That smile weakens my knees, but my love for her blooms in my chest when I see the sparkle in her stormy eyes.

"You're the worst."

I bring my knees up to the bed and straddle her thighs. Leaning down, I hover my mouth just above hers. She leans in to kiss me, and I pull back, thwarting her advances and watching her squirm.

"Fine, then I'm not kissing you," she says, clapping her thighs closed.

I chuckle and give in. My mouth meets hers in a slow, sensual kiss, and I nip at her lower lip before soothing it with the tip of my tongue. I love how impatient she is for me, and I feel her trying to turn our kiss into something more urgent, but I don't let it. I slide my knee between hers and slide it to the apex of her thighs. When my knee brushes her panties, she lets out a small whimper. She's so sweet.

"Fuck, I love you," I growl.

"I love you too," she pants out, her breaths picking up.

I push down my boxers and jeans and let out a sigh of relief when my cock is set free of the denim cage it's been pressed against. Her gaze drops, and she bites her lower lip.

Her painted nails wrap around my erection, and I groan.

"That's a pretty sight."

I grip her inner thigh and squeeze the soft, delicate skin before pushing her panties to the side and grazing my thumb over her wet pussy. I draw more of her arousal out and spread it around.

"You're so wet, sweetheart," I say, shoving two fingers inside her.

She lets out a gasp and then moans when I widen my fingers into a V, opening her up for me.

"Make love to me, Lonan."

"Pretty sure I'm not supposed to have sex with my bride the day before the wedding. But tomorrow afternoon, when you're standing in front of me, looking like a dream in that white dress, I want you to think about this."

I pull my fingers out and fist my cock, pushing my entire length inside her. Her mouth drops open, and as she writhes under me to adjusts to my size, I get even harder. Her head lifts, and she watches as I slide in and out of her. The sounds of her breathy moans and wet pussy mingle with the sounds of the outdoors. Birds chirping, branches settling—even the trees seem to pulsate with energy.

"You take me so well, baby."

"You give it to me so well," she pants.

I give her a cocky smile and shake my head. I'm the luckiest man alive.

When her legs shake, I know she's close. I thrust

into her as deep as I can. The gush of fluid that hits when she clenches around me only makes me fuck her harder through her orgasm. Her body pulses as she eats up every inch of my cock, her muscles tightening around me.

I explode inside her.

"Such a good fucking wife," I growl in her ear.

BRIDGET

It's my wedding day. My wedding day to the man who makes me feel seen, loved, and protected. I take one last look at myself in the mirror and smile. After trying a few dress shops, I couldn't find anything I loved. However, we found a seamstress that created the most beautiful backless gown from my mother's wedding dress. It's a masterpiece that has so much meaning sewn into each stitch. My bouquet is made of mostly creams and greenery from the woods. Still, there's one magenta peony I've added, reminiscent of the flowers from Lonan, and a reminder that no matter how far apart, we will always find each other again.

A tall tent sits off to the side of our forest sanctuary. Dad and I wait inside.

"How ya doing, kiddo? Nervous?"

"A little. Mostly happy, though. I'm so happy, Dad."

He pulls me in for a hug, and when we release, his eyes are misty.

"I remember seeing your mom walk down the aisle in this dress, and I remember thinking that I could never feel happier than I did at that moment. Years later, your brother was born, and a couple of years after that, you came along. That was a joy like no other."

He pauses and clears his throat, emotion pulling at his voice.

"After . . . we still had fun times, but there was always that shadow of your absence. But now? It's like we're whole again. I'm so proud of you and who you have become."

I give him another hug and squeeze him tight. "I love you, Dad."

Feeling my eyes start to burn, I look up, gently blotting away some of the moisture with a tissue.

"Come on now, don't start that shit. You'll get me going too."

"You started it." I sniff. He laughs and then I giggle. It's part nerves, part giddiness.

I watch through the small window and see Lonan. Holy shit, he looks good. A smile takes over my face, and my heart is wrapped in warmth as he walks my mother down the aisle. His family is my family. The bond he shares with my parents makes me love him even more. Next, Jack walks down, holding Liam in one arm and Audrey in the other. The love in his eyes when he looks at her is palpable from here. He hands off the sleeping baby to Auds, and she takes a seat in the front row. Micky walks down with Mads. The guests "Aww" when her fairy wings bounce with each step as she drops handfuls of lavender onto the ground with her little rustic twig wand tucked in her fist. Micky needs to wear more dusty blue because it's her color. Lonan's single teammates will be trying to get her number tonight.

The song that's playing quiets down, and Lonan turns away. That's our cue.

My dad takes my arm, and we make our way over to the closed doors at the end of the aisle. Lakes' forwards Sully and Conway open the doors as the processional plays. Dad gives me one last look.

"Ready?"

I nod and tuck into his elbow. Here we go.

As we take our first steps, Lonan turns around, and the look on his face when he sees me melts me to pieces. His tongue darts out to wet his lips before they curve into a smile that can't be contained, the one that slays me. I know mine mirrors his. I understand the happiness my dad spoke of just moments before. I can't imagine a joy greater than this one. It's more than anything I've ever felt before.

My feet continue to carry me forward, but time seems to stand still in this surreal moment of bliss. My dad lets go of me to embrace Lonan and give him a squeeze. He must say something to him because Lonan mutters a "Yes, sir" in return. I hand my bouquet to

Micky, and she dabs her eye with a tissue. It's rare for her to get emotional, so I cherish the moment. My dad turns back to me and wraps me in one more hug.

"Go get 'em, kiddo. I love you."

"Love you too, Dad."

His eyes twinkle when he pulls back. Jack gives me a nod and smiles like he's proud of me. When I look at my mom, she's got her head tilted to the side and her eyes shine with tenderness. This is love. It's real. *The good stuff.*

I take my place across from Lonan. He's so handsome. That's one hell of a suit. He takes my hand and yanks me closer. There are some chuckles from the guests, but right now, it feels like he and I are the only two people in this space. The officiant speaks, but I'm lost in Lonan's eyes and the way he's looking at me.

We repeat our vows back to the officiant, and when my husband slides the ring back on my finger, and I slide one on his, we say our promises to each other.

As the final words are spoken, Lonan pulls me close, and his hand cradles the back of my head as our lips connect. It's intoxicating.

"I will love you forever," he says against my lips.

"Forever," I promise.

No matter the circumstances, we would always find each other. This love existed before I forgot, before I remembered, and before we came to be what we are in this moment.

EPILOGUE II

THE MALDIVES

Birdie

Waiting is torture. I'm naked, but the sunset casts a warm glow in our water villa. I've been instructed to get on all fours and wait on the bed for him to come back from his swim. The sheets below my fingers are plush and downy. I think about the last time he took me from behind, and my arousal coats my thighs. Then I hear it. The steady, solid footfalls get louder as he approaches. I swallow, suddenly more scared than excited.

My back is facing the door, but when the knob turns, my heart races. My awareness of my exposure and self-consciousness kicks into overdrive. This is not the most flattering pose he requested. What the fuck was he thinking making me pose like this?

The door opens. Silence.

I'm naked on top of our bed, on my hands and

knees. Thankfully the lights are low, which will paint me to be more flattering than I probably am. Why is he so quiet? Is he just staring at me? I'm not supposed to turn around.

His fingers start at the back of my thigh, then run along my ass and up my spine, sending a shiver up to my neck. Finally, he walks around the bed and stands in front of me, tilting up my chin.

"Were you a good girl today?"

Oh fuck. I try not to show my excitement.

"Yes."

"I'd say you were a very good girl. Tonight, you and I are the only things that exist. Spread your knees."

I obey.

He walks around to the other side of the bed, and his wet suit slaps onto the floor. Feather touches kiss the back of my legs and thighs. The bed dips and my breath quickens.

"I love seeing you on all fours for me. You're so beautiful, baby."

Exhale. I feel safe again.

Then his warm mouth closes on my ass cheek and he bites. He literally bites me. I yelp, and he licks the same spot, soothing the sting.

"I've wanted to sink my teeth into your ass since the first time I took you from behind."

It sends a shock of warmth to my core.

"What took you so long?"

He's been longing for me, and I want to give myself over to him even more. Please him and submit to him.

A hand slides up the inside of my leg and he traces the heart-shaped birthmark on my thigh.

"So sexy," he mutters like he's making an open observation.

As his fingers draw higher, I gulp. And when his fingers swipe between my thighs, my back arches with need.

"So responsive to my touch."

He slides his strong fingers back and forth through my folds and the ache grows.

"Already so wet for me."

I tighten up as he continues the torturous strokes. My pelvis rises as my back arches even harder. My body already wants to come.

The moan that falls from my lips is louder than I intended.

"Please," I breathe out.

"There's my polite girl."

His footsteps move to the dresser and a drawer opens and closes. I hear what sounds like a package opening. Did he get a box of condoms? Why are we using a condom?

He returns to my pussy, rubbing my clit, making my knees weak. He inserts a finger, and I whimper, wanting to be filled more, he inserts a second finger, and it's an appreciated consolation for now. When he pulls his fingers out, he spreads my wetness over my asshole, and I startle.

"What are we doing?"

"I'm going to devour this sweet pussy tonight," he says. "But this time your ass is going to be filled when I do it."

He spits directly onto the tight knot, and I gasp. I should be disgusted but it's electrifying.

"Ready?"

I nod. .

He holds the plug in front of my mouth. "Suck."

Afterward, he stands behind me and pushes down my shoulders, lifting my ass in the air. The cold metal pushing into me sends chills up my back.

"That's it, baby, just relax."

I ease my muscles and blow out a breath. With each centimeter, it fills me up more. When I feel like I can't stretch any wider and I'm about to object, my ass draws it in deeper until it's securely in place. The taboo feeling is unfamiliar but arousing. Handing over control feels so freeing, and experiencing his desire for me this way is such a turn-on. It's fucking hot that he's about to have his way with me.

"Come here." I almost laugh at the phrasing because that's all I want to do.

He lies next to me and positions my pussy over his mouth, then reaches around my thighs and pulls me down to him. Fuck.

I suck in breath on impact, and he does exactly as he promised—devours me. He licks me slowly, flattening and flicking his tongue over me, when he pulls my clit between his lips, I know I'm not going to last long. The anticipation has been building for hours. He's latched onto me, and paired with the feelings of fullness, it's exhilarating. I can't help but grind harder against his face. My orgasm is growing and spreading through my body.

"Just like that, take what you need," he instructs as he slides a hand between us. He seals his mouth over me again, and when he spears two fingers inside my pussy and crooks them into that spot only he can reach, I relinquish my control. I clamp down on his fingers, and my pelvis undulates in a spasm as reach into his hair and pull, trying to hold on.

"Fuck, Lonan!"

He chuckles beneath me, and it only heightens the experience. His tongue flattens and laps up my arousal, savoring me. He looks up at me, and he's on the verge of smiling. God, I love it, how can a smile turn me on so much?

My legs quiver, and he gently lifts my hips for me.

I lean forward, crouched on my knees, my ass in the air, still trying to get my bearings.

He wraps his body over mine and whispers in my ear.

"My turn, Princess."

My eyes drift closed, and I bite my bottom lip to keep from grinning like a maniac.

His hand cracks against my ass, and I jolt up, instinctively grabbing onto the stinging cheek. He rubs his hand over mine, kneading the spot.

When he bends me back over again and slides his cock inside, I groan. Gorged with pleasure and so full.

"Lonan, make me come," I say breathlessly.

"Oh, yeah?" He sounds so overconfident.

"Please, I want to come just like this."

"Open your eyes."

I didn't even realize they were closed. When I open them, the tall mirror is in front of us and he's standing behind me.

He wraps a fist around my hair and pulls my head up to look at him. I catch myself in the reflection. My eyes are wild, and even in the dim light, I can see how flush my chest is.

He wraps a hand around at my breast and lifts me to my knees. Fuck, he feels even deeper than before. His hand lowers to my clit and he rubs small circles over the sensitive nub. His nose runs up the column of my neck. He reaches around my neck to collar my throat with his tattooed hand. He doesn't squeeze, just grasps me firmly in place.

I almost cry, the feeling it gives me is incredible. It's deeply intimate and trusting. I lift my chin, offering my throat to him. His fingers fan out, and he brushes over my pulse. The act is tender and dominating at the same time. *My favorite.* Then he rears back and thrusts into me, burying all of himself inside me. I sob at the full sensations lighting up every part of me. My mouth drops open at the erotic image.

"You're going to watch me fuck you. I want you to see how beautiful you are when you're filled with me. Look how sexy you are like this."

I gaze at my swollen lips, my rosy cheeks, my hooded eyes, and dark lashes. Reaching behind, I hook my arm around his neck and my breasts rise and fall with every pump of him inside me. I feel beautiful.

He runs his nose along my neck.

"You're such a good fuck." *Thrust.*

"So perfect." *Thrust.*

I gasp as he continues his praises, my ears ringing while he continues pounding into me over and over. My core clenches tighter and tighter.

I'm teetering on the edge, about to experience one of the greatest orgasms of my life. It's like life stands still. Until he whispers in my ear.

"Now be a good girl and come all over this cock."

Done.

My pussy almost ejects him after squeezing so tight.

"Fuck."

In the mirror, I watch that wicked smile appear on his lips, proud of his work. Rapture takes over his features. When my orgasm thunders through me, I fall over the edge and shatter into a million pieces. It's like no other. My knees lock up, and if he wasn't holding me, I'd double over.

"There it is, baby," he grits out before roaring a curse and coming with me. He grips me hard, and I know there will be handprints tomorrow. I can't wait to see my body marked by him.

Then he slowly slides out of me, and I collapse onto the bed.

"Hold still a second," he whispers. He reaches for the plug, and I practice trying to relax again. It feels like it takes some force, but once it slides out, my body misses the feeling of being stuffed and satiated. My body is exhausted.

We lie together as the sun melts under the horizon, and my mind drifts. Lonan presses a kiss to my hair, and a soft moan slips from my lips. We lie in silence, husband and wife, listening to each other breathe and falling into a warm slumber.

THE END

MORE BOOKS BY SLOANE ST. JAMES

LAKES HOCKEY SERIES

————

BOOK 1
Before We Came
Bridget & Lonan

BOOK 2
Strong and Wild
Freya & Rhys
(Summer 2023)

BOOK 3
In the Game
Raleigh & Barrett
(Fall 2023)

.

ACKNOWLEDGMENTS

Holy shit, I wrote a book. Last fall, I looked at my loving husband and said, "Hey. I'm going to write a book." He said, "Okay." And that was that. Now, lo and behold! Here you are, dear reader, holding my first book baby. Please be kind to her. She is new to this world and has much to learn.

This won't be short, I have a lot of people to be thankful for in my life, but I need to start with my readers—YOU. From the bottom of my heart, thank you for picking up my book and taking a chance on a new author. It means everything to me. Truly.

To my husband, who supports whatever crazy ideas I have, no questions asked—thank you for always believing in me. You are the most wonderful human I know, my soulmate and best friend. You find a way to make me laugh each day, and I love our life together. This book is for you. You gave me the courage I needed to continue. I can never express how much I appreciate you taking the reins on the house and kids when I lock myself away in the bedroom to write. I would not have finished this without you.

To my kids, if you ever find these books–
SURPRISE! Seriously though, I hope someday you can
be proud of your mom and what she spent so much time
on. Always remember, big feelings are okay, and I love
you so much.

To my editor, Dee Houpt. Thank you for helping me
develop my skills and pushing me to become a stronger
writer. And for your encouragement to keep my mental
health in check. I am so excited to keep working with
you on future books!

My beta readers! Emma, Shannon, and Jennifer. A
special shout-out to Emma and Shannon—thank you for
helping me develop this story and giving me honest
feedback—your raw input is invaluable! Never stop
telling me when something is shit. You both have
made this book so much better, and have given me faith
to continue writing. I cannot put into words how
much your support means to me. You were the first
people to read Before We Came, and I'm so excited
to continue working together on future books!

Thank you to Mallory, The Nutty Formatter, for
formatting this book and making it beautiful!

To Ohana, my pack of weirdos. I love you, but we
will never group-read this together. Thank you for
always holding space for me, for being some of the
funniest and smartest people I know, and for your
unconditional love and support.

To two of my favorite people, Megan and Katie. Thank you for being as excited about this book as I am. Your friendship means so much to me.

To Lisa, (chicken wing emoji).

Mom and Dad, if you've read this far, you did what I told you not to do. I warned you. I'm not mad, but I am disappointed. Mom, thanks for not judging me for writing smut. Granted, if you read this book, I'm guessing you didn't realize it was going to be this smutty. Dad, thanks for teaching me that I'm in charge of my own destiny. This is me trying to make something of it.

Everyone over at The Smuthood, thank you for the endless plot bunnies and creating such a welcoming community.

I would like to give a couple anonymous shout-outs that helped tremendously with my research: a retired detective from the Cleveland Police Department and a retired Minnesota Wild defenseman. Thank you for answering my questions, providing industry knowledge, and sharing your stories!

This is the part of the show where I shamelessly beg.

If you loved my book, please, tell your friends and followers. Recommend and share the hell out of it. If you already have, you have my endless gratitude. I hope you sleep well knowing that you are making some woman's mid-life crisis dreams come true!

Please help spread the word by leaving a review on Amazon, Goodreads, BookBub, StoryGraph, LibraryThing, Facebook Reader Groups, Booktok, Bookstagram, or wherever you talk smut.

I love to connect with my readers!
SloaneStJamesWrites@gmail.com

Want to join my Beta or ARC team?
linktr.ee/sloanestjames

Facebook Reader Group:
Sloane's Salacious Readers